SPHINX

DEATH WAVE CHRONICLES BOOK 3

ANDRE JONES

ALIEN
PRESS

ISBN: 978-0-6452512-0-3 (paperback)
ISBN: 978-0-6452512-1-0 (ebook)

A catalogue record for this
book is available from the
National Library of Australia

DEATH WAVE CHRONICLES

To save humanity, civilisation must be destroyed.

Nature is brutally harsh. She plays no favourites, and she rarely gives a second chance. Humanity had its opportunity ...

Now it's her turn.

———

The Death Wave Chronicles is a blend of mythology, 'weird science', fringe science and pseudoscience. Throughout the storyline — more so in some novels than others — I will touch on subjects such as Gaia myth, Earth chakras, the power of crystals, ley lines/earth energy grid, druidism, UFO's, aliens ... even Atlantis.

I hope you enjoy the read.

1

TYRONE STRADJEK MOPED ABOUT HIS APARTMENT. HE HAD JUST finished another frustrating vid-com with his grandfather, arguing over the direction Volaris was moving.

"This wasn't what I had envisaged."

"Opa. I am not my father. You both had similar tastes and skills; mine are different. I couldn't possibly continue Volaris with the same zeal as you, simply because I don't feel the same about art ... It's what got Father killed."

Their discussion went downhill from there. He checked his watch, wondering how that redheaded brat — Rhyllien — was faring with the first task he had set her.

"Zera, play news," Tyrone commanded his personal AI. "Search for Niger." The TV came to life and after a couple of seconds a report on Global News Network aired. It depicted aerial footage from a drone over the old mine. A couple of bodies could be seen lying in the dirt. The caption *Breaking news — mysterious death wave hits Niger* flashed along the bottom of the screen.

"Finally, some success." Tyrone smiled. "I didn't think the girl had the stomach." Now all he had to do was ensure she still considered her friends were in danger. Still, if he had to arrange for her mother to have an accident ...

In a rare and spontaneous display of trust, he decided to arrange for the next diamond to be sent immediately.

"Williams," Tyrone called as he opened his safe.

Williams knocked and strode through the door a moment later. "Yes, sir."

"I've got another delivery for Lightning Couriers." He handed him a small unmarked box, then picked up a document, reading the short list of names. He picked up a stylus and drew a line through Niels Franke. "Get them to send this to Joseph Hart of EpiQ Minerals."

"Like the previous order, sir? Rush delivery?" Williams pocketed the box, hearing the slight rattle within.

Tyrone considered for a moment; the girl still had to fly to Giza and do whatever she needed to do there first. He still had a while. "No, not the Premium Rush, whatever the next level below is should suffice."

"Very good, sir." Williams was about to turn, then hesitated.

"Something else?" Tyrone asked as he closed the safe and slid the picture back into place.

"Sir. These items are far too valuable to be kept here. Surely the Volaris vault would be better suited for such things."

"These stones are small and easily hidden on a person, and as you say, extremely valuable. I simply don't trust anyone else with them."

"I see, sir. As you wish." Williams noted the brochure on the small table. "Also, I'm pleased to confirm everything is prepared for the displays for the fundraiser this Saturday. I'm certain the auction will be a success."

"Good work. In fact, I was thinking of displaying the remaining pair of diamonds. No one has ever seen diamonds as large. It could be a huge drawcard."

"I see. I can arrange security here to be tightened; bring a few more over from Miramar."

"Excellent. With much of the Volaris vault empty, there's little point in them all being at HQ."

"I'll see to it, sir." Williams nodded, pivoted and left, closing the door quietly behind him.

Tyrone walked onto the balcony and watched the ocean for a few minutes, swilling the ice in his bourbon. With only a few remaining assets to be sold, the Volaris collection would be the end of the business that had built their reputation. Moving in a completely different direction, in which he'd have even greater control, he would be pinning his hopes in the new off-world mining boom. From the data obtained, he was glad he'd acted when he did, before it became astronomically expensive.

"And if the world's population is decimated, large scale organisation will be doomed on Earth anyway," he reminded himself.

"INCOMING MESSAGE."

Tyrone put the pillow over his head and rolled over, trying in vain to ignore the monitor as it beeped softly.

"Incoming message," Zera repeated.

He blearily looked at the clock. 02:17.

The pillow sailed across the room at the monitor, which toppled back against the wall. Tyrone sat up in his bed and yelled at the AI. "Damn it, Zera. Do you need an upgrade? What don't you understand about 'Do not Disturb'?"

"Emergency call, Tyrone." Sensing his agitated state, the AI used a softer tone.

"Put it through," he said eventually. Rubbing his eyes, Tyrone reached for his robe and sat on the edge of the bed.

"Sorry to disturb you, Mr Stradjek. We've lost the pod and the girl."

"What? Speak up man!"

"We've lost the pod and the girl," the voice repeated.

Tyrone stomped over to the monitor and pulled the pillow off the speaker. "Damn it, Simmons. How? Where the fuck has she gone?"

"Sir, we believe the pod has been hacked. We lost contact several hours into the flight. It was travelling east over Niger at the time, heading for the programmed coordinates in Giza, then ... just disappeared."

"And no trace at all?" Tyrone tossed the pillow back onto the bed.

"Nothing. The transponder signal has been cut completely. If there's any course change, we don't know it."

"So, you can't track it?" He paced back and forth, flustered at the early morning call, but more irate at the news. "Do we know who could do this? That AI pod was top of the line."

"Several entities come to mind—"

"And who's out to get me or knows what I'm up to? The Easterners? Did one of the mining corporations get wind of it? Maybe Franke sabotaged it?"

"If Franke sabotaged it, we'd still have the transponder. Those things don't simply cut out, there are too many fail-safes and if it crashed, even blew up, the emergency beacon would be pinging. As to who — a few corporations have the ability, but it's unlikely they'd worry about us. We aren't that big a concern."

"Not yet. What about ICON? Would those bastards get involved? They're not into mining, but we've crossed paths recently."

"If ICON is involved, perhaps they're merely doing it for a third party — someone who is into off-world mining and using them. Of course, it may have nothing to do with mining. Perhaps a corporation is after a cure. Or someone is simply after the diamonds."

Tyrone poured a bourbon and sat down, thinking. "You're certain the pod was hacked? Could this brat have done something?"

"As you say, it's top-of-the-line AI. I doubt she has the

knowledge to override the whole system at once. No, this is definitely from an external source with big money."

Tyrone cancelled the call, and commed Williams.

"Mr Stradjek? Yes?" There was the ruffling of sheets in the background.

"Williams, have we got a list of ICON interests and their partners?" He switched on the TV to get world news as he waited. There'd be no sleep tonight.

"Umm, I can get a list, sir."

"Send it. What about our kidnappers in the UK?"

"The kidnappers? Oh ... I just read a message from Simmons about the pod. Interesting—"

"Interesting? It's a shitfest, that's what it is! Now, about these kidnappers?"

"Last data I have is they're still in Reading, or the phone is, but it did move slightly before we lost it."

"How did we lose the signal? Was that hacked too?"

"Unlikely. I can only assume the battery is dead."

"Fuck! Can't anything go right for once? What the hell were they doing in Reading? Weren't they supposed to rendezvous in Maidenhead?"

"We've no information. Reading is on the way to Maidenhead. Maybe they're too sick to continue, or a double-cross?"

"Send a drone out to check," Tyrone ordered.

"Sir, we can try. Our influence over there is minimal, and any local assets have either been evacuated or are now dead."

"I'm sure you'll do what you can. Keep tabs on the phone at least. If it pings in a safe zone, I want to know. Have you anything at all to report about the pod before we lost contact?"

"Only notes from Simmons; just before arrival in Niger there was an indication of the door opening prior to landing. Could mean anything, perhaps a glitch ... but nothing to do with the hacking. Everything was nominal on departure."

"Is she after me? Does she know of my location?"

"Unlikely, in both—"

Stradjek cancelled the call when his tablet pinged; the requested list of ICON affiliates had arrived. It was long; some of the listed affiliates were shared between ICON and Volaris and several other organisations with mutual underhanded dealings. Some he couldn't care less about; others he'd be dealing with in the future, so it would be best to keep onside.

It amazed him how Williams managed to get all this information. "It will be worth keeping him when we transition to the moon," he decided. "Or maybe not ..." *He's very efficient ... maybe too efficient ...*

2

"IT'S ALL SO ... *ALIEN!*" RHYLL HAD NO OTHER WORDS TO DESCRIBE
what she was looking at. Everything inside the UFO control
room had a uniform appearance; only the slightly varied shades
of black gave it any depth or detail. *Black on black.*

"Any lighting?" She stepped inside warily, looking down as
her shirt glowed and tiny specks of dust particles that she hadn't
known were there stood out against the fabric. "Black light?"
Rhyll raised her hand, still unsure about the alien covering her
hand like a glove.

"Very close to ultraviolet."

It was an eerie feeling, having a voice directly inside your
head.

The control room was devoid of anything recognisable as
furnishings, and by her judgement, it took up half of the ship's
interior. The wall separating the rear half of the ship had no
visible doorway. There was a blocky structure against the opposite, curved wall. Rhyll touched the surface, wondering if it was
frictionless like the hull. She didn't even know *what* she was
looking at.

"The navigation console."

"If you say so." Rhyll could make no sense of the featureless surface. There were no monitors or gauges she could recognise, and no other doors apart from the one entrance outlined by a faint strip of light. Her eyes adjusted slightly, getting used to the dimness.

The interior became slightly more apparent when the light increased. *"That is the brightest I can make it."*

"Thanks. It's certainly better than before." Rhyll looked up. The entire ceiling now had a slight purple glow. "Do these aliens sit, or stand? Do they have legs—"

Part of the floor distended, forming a black bubble as she spoke.

"Erk." She stepped back, unsure.

"Your seat, and yes, they had legs as well as other appendages—"

"I don't need to know." Warily, Rhyll touched the bubble with her bare foot. It was softer than she'd expected, yet it appeared to be made of the same hard material that she'd been standing on. She reached out with her hand to push the *chair* experimentally.

"It's like a beanbag!" Rhyll said once she sat. When she looked to the console, the chair moved her closer. There was nothing like a viewport or window. With every surface a variation of dark shadow, it was hard to distinguish floor from wall from ceiling.

"Are we still in the hangar?" Rhyll realised part of her discomfort was she now had absolutely no perception of outside, even moreso than when she was a prisoner.

"We are stationary."

"Are the guards still there? What are they doing?" She was completely and utterly cut off from the Earth. It was not a sensation that appealed.

Like a curtain lifting, a viewport appeared. Rhyll could now see into the dim hangar through the hull.

The hoverpod lay in a crumpled heap against the far wall. Several more soldiers had arrived to join the others who'd begun to fan out, surrounding the flying saucer. There was no sound, but the bright muzzle flashes in the dim hangar indicated they were discharging weapons.

"Do not be alarmed. Primitive projectile weapons have no effect."

"Oh, yes, the frictionless surface." As she wriggled in the seat, the diamond dug into her thigh. She moved it to her breast pocket.

"Correct, among other things."

"Is everything primitive to you?"

"So far."

"How old are you? Where are you from?"

"As you measure time, I first became sentient 1.2 million Earth years ago. You have no reference to my origin other than Andromeda."

"Andromeda? The galaxy? How did you get here? In this craft?"

"The craft I journeyed on was destroyed emerging from a temporal rift."

"You were on another craft? Then how—"

"I was adrift in space until the crew of this craft detected me. We later crashed here."

"Is there another hangar? I only sensed the one."

"That craft was at another facility."

"Area 52? They said it was destroyed."

"Correct. In a failed attempt to conduct research on an anti-matter propulsion system."

"And the owners? The other pilots?"

"Are no longer functioning."

"Functioning? Oh ..." *Dead.* "But you survived?"

"I function. My self-repair capabilities are advanced, but very limited in this location."

"You mean in Area 53?"

"I mean this world."

"Oh." Rhyll tried to fathom all of this. "How long were you adrift in space?"

"The equivalent of 103.4 Earth years."

Rhyll's face paled at the thought of a century drifting aimlessly in space. If the things that had happened to her hadn't happened, she doubted she'd believe any of it. "I've only been missing for several days. My friends will be worried sick, but I can't contact them."

"Friends?"

"Dan and Nala. Good people." The glove remained silent. Rhyll waited, realising the silence meant it was working on something. There was a sudden booming hiss all around her. She winced, cupping her ears tightly and looking around worriedly. "What's that?" she yelled.

"An attempt at communication. Incompatible primitive interface—"

"He ... He ... l ... lo ... lo?" The volume reduced until it was bearable. The sound was badly garbled at first, but quickly resolved into audible speech.

"Dan?" Rhyll sat up, gradually recognising the voice. She looked at the glove in amazement.

"Rhy ... ll? Where t ... he hell are you?"

"Modulating signal now."

"You won't believe me. I'm in an alien spacecraft." She was relieved the sound was far less garbled.

"Quit ... pulling my leg. We almost died in a plane crash and I'm not in the mood. My phone just started making a crazy noise. It's weird. No number showed—"

"Plane crash? Why are you in a plane?" In the background she could hear the wail of sirens and people yelling, and thought about the plane they'd almost crashed into.

"Scenic Air Tours," Dan was saying.

"I'm missing for days, and you're taking a scenic tour? Where's Nala?" Feeling frustrated, Rhyll had to get up and pace.

As she tried to stand the *bubble* expanded and contorted, pushing her into an upright position. *What the—!*

"I'm here, *chica*." Nala could be heard over the background noise. "So glad to hear your voice. We were so worried—"

"So worried that you went on a tour?" Rhyll started pacing. It didn't seem to matter where she spoke, the sound was all around her.

"It was part of the plan to find you ... sort of."

"Your plan, or Dan's?"

"Hey!" She heard Dan protest. "Thurston said you had a drone with you. He traced the GPS to Sedona. We arrived—"

"That's where *I* am!"

"In Sedona? Seriously?"

"I did see a sign with Sedona Airport on it. How many Sedonas are there with a secret research facility underneath?"

"It's really not so secret," Dan laughed.

"You were kidding about the UFO thing though, right?" Nala asked.

"Oh ye of little faith. Just wait and see."

While she spoke, the hangar disappeared as the craft whisked up and outside. At no stage did she feel any movement. She was now looking at trees and sky. There was a blaze to one side, and she recognised the airport buildings to the far right as the same ones she saw near the car park.

"I took the liberty of tracing your friend's location." The craft quickly glided to a barely perceptible landing among the cars.

"You said a plane crashed. Did it catch fire?" Rhyll asked. The airport fire brigade were now in attendance.

"No. Those sirens you're probably hearing are for a substation that just blew up. We're okay."

"I blew that up!" Rhyll replied as the door irised opened. It was both fascinating and uncomfortable to see segments of the wall spin and retract into itself.

Surprised the walkway between the ramp and the entrance

was no longer frictionless, Rhyll stepped outside and looked around wildly.

"I'm in the car park," she said.

Two familiar figures moved away from the crowd, first at a walk, then they began running as they saw her, calling her name. Dan's loping gait suggested he might have injured a leg.

Other spectators of the fire turned to the shouts. Upon seeing the alien craft, they started yelling and pointing. Some people screamed and ran away, but a third of the crowd surged forward, now videoing the alien craft and not the blaze. Others were speaking earnestly into their phones and gesticulating.

Dan and Nala ran to the edge of the craft, sharing equally amazed glances between Rhyll and the spaceship.

"It really *is* a UFO!" Dan said, flabbergasted.

"He catches on quick, doesn't he?" Nala laughed. She jumped back nervously when a ramp started to emerge from the hull, then rushed up it to join the girl at the top.

Rhyll gave her a huge hug.

Dan strode briskly up the ramp, eyes as wide as his gaping mouth.

"Quick, follow me." Rhyll led them inside before the crowd got too close.

Her friends stared in disbelief at the interior, too stunned to be scared.

"How long have you had this?" Nala asked, looking around in fascination.

"About ten minutes, but I've been in Sedona for a couple of days."

"Black on black ... I don't see it catching on." Dan looked dubiously into the darker recesses. "Where are the lights?"

"The visual range of the previous occupants was different than yours." The sound of the alien entity was all around them now.

"What the fuck!" Nala and Dan jumped, looking around for the disembodied voice.

"Utilisation of audio is now logical for efficient communication."

"It's ok, it's ... a friend." She pointed to her glove.

"And here I was thinking you were starting a fashion fad for the new world." Dan looked at the glove curiously when Rhyll raised it. He was cautious not to touch it. "Where did you find it?"

"It found *me* really. I was in a lab looking for a diamond and this sort of ... melded onto me." She showed Nala. "I don't know why, though."

"I felt a worthy presence, and I sensed you were wanting to depart. It was a beneficial melding."

"Yes, but why me?" Rhyll asked.

"There was no other likely candidate until I felt your presence. My goal is to return to my place of origin, but I owe you a debt."

"I thought you said this craft wasn't capable of getting you to Andromeda."

"Correct, but it is quite capable of getting around this galaxy. I may find a more suitable craft, or even another temporal rift. In the meantime I will continue my repair. The components required cannot be located in this sector."

"You came from Andromeda?" Dan repeated, incredulous.

"It did. I can only assume getting to Giza in Egypt would be easy?" Rhyll asked.

"29.9772962 North, 31.1324955 East."

"What would that be?" Dan asked.

"The coordinates for the Giza Necropolis."

"That was a quick calculation," Dan acknowledged.

"It was already in the ship's nav-data."

"They have been here before, haven't they?" Rhyll stated, not sounding surprised.

"Correct." Two more bubbles sprouted from the floor. "Please be seated."

Dan jumped back. "What the hell?"

"It's okay, Dan. They're seats — like beanbags." Rhyll flopped into hers to show it was safe.

"I hate beanbags." Dan sat tentatively, as did Nala.

"Oh. This is great." Nala settled in comfortably.

"Does it do massage too?" When it started vibrating, Dan smiled. "I could get used to this."

"Greater efficiency can be achieved by integrating with the craft. Do not be alarmed."

The glove dripped off Rhyll's hand. She wasn't distressed, though from Dan and Nala's screwed up faces they obviously thought it looked gross. The entity now formed a dark lump of jelly and flowed across the floor, sliding up the side of the console where it flattened to almost nothing on the top.

Rhyll found her tongue. "That was ... *different*. If you're not a glove, what are you?"

"In your terms, I would be a Quantum Molecular Assembler."

Rhyll thought long and hard, shaking her head. "Nope. No idea. What about you two?"

Nala and Dan shook their heads, still getting over the sight of the dark lump squirming slug-like across the floor.

"My function is to modify matter from one form to another as the need arises."

"Like an alchemist?" Dan suggested.

"We will begin," was all they heard in reply.

There was no discernible engine start; no vibration or noise. The Sedona airport receded at an incredible rate.

"Wait!" Dan abruptly tried to sit up and was nearly thrown out of the chair as it contorted to assist him getting up.

"What is it?" Rhyll asked, concerned.

Dan regained his balance. "Our gear! We need to go back to our hotel and get it."

"For a couple of burner phones and a camera?" Rhyll looked at him like he was crazy.

"We really, really do," Dan insisted. "Can you take us to La Auberge de Sedona?" he spoke towards the console.

Rhyll turned to Nala in confusion. "Seriously?" she mouthed.

Nala shrugged with a wink.

"L'auberge de Sedona."

"Yes. I'm not sure of the address, but — Oh." Dan looked stupidly at the resort's car park through the viewscreen.

The door irised open, letting in the cool night air.

Seeing what happened to Dan when he stood up, Nala made to climb out of her chair; it expanded and contorted. She calmly stepped over and nudged Dan, who was staring dumbfounded out the door.

"We'll be back in a few minutes," she called over her shoulder to Rhyll.

The ramp extended to the ground for them.

While she waited, Rhyll looked about the interior. "I assume once we get to Egypt, you'll be wanting to go your own way?"

"Only once I reach full functionality will it be possible to return to my origins. What you see here is only an insignificant portion of my full capabilities."

"I see."

"However, since you assisted in my freedom, I am at your service."

"That's great to hear. With your ability and this craft, I can complete my task much more quickly."

"Efficiency is part of my design parameters."

"Do you know what's happening here? What my task is?"

"I am aware of the information received on all frequencies, which gives me insight into your tasking."

"What do you think?"

"I think a culture that goes about destroying its own habitat is foolish; a culture that does this does not deserve the privilege of travelling to other worlds until it matures sufficiently."

With the reflections of a million-year-old entity coursing through her mind, Rhyll spied Nala and Dan returning briskly through the car park. They clambered up the ramp and strode inside. Rhyll again noticed Dan had a slight limp.

"Sorry about that." Dan was all smiles, placing a bulky bag as well as his backpack by the back wall. "Egypt, here we come."

"Boys and their toys." Rhyll rolled her eyes.

"Hey, I've been thinking; Quantum Molecular Assembler is a mouthful. How does Q sound for our new alien friend?" Dan asked as he flopped into the chair.

"Pfft." Nala placed her bag behind her seat. "As long as you don't start calling me *R*, or Nala *N*."

"He started a long time ago; don't forget he already calls your mother *Mrs E*."

"It's efficient," he argued.

The ramp had already retracted, and the door silently spun closed. Through the viewscreen, the resort receded rapidly as the craft moved at lightning speed. There was no sensation of movement. The craft had turned so the view was forward and looking down.

Uncertain what to expect, they all nonetheless gasped when the craft rocketed through the atmosphere.

"How fast can this thing go?" Dan asked.

"Velocity is relevant to requirements and dependant on location. Greater speeds are achieved the further the craft is from gravitational forces."

"No heat from friction?" Dan asked. He'd expected the hull to glow from such a high speed through the atmosphere.

"The hull's almost frictionless," Rhyll told him. Like the others, she was both mesmerised and terrified, trying to take it all in.

They were beyond the atmosphere in a matter of minutes. The trio stared outside, gobsmacked at their first sight of space: the inky blackness, the brilliance of the stars, the moon in its last quarter, and the Earth curving below in shadow with the major cities clearly visible by their lights.

"It's beautiful, isn't it?" Nala gasped in awe.

Rhyll nodded. "And worth saving."

"And it isn't flat," Dan chuckled. He had pulled his camera out and was busy snapping pictures.

"Might be easier if you record it," Nala suggested.

"Of course. I can get stills off vid." Dan smiled at his absent-mindedness. He set his camera on the console to record the screen. "I must remember to replace my tripod," he muttered.

Overlaying the vista of the Earth below, a range of alien symbols appeared on the screen like a heads-up display.

"Does that show the speed and altitude? We can't read it," Dan stated.

"Correct. I will adjust..."

"Wow," Dan gasped when the symbols changed to Earth standard. He tried to do the math in his head. "That's over twenty thousand kilometres an hour!"

"5.79288 kilometres per second for optimal trajectory, reaching an altitude of five point five thousand kilometres."

The girls were also reading the display in awe.

"Minus a hundred and thirty; I might need a couple of jumpers outside." Nala shivered at the thought of it. "I wonder how hot it gets in the sunlight?"

"Wearing anything other than spacesuits would be fatal. This craft has several suits that will be suitable for your body type."

"Speaking of sunlight, here comes the terminator," Dan noted.

"Terminator?" Rhyll asked him.

"He's trying to show off. It's the line separating night and day." Nala pointed to the oncoming brightness.

Dan laughed when Rhyll stuck her tongue out at him.

The screen dimmed as a filter materialised to shut out the intense glare of the sun.

"Good morning," Nala said softly.

"There you go; one hundred, one-fifty ... two ... two-fifty-six degrees Celsius," he read as the craft crossed the terminator into broad daylight.

The unmistakeable landmass of North America drifted south, with Hudson Bay now below them.

"Why are we flying north?" Rhyll asked. "Egypt is further south."

"Due to the curvature of the planet, this is the most efficient route."

"How long before we get to Egypt?"

"Arrival will be in thirty-six minutes."

The trio watched, mesmerised as the southern tip of Greenland, then Iceland and the North Atlantic Ocean came into view.

"I wonder how things are in England since we left?" Dan muttered when he saw the United Kingdom.

In a corner of the screen in front of him another image materialised, this time showing a news channel. There was a mass of people in the streets of London. Many police were in attendance, standing side by side with the various corporate militia.

"I can't believe it!" Nala shook her head. "You're in space for the first time ever and all you want to do is watch the news?"

"Hey. Don't blame me. I was just wondering. Q put the TV on," Dan defended himself.

"I was merely attempting to appease your curiosity."

The news broadcast continued, though muted, flashing to other hotspots around the world.

"Doesn't look like anyone is rioting this time," Dan observed.

"Looks more like someone's holding a rally. Shit!" Nala exclaimed. "Are you seeing this, Rhyll?"

Despite Europe now passing below, Rhyll was silently staring at the TV display.

There were crowds of people, but as Dan said, they weren't rioting. Dozens of placards were waving with her image clearly shown. Many signs with *Protector of the Earth*, *Messenger of Gaia*, and *What have you done with Rhyllien?* were also frequently displayed.

"At least they spelled your name right," Dan noted.

"What's going on?" Rhyll's face reddened at what she saw.

"Q, can we have volume?" Nala asked.

"... crowds gathering, all chanting the name of the mysterious redhead seen here at the Samhain Festival at Stonehenge." The news showed clips of Dan's video interview, Rhyll kneeling with the lions and walking among the druids. "Miss Rhyllien Ellis hasn't been seen since. Many now believe the corporates might have her in custody."

The images changed to other venues. One in particular had a large, snow-capped mountain as a backdrop.

Rhyll gasped. "That looks like Mount Shasta. I've not even been there yet."

"I said you'd be a force to be reckoned with. Now you've got a world-wide following!"

Rhyll fell back into her chair in disbelief. "Why?"

"Isn't it obvious?" Nala knelt beside her. "Your message is getting out, being listened to far more than what my grandfather could have achieved. He'd be proud of you."

"Proud? Of me?"

"Of course, for doing what he couldn't: saving the lives of those that matter, the ones that will live on as stewards of the living world, the future guardians of nature."

"I ... I don't know what to say ..."

Nala looked to Dan for a moment.

"There's plenty of time. I'm sure something will come up," he said.

"In the meantime, you've got the fourth diamond to place," Nala encouraged, scowling at Dan.

"Yes." Rhyll wiped her face. "It'll be all for nothing if I don't." She moved her eyes from the screen and looked out the viewport, and changed the subject. "Unless Stradjek is a complete imbecile he must know you guys are no longer captives. That leaves my mother as the only possible leverage. He'll no doubt wonder where I've been for the last few days. Once we get this done, we should go and get her."

Nala reached out to hold her hand. "I'm sure she's fine with Cat and Ileana as protection."

"The speed this thing goes, we can get to Brazil in no time," Dan said as they raced across the Mediterranean, leaving Greece and the Aegean coastline behind.

"If only we found this craft in the beginning, we'd be finished by now," Nala said.

"But think of all the fun we'd miss out on," Dan joked.

As the craft began its descent, the coastline of northern Africa came into view with a glimpse of the vast expanse of the dry interior to the southwest. At no stage in any of the flight did the passengers feel the slightest bit of motion.

"Looks like the ride's over." Rhyll climbed out of her chair.

"It was spectacular." Nala stood and stretched.

Seeing the look of disappointed on Dan's face as he stood beside her, Rhyll was waiting for him to say: "Can we go again?"

"What's that?" Dan asked instead, pointing to a large green area below.

"That's the Nile delta, the food bowl of Cairo, not that there's much left with the sea level rise and tidal effects."

They swiftly approached the sprawling city.

"And there are the pyramids," Nala said, standing on Rhyll's other side.

"29.9772962 North, 31.1324955 East. The Giza Necropolis. We have arrived."

3

SKY CITY SAT ON TOP OF THE ORIGINAL SPACE ELEVATOR ANCHORED
to Galapagos Base. Being the hub of off-world travel and transport, it was now a hive of activity. The top floor of the orbital
was permanently inhabited by some of the most powerful
people on — or off — the planet.

ICON, one of the most influential corporations with its financial resources and interests with the lunar and Mars colonies as
well as asteroid mining, could afford a permanent headquarters
here.

Theodore Howards, Chairman of the Board, greeted
everyone and called the meeting to order as soon as everyone
was seated. Eleven of the thirteen senior board members of
ICON sat around the large table. Facing them was a bank of
monitors; two absent members were on screen. After some
general business, Howards turned to the man on his right and
said, "Lucas, what's next on the agenda?"

"Gentlemen." Lucas cleared his throat. "Item 8 — Volaris and
Tyrone Stradjek's foray into off-world mining." He then activated another monitor. It blinked on, but only a dark silhouette
appeared.

"Surely this is but a minor concern?" said Joseph Hart,

licking his lips nervously. From his position at the other end of the table, he added: "Akin to a mosquito attacking an elephant."

"Normally I'd agree, but Stradjek has stumbled onto a plan to rid himself of competition; preliminary results suggest that it's very effective," Lucas said. "Joining us this morning is the informant we have in Stradjek's employ."

"Mosquitos do kill more people than anything else on Earth," the new informant said. "At least they did, until this death wave hit." The monitor only showed a silhouette of a male against a plain white background.

"What do we call you?" Howards asked.

"*Bill* will suffice, Mr Howards."

"Very well, Bill," Howards agreed. "What's Stradjek doing now?"

"Other than selling off his assets on Earth, I have information Stradjek has sent a valuable red diamond to his next target."

"Valuable diamond? Is he crazy? Why is this a concern to us?" Howards asked.

"His next target is Joseph Hart. The diamond should have arrived by now."

The members turned to Hart, who laughed nervously, almost spilling his wine.

"Is this true, Joseph? Have you received it yet?"

"I was going to tell you. It arrived a little over an hour ago." Hart pulled the massive red gemstone out of his pocket. "I haven't been able to have it appraised yet, but I'll gladly accept this trinket of Stradjek as his farewell gift. Perhaps we can dispose ourselves of him now?"

"Leave him, Hart, he's of no consequence. This diamond, however ... May I?"

Hart reluctantly passed the gemstone along. It had to go to several other members first before it reached the most senior member at the far end of the table.

When it reached him, Howards looked at it with intense

interest. "Bill, do you know the value of this *trinket*?" he asked, addressing the shaded figure on the monitor.

"Until this emerged, the most expensive red diamond had been found in Australia. It sold for over twelve million dollars — almost a million a carat — but that was US dollars, many decades ago. This stone is better quality, with a weight of forty-eight grams, which comes in at two hundred and thirty six carats. In Global Credits, it's a cool half-billion."

"Astounding! And Stradjek simply *couriered* it to Hart? Is he mad?"

"Mad? Not quite, but he's determined to gain a strong footing in off-world mining."

"And how does he propose to do this? If it's bribery, he's gone about it the wrong way." Howards chuckled, as did the other members. With obvious reluctance, he handed the stone to Lucas, and it was passed from man to man until it reached Hart, nervously waiting for its return; the little man at the end of the table barely controlled himself from snatching it when his neighbouring board member took too long with it.

"Sir, have you heard of this death wave?" Bill asked.

"Of course. It's very bad for business. Chaos in the streets, and people aren't going to work. Whole factories are idle and deserted!"

"This red diamond Stradjek sent, it belongs to the girl believed to be involved with the death wave."

"I, for one, do not subscribe to this nonsense. Is this the one who recently escaped from Area 53? How could she possible own a half-billion GC diamond?"

"I can confirm it is the same girl, sir. The first time these stones came to our attention was when she was found wandering the Erdany mine in Brazil. It turns out she had seven diamonds of the exact same size. The only difference is their colouring."

"Seven! But it isn't a diamond mine," one of the other board members exclaimed.

"Tin, mainly, and not much of that," the dark figure nodded.

Howards cast his eyes over a document Lucas had handed to him. "I have the initial report. Area 53 suffered a series of electrical failures — surely she was lucky and simply took advantage of the situation. Street smart she is, I'll give her that," he said.

"She paid a visit to Niels Franke in Niger to retrieve the blue diamond Stradjek sent earlier. The Niger operation is now finished, and according to our intelligence, Franke and his staff are also dead."

"Has this been verified?"

"On the news reports and by hearsay from the locals. They are now evacuating the area. Understandably, no one is willing to approach in person. Drone footage indicated evidence of bodies—"

"*Evidence?* Not the *actual* bodies?"

"There are signs of wild animals scavenging for easy meat."

"Hmm. And these other diamonds?"

"When we got hold of her, there were four left—"

"Is this girl simply losing them?"

"According to her recent news clip, she has a purpose. We don't know for certain, but believe she has left them at specific locations in the UK and Brazil, possibly Lake Titicaca."

"We lost men there, and earlier in a small town near the mine."

"That would be São Lucas. Whenever she feels threatened—"

"Then why is she still breathing?" Hart spoke out. "Surely she's a threat to us all — a clear and present danger. She should be dealt with accordingly!"

"It's okay, Joseph. There's no way she can get to Sky City without us hearing of it," Howards reassured everyone, then spoke to the vid. "Bill, I gather you're referring to this 'nature's retribution' crap? This death wave?"

"Retribution, yes; crap, not entirely. While millions have died mysteriously, there is much evidence indicating her actions are in fact saving people. When she accomplishes her task, people have been surviving the death wave — some around Lake Titicaca and in Manaus ... Those druids at Stonehenge, as well. Equally, when she's in danger, there have been mysterious repercussions."

"Superstitious mumbo-jumbo." Howards drummed his fingers on the desk in annoyance.

"Can't argue with the facts, sir."

"What else can you tell us about her?"

"Not a great deal more than what I'm sure you already know. We lost her when our hoverpod was hacked, while she was enroute to Giza ... but I suspect you know that already."

"Very well. We'll take your advice into consideration. Thank you." Howards motioned for Lucas to end the call. The silhouette of Bill blacked out. "So, gentlemen, what are your thoughts?"

The board members conferred with one another.

"Let's go around the table. Chang, why don't you start?" Howards said, speaking to one of the members on the vid.

"I trust increasing profits. I don't see that happening in this situation," Chang stated.

"Phelps?"

"The same. How can we be cowering from a mere teenage girl? We have many resources to utilise. I say we do."

As each member spoke, it became clear the feeling of the board to prevent any further interference into their organisation's activities was mutual.

"So, then, we vote on what to do with this child: let her continue, or end this charade?"

The hands went up. The decision was unanimous.

"So be it," he said after the count. "Lucas, tell me what happened in England."

"Sir, we believe our Reaper was somehow infiltrated with water. Drone footage shows a large rend in its side. The moment the circuits shorted the droids also stopped, as they are linked."

"What can we do in future?"

"You must understand, sir, these are highly sophisticated vehicles designed for the most arduous conditions—"

"And yet, two ordinary civilians crippled one along with its entire compliment of androids."

"There are only so many contingencies we can plan for and still have a functioning machine."

"Therefore hacking into the Reapers in Cairo will have little benefit?"

"We proved we could do it when we hacked into the hover-pod, but in Cairo we have a different problem; nothing electrical works there now. For some inexplicable reason, there's blanket interference."

He paused, then turned to another aide. "Phillips, tell me what happened in Area 53."

"They suffered a series of power fluctuations. It started small, then grew in size until the Sedona Airport substation blew. We believe a UFO had been activated and caused the trouble there, sir. It flew out shortly afterwards."

"Not caused by the girl — this Rhyllien?"

"How could she, sir? She's just a kid. We've the best scientists working on this—"

"And this *kid* just happened to be in a position to use this situation as a means of escape? Does that not strike you as coincidental?"

"As to that, sir, Area 53 — much the same with Warehouse 13 — deals with many strange phenomena of which we have little understanding. Not forgetting the EMF shielding is mostly experimental, there were also irregularities with some of the suits shorting out."

Howards pushed his chair back and paced. "Alright, what we did learn about this girl in the short period we had her?"

"She has an extremely dense bone structure, with a unique crystal matrix throughout; her blood type is now Rh-null whereas it used to be A-positive—"

"Can that happen?"

"Never, sir. Neither can the bone structure—"

"So the results are flawed? Cross contamination, perhaps?"

"There are less than sixty people on the planet with this blood type, and none of them are in Area 53. There was no chance of cross contamination."

"Continue."

"Medically, sir, that's it," Phillips finished his report. "Oh, this informant, Bill, is not entirely correct about the girl — if anything he said can be believed."

"How so?"

"You can imagine how stressed out or threatened the girl must have been to endure the research and probing, yet there is no death wave there."

"Isn't that down to our EMF shielding experiment?"

Phillips paused. "That is a possibil—"

"And what explanations have you for the impossibilities? What do they say about her age?"

"While any records of her we can find have her born on the first of April 2005, all indications are her chronological age is sixteen-and-a-half years."

"A fifty-three-year-old teenager? Preposterous. They obviously have the wrong records; incorrect blood type, incorrect date of birth ... and you call these top scientists? Am I surrounded by amateurs?"

"Sir—"

He waved Phillips silent and turned to Lucas. "I want a list of possible scenarios to deal with Cairo within the hour." He then addressed the members. "Once I've seen all the data, I'll determine the next step and let you know. In the meantime, do what you deem best to fortify your position on your holdings, just in case. There are too many *irregularities* occurring. While we have ample resources and capital, these evacuation orders are a hindrance to further profits. We must devise a way to get back to normalcy; failing that, how to make the most profit out of it while we can."

"And Stradjek?" Hart asked.

"A gnat. We'll squish him soon enough, but he's no concern. Good day, gentlemen. I'll keep you appraised of any more developments. Lucas, stay." Howards watched the board members as they stood, nodded and left individually or in pairs; Chang and Phelps on comms went dark.

Howards turned to his aide. "This informant going by the name of Bill. He is trustworthy?"

"As far as any informant is, yes sir. His intel has been one hundred per cent accurate so far."

"Do we know who he is yet?"

"Working on it, sir. Possibly to do with Volaris, or one of their close underworld associates. He's quite canny. What we do know is he's well-resourced."

"That's good. If we have trouble finding him, others will also — and that is his main benefit; we could use him to slip into other organisations if he works out. However, it's not Tyrone who concerns me; I know his grandfather. Viktor's a wily old coot. We need to get a handle on his situation."

"He's a resident at Inspiration, the lunar colony now. His ailment is getting worse."

"Keep tabs on him. Let me know his movements: who he sees, who he speaks with."

"Very good, sir."

4

THE ALIEN CRAFT LANDED WITHOUT A BUMP, SCARCELY KICKING UP any dust, in the centre of a large roundabout between the pyramids and the Sphinx. Abandoned market stalls surrounded the perimeter.

The massive pyramid was in front of them, and the edge of urban sprawl was about a kilometre away to the east, starting at the base of the slope.

"Fuck. There are Reapers down there!" Dan said, his gaze sweeping across the arid scene presented on the curved wall inside the spaceship. "Can you enhance the image and scan left to right?"

The built up area suddenly blossomed with detail as the view zoomed in and drifted to the requested direction.

Nala clenched her hands when the androids and eight-wheeled vehicles appeared on the screen. "We had a very bad run-in with Reapers previously," she told Rhyll.

"They aren't moving at all," Dan noted.

"There would be a lot of bodies. Living this close to a chakra point, there'd be little warning." Rhyll sounded forlorn, looking dejected at the potential loss of life.

The minutes dragged on with no visible change.

"Let's get this over with." Rhyllien turned towards the door, which irised open.

Even though it was mid-morning, the air was hot and dry. Dan and Nala felt it the moment they crossed the threshold, and took a while to adjust. Rhyll didn't appear disturbed at all as she scanned the surrounds, noticing the ramp was already extended.

Numerous flocks of birds circled in the sky, and they could hear cawing echoing in the otherwise empty, silent streets.

"Are they vultures?" Nala asked.

"Those are." Rhyll pointed to a gathering of large birds further downhill feasting on several bodies. "But there are a few hawks and eagles. It's a smorgasbord for them."

"That's gruesome." Dan pulled his camera out and started taking pictures. "Damn. My camera's playing up," he said after checking the settings. "It's not uploading to the cloud."

"Perhaps it's something to do with the area. We've experienced electrical interference in all other death wave sites," Nala suggested.

"Never this bad, though," Dan griped.

"Maybe that's why the droids aren't moving," Nala suggested.

"That can't be a bad thing."

Rhyll abruptly turned towards the northeast. "Do you guys hear that?"

A drone appeared in the distance. It was heading directly for them.

"I'm pretty sure it would have noticed the UFO," Dan stated.

"We should find cover and see what happens," Rhyll said.

"Probably too late," Dan said, shrugging his pack over his shoulder.

The trio ran to the nearest stall, its cloth awning providing shade and a level of concealment. They peered out from under the canopy as the drone came closer and hovered above them.

"It doesn't appear to be paying attention to us at all," Rhyll said.

"More like it's focused on the spaceship," Nala agreed. "See how the camera lens is not pointing directly down?"

Dan's camera clicked several times.

"Let's get behind this display table before we're seen," Rhyll suggested, as they would be in full view of the drone when it was on the other side of the UFO.

"I wonder how high this death wave or the electrical interference goes?" Dan squinted as the drone began circling, the nose remaining centred on the alien craft.

"Shit. Here come more drones," Nala pointed.

From various sections of the city, several dots in the sky were making a bee-line to their location.

"We'll be spotted for sure now," Rhyll muttered.

They tried to conceal themselves as the drones drew closer.

"Hey, look. The UFO's leaving!" Nala called out.

Rhyll and Dan glanced over the display of gourds to see the spacecraft moving to the south, the drones following but barely able to keep up.

"Q's drawing the drones away!" Rhyll exclaimed.

"He is?" Dan looked at her. "Do you think he's bailing on us?"

"Hardly. When does Q ever go so slow? He'd be in space in seconds if he was really going to leave us."

"We better make the best of the diversion, then." Nala crawled out from her hiding spot. "Where to, Rhyll?"

"Where to?" Dan interjected. "Look where we are." He pointed. "I say we go to the Great Pyramid. It's closest."

"It might be the closest, but the entrance is on the other side. The nearest entrance is Khafre's pyramid." Rhyll pointed.

Dan turned to where she was looking. "Or we could go there instead."

"Great idea, genius," Nala said as Dan helped her up.

The sky was clear of drones now, and no familiar buzzing sound came to their ears.

"Ready?" Rhyll waited for their nods, then started jogging to the dark entrance on the pyramid's northern face. "Watch your footing. The area isn't level."

They covered the two hundred metres quickly, aided by a section of the paved pathway closer to the pyramid's base. Rhyll stopped. There was an entrance directly in front of her, and another about a dozen metres up the wall.

Dan grimaced at the threat of an arduous climb over massive stones, and said: "Please choose the lower entrance."

"Do you know where this goes, other than *down?*" Nala asked, looking tentatively inside the entrance. The sunlight only made an impression for a short distance, after which was only darkness.

"This is Vyse's entrance. It's supposed to go to the queen's burial chamber, and further in it rises to join with Belzoni's entrance, which angles down to a junction."

Dan brought up his camera. After a few attempts, he swore. "Damn battery's flat now. Damn this electrical interference!" He was about to sling it over his shoulder but Rhyll reached out her hand for it.

"Anything that's stopping those Reapers and droids is fine by me." Nala looked back towards the city skyline just in case.

Rhyll held the camera while she spoke. "I can't say how long the interference will last, but they might reactivate once it stops. Like back in Brazil: anything electrical stopped when the death zone spread, but batteries can still be charged."

"So no tablet, no phone, no internet for you, Dan," Nala teased.

Dan considered. "Nup. I can deal with that. In fact, we could use the opportunity to smash open every Reaper van and hose water into it. That *will* stop them."

"It's still a good plan." Nala nodded with a smile.

"How long will we be here?" They both looked to Rhyll.

She handed back the camera, the light indicating full charge. "I don't know. I thought the previous chakras were at Stonehenge and the tor, but they turned out to be only in the *vicinity*. The one constant to all this is everything's been underground. I'm feeling nothing here to indicate where to go. There's so much interference we could be here for days. I'm not familiar with the area at all, and my father was always wary of traps and misdirection in some of these ancient sites. Perhaps we'll find something in his notes."

"Nothing in your visions?" Nala asked.

Rhyll shrugged. "I haven't had any visions for a while, and nothing I see here gives me a hint. Perhaps a good look around will trigger a clue. We may as well start here." She pulled out a phone from one of her many pockets, activated the torch function and started down the angled passage cut into the bedrock. "At least I can recharge the batteries when needed."

Although covered in drifts of sand, a long, narrow wooden ramp had been installed for the ease of the tourists to descend into the earth, but the uncomfortably low ceiling forced everyone to stoop. At the bottom, just beyond a portcullis, the passage levelled out. Nala and Dan groaned as they stood upright, even then Rhyll didn't seem to be in discomfort as she moved on.

"I hope that damn thing stays up," Dan mattered looking over his shoulder.

About ten paces later the corridor expanded, with a rectangular alcove on the left about five metres long and two metres wide. Opposite was another descending ramp.

"Far enough away from outside that there's no sand here," Rhyll noted as the others followed. They descended another ten metres before the passage ended at a larger chamber. She shone her torch around the interior, but it was completely empty and devoid of any hieroglyphs or inscriptions.

"Is this where Khafre was buried?" Dan winced, arcing his back slowly as he looked around with interest.

"Some refer to it as the Queen's chamber, but nothing was found. By the time this place was searched — at least on record

— it was empty. In Khafre's chamber there's writing indicating it was looted centuries beforehand."

"Early tomb raiders?"

"You could say that," she replied as she walked around the walls, noting the salt encrustation.

"Just like in the passageway." Dan ran his hand over it. It was cool to touch, leaving minute salt crystals on his fingers. He wiped the residue on his trousers.

"Do you feel anything different?" Nala asked, watching her walk around.

Rhyll shook her head. "If anything, it's worse."

"Worse?" Nala asked.

"It's hard to describe. Louder ... or stronger. The point being, I've still no idea."

"I guess it would have been too easy otherwise."

Dan laughed. "Well, we wouldn't want *that* then, would we?" He was using his phone torch now.

"Let's move on. I don't know how long Q will be away, and we've still got the other chamber to check."

They followed Rhyll. At the top of the ramp she turned right and continued along the horizontal passage. After about twenty paces it angled up. This ramp levelled out into a longer tunnel junction.

"If you went that way you'd end up at the higher entrance. If you went that way you'd end up at the higher entrance." She pointed to where another ramp joined the tunnel. It was blocked by a large, rusty grill.

The walk to the main chamber was less spectacular than they expected, although there was the carved granite sarcophagus at the far end, picked clean after all the years of public scrutiny.

"There's no change here, either," Rhyll informed them as they curiously examined the sarcophagus.

"Would your father's notebook have any clues?"

Rhyll considered for a moment. "Not that I noticed, but Mum

would have a better idea: she knew how he thought. I think we should head back and see what's happening out there."

Other than Dan's torch going flat and grievances about the low height of the passages, the return to the lower entrance was uneventful. They waited in the shadows, listening and watching for any sign of the spacecraft's return.

"Can you guys hear anything other than the wind?" Rhyll asked after a few minutes.

The others shook their heads.

Rhyll lay down on the ramp and glanced out carefully, but there were no drones in sight. "Nothing, and no flying saucer yet," she confirmed as she used the railing to help stand, then climbed the short distance to the surface. Nala and Dan were a few steps behind her.

Since they weren't in a hurry, Rhyll described what they were seeing. "That's the western cemetery, also called mastaba tombs." She pointed to a network of weathered rectangular structures several metres high and twice that in length, all with sloping sides and flat rooves. There were rows and rows of them.

"Who's Mastaba?" Nala asked.

"It's not a 'who', just the name they gave that particular design."

"Are we heading to the Great Pyramid now?" Dan asked.

"What do your father's notes say about it?" Nala asked.

"Not too much more than what is publicly known, as far as I can tell. I've only been here once, and that was years ago; who knows what new discoveries they made in the last few decades. Let's see ... in 10,450 BC the pyramids lined up perfectly with the stars in Orion's belt, and this will recur every thirteen thousand years; many of the measurements correlate with the golden number and pi — before we knew of them; it has eight sides, not four—"

"Eight?" Dan squinted at the pyramid bathed in harsh sunlight.

"Each face is slightly indented precisely down the middle, forming the only eight-sided pyramid."

"By accident?"

"Highly unlikely all four faces being so precise was an accident. You can't see it from the ground, only from the air at dawn and sunset on the spring and autumn equinoxes when there's a shadow cast for a few minutes, which gives more weight to the theory they were built for astronomical reasons. Has anyone been able to replicate the building method yet? Last I heard, modern engineers had no clue."

"There's been no change on that front as far as I know," Nala answered.

They kept walking, only the sound of boots to be heard.

"Here's Q." Rhyll pointed to the horizon, where the shape of the UFO raced towards them. "Let's go." She started jogging.

In moments, the craft landed. The door spiralled open as the ramp extended.

"So good of you to return," Dan huffed as he ran inside.

"It seemed logical the drones would follow me, allowing you to move unnoticed," Q informed them. "However, the drones will return shortly. Did you have success in your mission?"

"There's far too much electrical interference; I couldn't sense the crystal platform," Rhyll said, explaining her failure. "I think we need to get my mother from São Paulo. She knows the Necropolis better than me. She might have better luck deciphering my father's notes."

As Rhyll was talking, the ship rose. It was soon in the upper reaches of the atmosphere and angling to the southwest. The yellow, arid Sahara Desert swept beneath them. In a short time the barren landscape turned into a band of verdant green as the craft shot over the southern coast of West Africa. The South Atlantic Ocean glistened below.

Rhyll turned to Daniel. "I noticed you're limping."

"Blisters, from running in wet shoes. They were healing okay, but I reckon I've opened them again; probably those stupid ramps."

"While we have a moment, give me your foot."

"I probably should change socks." He started to undo his laces.

Rhyll laughed along with Nala. "You can keep your boots on." She put her hand on his foot when he lifted his leg up and rested it on her thigh, closing her eyes for a few moments.

She surprised herself, when she finished after only a short period.

Dan placed his foot back on the deck and took a few experimental steps, nodding to Rhyll. "Feels like the blisters are gone."

"Perhaps they weren't as bad as the previous injuries I've had to deal with, but I'm feeling as weary as then."

"Maybe it's like training: the more you do of it, the better you become at it," Nala offered.

"Either way, I'm not complaining." Rhyll moved over to her pack, rummaged around and pulled out a flask of water. It was nearly empty. "Anyone happen to have any water or food? The last thing I ate were stale chips."

"I think we have something." Nala hopped up and went to her pack.

While she waited, Rhyll realised her mother would have no idea what was happening.

"Q, would it be possible talk to my mother, Professor Imogen Catherine Ellis? She should be in the Sau Paulo Univers—" Rhyll stopped, hearing the same hiss she'd noticed when the alien first contacted Dan and Nala, then her mother's voice came over the speakers.

"Hello?"

"Mum? It's me!"

"Rhyll! Darling ... Where are you? I was so worried—"

"I'm okay. I've got Nala and Dan with me, too." Rhyll quickly gave Imogen a brief rundown on the recent events. "When can you be ready to leave? It won't be safe for you now."

"You know I have Cataleya and Ileana here to look after me?"

"Hey, chica," Cataleya called in the background.

"I do, and that's fantastic, but we need your help in Egypt."

"Egypt?"

"I'll explain later. We're on our way to pick you up."

"Pick me up? How?"

"Something else I'll explain later."

"She'll be ready whenever you get here, chica," Cat said with confidence in the background.

"Are you at the uni?" Rhyll asked.

"Yes. Cataleya insisted I move onto the campus where the security makes it a bit safer."

"I have her location," Q's disembodied voice said. "We should be there shortly."

"I'll call when I arrive. See you soon."

Nala handed her a bottle of water when she finished talking. Her eyes lit up when Dan handed her a muesli bar.

"Sorry it's not organic," he said. "I grabbed them as we left the resort."

"About that ... You both still need to tell me what you guys were doing in Sedona in the first place."

No sooner had the three returned to their bubble seats to talk when the craft began angling down, but between them, her two friends managed to give a very brief account of what had happened to them after the kidnapping incident.

5

In an amazingly short span of time, South America's landmass loomed. The ground grew in size and detail as the craft descended. The lights of the city steadily brightened as they approached, while the speed on the screen quickly reduced.

"Precise location of previous communication device has been obtained," Q informed them.

As the city grew larger, it looked like they were aiming for an area slightly west of the central district.

"That must be the university sector." Rhyll stood and began pacing the narrow area behind the three seats. "Can I contact her again?" she asked Q.

The familiar hiss started.

"Rhyll? Why doesn't your number appear?" Imogen's answered the call.

"You'll see soon enough. Is there a large car park or clearing near you?"

"Yes, both—"

"Great. We'll be there in a couple of minutes."

"But campus security—"

"Won't see us coming. Watch to the northeast, and look up."

The passengers saw a river snaking through the city. A busy

roadway came to dominate the screen, followed by a group of buildings.

So sudden it almost made them jump, the vista on the screen changed from what lay ahead to a vision of the ground directly below, giving the impression the craft was about to crash.

A dimly lit car park adjacent to a field resolved from the pre-dawn gloom. Three figures were standing on the edge of the field, staring at the alien craft as it landed in front of them.

"It's going to get cramped in here," Dan noted, seeing the three extra packs.

"I'm sure we'll cope, even if we all have to stand." As Nala leant forward, the chair gently nudged her upright.

The door was barely open before Rhyll ran outside and down the ramp. She was in her mother's arms in moments.

"Nice haircut, *chica*," Cataleya greeted her with a friendly ruffling of her short red curls. To Ileana, she nodded in the direction of the craft. Together, they warily walked towards the ship and left the reunion in peace.

"Olá," Nala called from the rim of the craft. Dan stood behind her and gave a quick wave.

The two Brazilians stared at the dark ship in disbelief.

"Great to see you both again," Dan greeted them as they filed up the ramp.

"And you, *cabrão*." After a brief hug with Nala, Cataleya slapped him on the back.

Ileana did the same with a soft chuckle.

"Cabrao ... That's good, right?" Dan asked Nala quietly over her shoulder.

"Oh, yes. Best buddies now." Nala winked at the two newcomers. "Shall we go inside? See where we can stow your gear." Nala stepped past Dan and led them in, laughing at their expressions when they saw the interior.

"*Caramba!*" Cataleya exclaimed, stopping abruptly.

"*Que isso?*" Ileana walked into Cat, knocking her forward.

Dan stood in the doorway behind them, joining in with

Nala's mirth. He decided it wise to remain silent though: the girls were armed.

"This is bad on the eyes," Cat said, regaining her composure swiftly.

On the screen, they could see Rhyll and Imogen talking animatedly as they walked to the ship.

"Hi, Dan," Imogen said as Rhyll carried her pack up the ramp.

"Hey there, Mrs E," Dan greeted her. He moved to the side to allow them to enter.

"Wow," Imogen said. "Impressive." She walked in as Cat and Ileana moved further from the entrance.

"Lovely to see you again, Nala."

"Likewise, boss."

Imogen chuckled. "And that's the last time you call me that."

Nala came forward and gave her a brief hug. "Right you are, Imogen."

"So then," Imogen started. "Off to Egypt you say? It won't be pretty. I've been in contact with some colleagues there. The city is so close to the affected area, it wiped out many people before the authorities got into action."

"We know. We were just there, and it was bad." She told them of the tragic scene and about electrical interference. "I've not been able to locate where to place the diamond. I need your help; you know Giza far better than I."

"Not because you missed me?"

"What? Of course I—" Rhyll started, before realising her mother was teasing.

"The trouble is, with Nala and Dan escaping, and me MIA the last couple of days, Stradjek will be nervous. I'm thinking we need to find him and grab the remaining diamonds before he does something stupid. Both tasks are a priority and can be accomplished quickly now we have use of this ship."

"And where did this thing come from?" Imogen gazed curiously around the now crowded cabin.

"A not-so-secret base in Sedona, Area 53," Dan said.

"We've plenty of time to explain on the way." Rhyll turned to the console and spoke to the ship. "Are you able to locate a Tyrone Stradjek? He works for an organisation called Volaris."

The familiar hiss started.

"No. Stop! I don't want to call him," Rhyll blurted. "I only want his location."

The hiss faded.

"There are seventeen Stradjek's locata—"

"What the hell is that?" Cataleya regarded the darkness where the voice seemed to emanate with suspicion.

Ileana also looked uncomfortable surrounded by all the inky blackness, her hand tense on the gun in the holster.

"Oh, you mean the voice?" Rhyll thought how to answer. "Think of it as voice-activated AI."

Dan grinned. "Yeah, that's *Alien* Intelligence, not Artificial Intelligence. We're calling it Q."

"You *are* in a UFO, after all," Nala added.

"Sorry. This is all ... *arrepiante* ... creepy." Cat put her hands in her pockets and tried to relax.

"It is," Nala agreed, "but wait until you get into space!"

Q continued, "Fifteen Stradjeks are located in what you call the Red Alliance; one is off-planet and the other is in the Central Commonwealth States, Miami."

"I was in Miami on assignment last month," Dan said.

"When was the last time you heard from him?" Imogen asked her daughter.

"Before I went to Niger. When I left, I only spoke briefly to some guy who sent the Giza coordinates to the pod. Then I fell asleep and woke up in some lab in Area 53," she told them. "Q, are you able to retrieve messages from my lost phone? It's been several days, I'm sure he would have tried to contact me to gloat ..."

"What was the numerical code for this device?" Q asked.

"I don't understand." Rhyll looked to Daniel to shed some light.

"Your phone number, perhaps?" Dan offered.

"Oh." Rhyll recited her number.

"Observe the console," Q said, as a list of her missed calls and messages were displayed in bright blue. "The call is also traced to Miami."

"Must be where Tyrone is, at Volaris HQ," Dan surmised.

"How do I read that new message?" Rhyll pointed to the last unopened message. The date stamp was 19:43 on 1 October. "That's several hours after the pod was hacked and hijacked."

Text popped up below the date, in slightly darker blue: *Well done on your first task. I'm very surprised you actually went through with it. I'm texting due to the weak signal your way. By the time you read this, Joseph Hart should be in possession of your red diamond. The coordinates will be entered into the pod's AI. I'm looking forward to hearing about the success of your next task. Think of the lives you'll be saving.*

"Anyone know who Joseph Hart is?" Rhyll asked.

"I heard the name on the news recently," Imogen said. "Hart's a board member of ICON, and he's got something to do with mining. I think his company found an asteroid with extremely rare metals."

"That sounds right. Stradjek wants me to remove mining competitors."

"ICON keep cropping up. Another bunch of bastards that need attention." Dan turned to Cataleya and Ileana. "I'm pretty sure they were the ones financing those who tried to kidnap us in Manaus, and attacked us in the Andes."

"Then they should definitely be paid a visit," Ileana said, echoing Dan's sentiments.

"Not sure what we can do as they are a huge corporation."

"'If you think you're too small to make a difference, try sleeping with a mosquito,'" Cat quoted.

"David and Goliath-like?"

"Exatamente." Cat nodded.

"Well, they all have it coming, especially Stradjek after what he's done to us," Dan said.

"Okay, we now know where Stradjek is, what about Joseph Hart?" Rhyll asked her mother. "Did you hear that on the news report?"

"I've no idea about Hart, but I've been keeping tabs on Volaris since Ken — since you disappeared — and know their head office is in Miami and that Tyrone lives here too."

"Q?"

"There is a Joseph Sebastian Hart, of EpiQ Minerals, located in Sky City. EpiQ Minerals recently put a claim on asteroid *Specter6*."

Imogen nodded. "That sounds familiar."

Dan whistled. "Wow! That's the platform on top of the space lift."

"Space lift? Sky City?" Rhyll questioned. "Please assume I haven't been absent for three decades."

"Hey Q, better help us out here," Dan asked.

The alien explained. "A space lift it is a capsule capable of travelling along a tether between a planet's surface and an orbiting platform. There is a tether comprising long filaments of graphene nano-tubes woven together to form an extremely strong, tensile cable. Many of these cables braided together form the main tether of the structure. A platform — your Sky City — positioned in a geo-stationary orbit 35,786 kilometres above the equator is optimal."

"And the base tower is off the Galapagos Archipelago," Dan continued. "It's a sort of elaborate space station. I've always wanted to see it, never thinking I'd get the chance."

"Why the Galapagos Archipelago?" Rhyll asked. "Last I heard it was the last most pristine areas in the world. Don't tell me they've ruined that, too."

"More than likely," Nala stated.

"There are very strict ecological rules with severe penalties for any breaches; it's one of the few policies that has a majority world government agreement. Its location is because of its access to North America, and being on water is more geopolitically stable than other equatorial landmasses," Imogen said.

"A surprising accomplishment for a primitive culture, both technically and politically," the alien said.

"We will go wherever we need to go," Cataleya said firmly.

Rhyll looked gratefully at them all. "Thank you. I know it's a lot to ask—"

"There is no need for thanks, *chica*.' Cataleya put her hand on Rhyll's shoulder. "I said before, what you can do is awesome and unusual. You do what you do; we can help in other ways ... even *with* Dan."

"Gee, thanks." Dan smiled good-naturedly.

"We'll teach you everything you need to know," Ileana said to him.

"Dan did take out a Reaper van single-handed," Nala said, coming to his defence. "And managed our escape from another Reaper attack."

"I hear those vans are quite formidable and hi-tech." Ileana slapped his shoulder. "Well done, amigo."

Dan blushed at the unexpected compliment.

After a brief discussion, they agreed once the diamonds were retrieved, they could forget about Stradjek and ICON and concentrate on placing them around the globe. Once accomplished, none of them would be a concern.

"Deserved or not, I'm not comfortable with seeking revenge," Rhyll stated. "The death wave will soon be taking out those who don't fit into the Earth's future."

A COUPLE OF HOURS LATER, THE UFO HOVERED A THOUSAND metres above Miramar. Even late at night, there was a lot of traffic on the main roads, but the urban areas were generally much quieter.

"There certainly are a lot of roads," Nala observed. "Are those dark lines canals?"

"Much of the area is reclaimed from the everglades," Imogen said. "They're used to help drain the water."

"Maybe they should've built elsewhere instead of ruining a massive amount of wetland area. Imagine how much wildlife habitat has been destroyed." Rhyll stood tense, staring at the view on the screen.

"The foundation for all this started back in the late 1800s," Imogen told them. "It was farmland, mostly sugarcane. The canals were initially built for irrigation, but what Dan said is truer nowadays. And over the last couple of decades, levees were established to keep the rising sea levels out, and large pump stations near the coast to remove excess stormwater."

"And where exactly is Volaris?" Cataleya asked, looking closely at the street layout. She wasn't interested in the history, just ensuring the next task was accomplished successfully.

"Here." Imogen pointed after a pause to get her bearings. "On the corner of Red Road. *The Reagan Turnpike*."

There was a largish structure, though not a skyscraper, surrounded by parkland and smaller buildings.

"All this water looks like a marina." Nala pointed to the surrounding urban area. The canals led to larger, darker areas.

"With so much water, developers thought it a great sales pitch for everyone to have waterfront views," Dan offered. "My uncle has a place much like this, but further south."

"We need to work out the best way to get there, and then to get away." Cataleya considered the layout of the terrain.

"With these canals, and that one so close, maybe we can use a boat?" Ileana suggested.

"It's a thought." Cat studied the view more. "Do we know where Stradjek lives? Is he nearby?"

Q's voice surrounded them. "His last location is the Carlton-Ritz Key Biscayne on North Club Drive."

"No doubt asleep, considering the time," Dan suggested.

"No, I have his residential address as Ocean Tower Four. He must be socialising."

"He lives in an apartment building? Any precise location?" Cataleya asked.

"East side. Top floor."

Dan agreed. "Knowing Stradjek, he'd have the penthouse."

"An apartment is good. People rarely lock their balcony doors," Ileana stated. "Penthouse is even better. How far is it?"

"Thirty four kilometres southeast."

"We will need him for access to the HQ. His keys, pass ... something."

"My digging into Volaris over the years has given me some idea of what you can expect. This organisation is also heavily involved with major crime — the arts and antiquities is a facade for legitimacy. Getting into the HQ won't be easy."

"If only we had some sure way of overriding high level security systems ... perhaps something like a Quantum Molecular Assembler."

"You want to take Q?" Rhyll asked.

"It was just a thought. You need these diamonds to save lives."

"Are you able to help, Q? We've asked so much already ..."

"I sense the urgency in you and in your task. Part of my programming is to ensure safety. If I can assist, I will."

"But haven't you got to repair yourself?"

"For this, my minimal functionality will be more than sufficient. And you forget, I was old before your kind left the trees. This is but a blink in my existence."

"Great." Dan smiled in relief.

"So, we don't need to visit Stradjek at all?" Nala asked.

"Looks like it. Mind you, it would be nice to see the look on his face when he discovers the diamonds missing."

"Okay, that should make things easier, then," Cataleya said. "Only one operation, not two. What can this ... What can Q do?"

"We're so primitive in comparison," Dan said, "that as far as we're concerned, it can do anything."

———

THE CRAFT LOWERED TO A METRE OFF THE VOLARIS HQ ROOF, hovering in much the same manner as it had in the Area 53 hangar.

"Q, what can you tell us about the interior layout?" Cataleya asked the alien.

"Five levels above ground; two floors below ground. The rooms are located both east and west side with a passage running north to south down the centre. There are stairways at both ends of the passage. The upper two floors are on a completely separate power supply, with its own security."

"That's weird, doubling up on security. I can understand redundancies, but two completely separate systems?" Dan pondered aloud.

"Is there anything indicating a vault?" Cataleya asked, after taking the details in.

"The sub-basement has a section of thick metal construction." Q zoomed in and highlighted the area in question.

"I reckon that's it," Dan said.

"Génio." Ileana smirked, punching him.

"Why does everyone do that?" Dan muttered, rubbing his shoulder.

"Hmm." Cataleya ignored the other two. "Nothing on the upper floors?"

There was a pause. "There does appear to be a small area with increased level of security on the upper floor. Observe."

The screen enlarged. On the schematic, they could see the vague outlines of rooms, furniture, and the heat signals of the occupants.

"You mean those?" Cat pointed to a large, dark area.

"It looks like a safe," Ileana offered.

"I agree," Cat nodded. "Not large enough for what I would call a vault. The sub-basement it is, then." She turned back to the group while Ileana prepared the weapons. "Nala, I checked your records. I see you've had National Service. Are you armed?"

"Only with this, but it's out of ammunition." Nala pulled the kidnapper's gun they'd collected from her pack.

"A Glock 9mm. Good, our ammunition will fit." Cataleya dug into a pocket of her pack and handed her a full magazine. "A gun out of ammo is a paperweight."

"I thought I was staying here," she said, accepting the clip.

"You are. This is in case there is trouble," Cataleya continued. "Imogen and Rhyll are also staying — too vital to risk any injury."

"What about me?" Dan asked with anticipation.

"I'm told you are good with tech?"

"If not, you should remain here too."

"I believe I am sufficiently qualified in tech, but I will require mobility," Q said.

The Brazilians stopped, looking uncomfortable when they realised one of them would have to carry it.

"Looks like Dan is coming after all," said Cat, her normally commanding voice sounding relieved.

"Welcome to the party, amigo," Ileana chuckled.

Dan's face paled, looking equally discomforted at the prospect of his hand being covered like Rhyll's.

"We'll be fine in here," Rhyll said to reassure everyone, knowing some of the abilities of the alien craft.

"Then make sure you stay inside. You too, Professor Ellis." By her tone, no objection would be considered.

Dan hadn't moved yet, still coming to terms with being relegated to carrying the alien slug.

"Daniel?" Rhyll tapped him on the arm. "Put your hand on the console," she encouraged.

Dan complied, cringing at the initial contact.

Cat and Ileana gasped, seeing the slug-like motion of the dark lump across the console.

"Does it hurt?" Ileana asked, when Dan's hand was black and glistening.

He shook his head, apprehensively looking at his gloved hand.

"Once we depart from the craft I will only be able to contact the entity known as Daniel," Q's voice resonated around the interior.

"H-how?" he asked, then his face went white and his eyes widened.

Rhyll laughed, realising he was hearing Q in his head.

"That's ... great ..." He said the words, but his tone didn't reflect the sentiment.

"That reminds me." Cat fetched one of the commlinks from her gear and handed it to Rhyll.

"Do any of the stairways go to the basement?" Ileana asked.

"They do not. The stairs stop on the ground floor. Access to the basement is via a separate stairway at the centre of the ground floor."

"And no doubt full of guards," Ileana said.

"There are several life forms present on the fourth floor," Q confirmed.

"You know this?" Ileana asked, surprised.

"Evidently. There are also two entities presently descending the north stairway and two on the ground floor."

Cataleya looked impressed. "That is very handy to know."

"Patrols," Ileana noted.

Dan studied the black glove again. "I told you Q was amazing."

"Can you tell what other sort of security they have other than guards?"

"I will need immediate contiguity for precision," Q said to them.

"It will need to be much closer to determine what the security measures are," Imogen translated for them.

"Right. We will go now," Cataleya ordered, unholstering her gun. "I would very much like to get in and out unseen. Daniel, do what you can to be a ghost."

"Do I get one of those?"

"No." Cataleya pivoted and walked outside into the night.

His face pale enough to look like a ghost, Dan followed.

Nala smiled and waved to him as he walked by. "If you don't come back, I'll take care of your bag for you," she whispered, winking.

Ileana walked behind Dan, chuckling.

GAINING ACCESS TO THE LOWER LEVEL WAS SURPRISINGLY EASY. Q was able to notify them if any patrols came close, and hacked into any of the security systems hindering their progress.

Cataleya remained alert. She didn't like things when they were too easy.

When they reached the foyer, Q cut the lights long enough for them to stealthily make their way from one stairwell to the next. This entailed moving close to the Security desk where one guard was punching buttons and turning dials while swearing at the patrol via his radio. The other guard hurried off — presumably to the switchboard.

Once the trio were safely downstairs, the lights returned.

They reached the vault shortly after, and Q again proved invaluable by disabling the security systems.

When the vault doors swung open ponderously on its hinges, they were completely taken aback by its emptiness.

"Merda!" Ileana hissed.

_____

6

"HAIL THE LIGHT."

"Let the Light be your Guide," Williams intoned the response.

The male voice was electronically modified and the screen darkened to hide identification, the way it had always been ever since these conversations started twenty years earlier. Never in that time was there a hint as to who he was speaking with or where they were calling from. The only thing he knew was the speaker was part of the Illuminati, and was well-resourced both financially and with intelligence.

"Benjamin, what progress have we made?"

"Sir, the real diamonds are safe and their replicas are now ready to go on display," Williams addressed the silhouette on screen, licking his thin lips. This was the only person after his mother to call him Benjamin.

"No one has noticed the forgeries?" the voice asked.

"After their initial appraisal, Stradjek hasn't let anyone near them—"

"Except you."

"Correct. He trusts me."

"And you've done well to cultivate his trust. I can foresee a bright future for you with us."

"My only wish is to serve the Light. You've done much for me since my father's death. It's the least I could do."

"And the diamonds? Where are they now?"

"Enroute to Sky City as we speak."

"Via fast messenger?"

"That would create too much expense and interest, especially to Sky City. It's in a normal, corporate pouch via the space lift. It should be there in the next day or so."

"Security measures?"

"Other than a tracker and clear warnings of the consequences of interfering with corporation property, there's a contact poison on all the diamonds and the interior packaging."

"And when it arrives? What then?"

"Once the package passes through the scanners, I will get notification. I'll signal via the normal, secure channel. This way there will be no direct connection to you and the package should things go awry."

"And this contact poison? How does one avoid it? What is the antidote?"

"You could always use gloves and a gas mask. However, get someone you trust to drop the whole parcel in a strong alkaline solution before unwrapping. Immersion for thirty seconds will nullify the poison's effects."

"And what is its effect?"

"Subtle but lethal. The poison is both colourless and odourless. Once it comes into contact with the skin, the victim will suffer dizziness and shortness of breath, and heart attack within the hour — give or take a couple of minutes, depending on his or her health."

"And the antidote?" he repeated.

"If it can be applied before the dizziness, adrenaline straight into the heart. But if applied after the dizziness, there's still an eighty per cent chance of death."

"Impressive. I hear you now have the ear of the ICON board."

"I ... I felt feeding them certain intel would aide in the plan."

"I approve, though I should have been notified. You are not the only asset we have, and your actions could have compromised us."

Williams bowed his head. "My abject apologies. I will consult with you in future. It will not happen again."

The screen went blank and silent.

Williams wiped everything down, checked his watch, then left the boardroom to join the auction reception.

———

"HARRISON, HOW ARE YOU? SO GOOD YOU COULD MAKE IT," Tyrone said for the umpteenth time that evening. If he wanted their credits, he'd have to put up with their platitudes and false smiles.

"This is a damn fine function," Harrison said. "You still got that fellow, Williams? I can take him off your hands if you want."

"Yes, still here. Yes, he did a great job in organising all this. No, you can't have him."

Harrison moved closer. "What's this about unveiling the most incredible diamonds the world has ever seen?"

"Ah." Tyrone winked. "You'll have to be patient." He looked at his watch. "Thirty-five minutes to go, then the auction will commence. But the diamonds aren't on sale, just on display."

"Strad, my boy, *everything's* for sale—"

"Good evening, Mr Harrison." Williams stepped over to save his boss. "So pleasant to see you again. I should point out that Georgette is already hovering around the buffet."

"Is she now? I better save her from temptation, or that'll be yet another diet gone to waste. She'll blame me, of course!" Harrison ambled through the crowd to his wife.

"Thanks for the rescue, Williams. I might get some fresh air for a minute."

"A happy boss is a paying boss."

"Good point. I'll keep that in mind." Tyrone headed to the balcony, grabbing a champagne from a tray on his way.

Guests had been arriving for almost an hour, dressed in their finest clothes and latest fashions for the paparazzi waiting on the curb in front of the entrance. The newspapers had already called it "the function of the decade", so everyone who was anyone was in attendance: movie stars, sports personalities and even a few rock stars, as well as TV celebrities. Stepping from their limousines, they were surrounded by crowds of both professional and amateur photographers seeking the picture of the year.

As long as they bring their credchips, Tyrone thought as he stepped outside into the fresh air. He had to admit, like Harrison had noted, Williams *had* done a fine job in organising the fundraiser.

Security was tight, with strict orders: interviews were to be undertaken in the foyer outside the reception hall; no cameras were allowed inside before the function's commencement. Most of Volaris' artefacts had been cleared from the vault for this fundraiser. The function centre of the Carlton-Ritz was ideal, and the top floor function room was certainly large enough.

The convenience of this particular venue was a delight to Tyrone — a mere stone's throw from his apartment. He turned from the view of the Atlantic and casually gazed across to Ocean Tower Four. The shattering of his champagne flute on the tiles made the patrons jump and stare at him. Some of them turning to follow his shocked gaze.

There was a large, dark shape hovering above the nearest building. A woman screamed; her partner fainted.

Stradjek ran inside, bumping into the guests as he barrelled his way to the nearest security man.

"My apartment's being broken into. Get men over there now," Tyrone almost shouted. "Move, man!"

The guard immediately issued orders over his comm. "They're on their way, Mr Stradjek," he said.

"What is it, sir?" Williams rushed over, briefly looking at his watch.

"Th-there's a ... a p-pod hovering over my apartment." Tyrone couldn't bring himself to say *UFO*.

"A pod? Over *your* apartment?" Williams quickly followed Tyrone as he raced back outside.

Below, several security men raced across the roadway and gardens separating the buildings.

Many of the guests were now strolling outside to see what the fuss was about. The large balcony was becoming crowded.

"This is like that one we saw at the Area 51 museum," one of them said over the loud mutterings and gasps of shock.

"Nah. This one is smaller and darker," another argued as the guests started recording the sight.

At first, Stradjek thought the screaming and yelling he heard from inside was from some of the more sensitive guests seeing the alien craft.

Then the gunfire started.

———

"THERE'S NOTHING HERE," RHYLL SAID, EXASPERATED.

"Then where could they be?" Dan asked, equally stumped. "We searched the entire vault; it was empty. This was the next best place." He joined Nala, who had slumped onto the plush lounge.

"Which would explain the minimal guards," Cataleya said, coming back from searching the other room.

Rhyll closed her eyes and relaxed. The alien craft was a marvel in so many ways, but much like when she was inside

Area 53, she had been completely shut off from feeling the Earth and nature. Now her senses could run free.

Everyone waited quietly, Cataleya by the balcony and Ileana covering the front door, even though Q would no doubt let them know if anyone was approaching.

"They are ... I can't tell." Rhyll slowly turned one way then the other, like a compass finding north. "I can't sense them at all!" Her frustration was evident.

"Maybe this will help." Nala held up a brochure. "It was on the coffee table."

"The Carlton-Ritz?" Dan asked, incredulously.

The group moved closer to see the glossy page with the details of the Volaris Corporation Fundraising Auction.

"That explains many things," Cataleya started.

"Yes, why there was nothing in the vault; why the guards here were so lax—"

"It might explain why the diamonds aren't here, but not why I can't sense them. Especially if they're so close," Rhyll said.

"Maybe some security measure?" Dan suggested. "You said in Area 53 your senses were cut off. Could he have them in a sort of Faraday cage?"

"I guess we'll have to go and find out."

"Surely Stradjek wouldn't sell them?" Nala asked. "He knows what will happen if you don't finish your task."

"To be honest," Imogen said, "he would." She smiled knowingly at their disbelieving looks. "He's a greedy sod. It probably occurred to him he could become much richer if he sold them to the highest bidder. If the money is high enough, you'd be surprised what greed can do to even the most reasonable person."

"And don't forget, Tyrone wasn't all that reasonable to start with," Dan added.

"It means little to him. He will assume Rhyll will still track them down. The result will be the same, people will die, but he pockets a tonne of credit. I've also read an article he's moving to the moon. He's already sent his grandfather there."

"So that's what his alternate plans are," Rhyll wondered out loud.

"What a low-life," Nala muttered.

Shots rang out through the darkness.

Cataleya was instantly alert. Her gaze swung to the Carlton-Ritz across the road. She pulled a monocular from a pouch strapped to her utility belt. It took a moment to focus, but then she saw the disturbance.

"Looks like a robbery," she informed them all. "I see ... five ... eight .. at least ten armed men. Four are moving the guests to the balcony, the others look like they are bagging the display artefacts."

"Can you see the diamonds?" Imogen asked.

"I cannot see much detail, but if the diamonds are there, they will find them." Before anyone said anything else, she added, "Back to the ship, pronto."

Ileana checked the corridor. When it was clear, she waved them to follow and jogged to the stairway.

"Q says people are coming," Rhyll called out as she left the apartment.

As Ileana opened the exit, she jerked back hastily. The door-frame splintered with the impact of several bullets.

"Shit." She slammed the door. There was no way to lock it.

"How many?" Cat asked.

Rhyll replied, "Five in the stairs; four in the lift."

"Police?"

"Security," Ileana said.

The elevator chimed.

"Back to the room!" Cat knelt by the wall and took aim at the lift halfway down the corridor.

Nala was at the rear, then Dan and Imogen. Rhyll, who had been behind Cataleya, pivoted and ushered them back.

The moment a leg appeared from the elevator, Cataleya shot

the kneecap. The man screamed and fell, his gun firing as he hit the floor. She dived to the carpet as an arm came out and fired random shots along the passage.

Cataleya snapped a shot back as the prone gunman was dragged back into the lift. From her new angle of sight, there was no one visible. She fired several rounds down the corridor to dissuade further attacks. Now clear of obstruction, the lift doors slid closed.

Splintered with a burst of bullets, fragments of the exit door rained down on Ileana. She ducked briefly, then blindly fired several shots through the door as she scuttled backwards, eyes rivetted to it.

"Ileana. Keep moving back. I have both covered." Cat's gaze flicked between the elevator and the exit. When she saw the door handle move, she fired a few rounds at it, and heard a howl of pain in response.

Ileana made it back to the room. "Your turn," she called from the doorway.

Cataleya turned and, keeping low, scrambled to safety as Ileana fired two shots.

"Now what?" Dan asked.

Rhyll answered, "Q can get the craft level to the balcony, but he needs to be in contact with it."

"Off you go, then," Cat ordered. "Imogen, go into that room until I call you."

"I—"

"I'll escort her," Nala offered, grabbing Imogen's arm. "C'mon, boss. You haven't paid me for this week yet."

Rhyll headed out to the balcony to see how she was going to climb up.

Dan looked flustered, unsure about anyone climbing to the roof from a tenth-floor penthouse. "How are you getting up there?" he asked her.

"I'm not, actually." Rhyll held Q, now a lump in her hand. "Remember, this was your idea," she said to it. Reaching back, she lobbed the alien blob as hard as she could up and over the edge of the roof.

"Alien tossing?" Dan looked where Q had disappeared over the roofline.

"It needs to be in contact with the ship; it said the hull would suffice."

"No arguments from me." Dan shook his head.

"Stay here and wait for the ship. Call us when it's down." Rhyll raced back inside.

"Sure thing." Dan nodded, then turned to observe the robbery across the road while he waited.

"Ship's on its way." Rhyll re-entered the apartment to Cat's surprised look.

"Rhyll—" Cat started.

Rhyll touched the nearest wall. "I've darkened the corridor."

"You can do that, too?"

"Apparently." Rhyll shrugged. "Something I picked up in Area 53. Like I know those guys from the stairwell are now coming slowly along the corridor."

Silently, Ileana opened the front door a crack. It was true, the corridor was in darkness, even emergency lighting was out. She reached out and blindly fired several shots, then closed it hurriedly. There were grunts and thuds as men fell or dived to the floor. Shots were fired in return, but the solid door stopped anything penetrating.

"That maybe gives us a minute or two. What about the men in the lift?" Cat asked.

"I shorted the lift doors as well. They're trapped for now."

"Oh ... great." Cataleya looked at Rhyll's right hand. "And Q?"

"I tossed it up on to the roof. Climbing would be too slow and hazardous."

Cat nodded. "Did it—"

"The ship's here," Dan called from outside.

"Good. Before we go, give us a hand to block the door." Cat

indicated the lounge. Together, the three of them managed to slide it against the front door, then they moved out to the balcony.

They met Nala coming out of the other room with Imogen.

Outside, the ship hovered next to the balustrade, the ramp extending to the tiled floor.

"We should have done this the first time," Dan called from the circular entrance.

"A lesson learnt for the next time," Rhyll said as she entered. "Where to now? The roof of the other building?"

"We can't go to that balcony, either. Those people will freak out. They'll run inside and possibly get shot. *We* might get shot!" Dan said.

"The roof is my recommendation also," Cat decided. "Then down the stairs as we did here."

Without effort, the ship slowly spun as it glided the short distance to the building on the next block.

7

"What's the plan, boss?" Ileana asked.

"Rhyll?" Cataleya passed the question on to the young girl.

"Me? Oh, Q might have an idea."

"The balcony has automatic shutters for severe weather; I have closed them. The guests are now safe, separated from the robbers. I have also deactivated the lifts, security systems and lights."

"I thought it needed to be in direct contact with the building?" Dan wondered aloud.

"Not when inside the ship. I can utilise the ship's equipment to do things remotely," Q told them.

The UFO was now above the roof of the resort building. They saw the fire escape directly in front of the ramp.

"There's no one manning the stairs," Rhyll informed them. "Finding the diamonds is the priority."

"And Tyrone?"

"Only if he gets in our way. With the diamonds back in our hands, and everyone here safe, he's reduced to a minor hindrance."

"He wasn't so minor before," Dan argued.

"We know things now that we didn't know earlier. I've learnt a few tricks, too."

"And it's like Dan said in Somerset, we'll be safer inside the death zone where he can't touch us."

"We have to come out eventually—"

"Enough," Cataleya intervened. "Worry about that later. As Rhyll said, we get the diamonds. If anyone gets in our way, we'll use our guns."

"About time we had some fun," Ileana joked.

"I've got a taser, too," Rhyll remembered, and fished it from her pack.

"Good. Ana, Rhyll and I will go down. You three remain here," Cat said to Nala, Imogen and Dan.

As they gathered on the roof to enter the stairway, they heard sirens getting louder.

"Q says there are drones approaching as well." Rhyll raised her hand and spoke to Q. "I think you should stay up here and monitor the situation. Using the ship's sensors will give us all an edge."

"I concur." Q oozed to form a lump in her palm, and she tossed it back through the door.

Ileana took off her comms unit and tossed it in after it. "So it can hear what is happening, unless it can read minds."

Rhyll shook her head. "No. Like me, it can sense energy fields, but the ship augments this so much more."

"I'm coming too," Imogen spoke up. "Volaris has stolen many ancient artefacts over the years. Unless anyone else here is a professor of antiquities, I need to look for myself."

"How about you come down after we make things safe?" Cataleya suggested.

"No time, not with the police coming. I'm sure we'll cope." Imogen moved confidently to the door. "There's only ten of them."

Nala and Dan came down too.

With no time to argue, Cat held her tongue, nodding to Ileana to lead. "Nala, you stay at the rear with Imogen."

"Sure thing. If anything happens to her, I won't get paid." Nala moved closer to her boss, giving her a nudge. "I should ask for a raise." She winked as she drew her Glock.

"What are my orders?" Dan asked.

"If anyone shoots at Imogen or Rhyll, your task is to get in their way," Cat hissed over her shoulder, "or you can keep Q company."

Ileana opened the door and moved into the dim stairwell. One after the other, the group moved in.

"You didn't strike me as the mercenary type," Imogen said softly to Nala as they stealthily followed.

"That's more like my sister's type," Nala muttered.

"You hardly mention her," Dan said over his shoulder as they moved into the stairwell.

"There's nothing to say. She's the exact opposite of me." Nala's tone indicated it wasn't open to discussion.

As Q indicated, the stairway was clear of people, but they could hear loud talking further down. Ileana swiftly moved down the stairs. Behind her came Cataleya, Rhyll and Dan, then Imogen and Nala.

"The function room doors are also locked electronically. I think the men are calling to each other through the door; there are two out in the passage," Ileana whispered.

"Hand me that taser," Cataleya whispered to Rhyll. "And stay here." As an afterthought, she gave Rhyll her commlink. "So you can speak with Q."

Ileana holstered her gun and took the taser Cat passed to her. As quiet as a mouse, the two soldiers slipped through the door into the dark corridor. There was the faintest crackling sound. A few gunshots were heard, but muffled.

A heartbeat later, Cat's head popped back. She motioned for them to follow.

The plush, carpeted hallway stretched half the length of the building to a point where an exit sign indicated another set of stairs. There were two double doors leading into the function room and an elevator opposite each door. Two men lay unconscious against the wall.

"How close do you need to be to accurately sense the diamonds?" Cat asked quietly, standing by the nearest door.

"I should have been able to do it already. I still can't."

"How many men inside?"

"There's twelve people — three of them are women," Rhyll responded after the briefest pause.

"Male or female, makes no difference," Ileana whispered from the other side of the doorway.

"We have one smoke grenade each," Cataleya informed them. She held the one from Ileana's pouch as well as her own. "Can Q unlock this door?"

Cataleya dropped to her knees by the doorframe.

"Done," Rhyll replied a heartbeat later after making the request

Ileana carefully twisted the handle. The talking grew louder as the door opened enough for Cat to lob the two grenades in. Ileana closed the door while Cat crawled back. A moment later, there were two loud pops. Shouting erupted, followed by a lot of coughing and wheezing.

Sneakily, Ileana held the taser to the door handle. Seconds later, when someone grabbed it in an attempt to escape the smoke, they got a powerful shock. Ileana ducked back as someone fired a couple of rounds through the door.

Cat donned goggles and nose filters. "We'll give it a minute." Her voice took on a more nasal quality.

Rhyll moved along the wall between the two doors. "Still sensing nothing."

"Stay put." Cat nodded, then tapped Ileana on the shoulder.

Ileana, also wearing goggles and nose filter, pushed the door open again. Stealthily, the pair snuck into the dark interior. The only light source was from the streetlights, but they were well below the level of the balcony. Several dark figures were moving around in the thin smoke.

As they entered, some of the smoke wafted into the corridor. Dan, being the closest to the door, moved back quickly, suppressing a cough. With the door now open, a lot of the previously muted coughing and swearing could be heard clearly. There was the sound of zapping from the taser, then gunfire followed, as well as screams of pain.

"No smoke alarm?" Nala asked.

"All electronics have been deactivated," Rhyll reminded her.

A shadow, hunched over and coughing, suddenly staggered through the doorway into the passage.

Before he could raise his gun, Nala jumped forward and clubbed him on the back of the head with the butt of her pistol. The figure slumped to the ground, dropping his gun and a bag. Nala pocketed the gun, standing by in case someone else came through.

Dan nervously pulled the bag away from the man's grasp, then handed it to Rhyll. She moved back with her mother and they carefully went through the contents, searching for their stolen artefacts.

Rhyll looked up suddenly. "There are a number of people coming up the stairs."

"Which stairs?" Nala turned to face the nearest exit.

"Both. I think they're police."

"Right ... so we're trapped!" Dan stated.

"We've got an alien ship and a million-year-old alien as an ally. I wouldn't give up yet."

"Psst," Cataleya called from the door. "Better come in quickly if you want to look for your diamonds." She handed them each some torn tablecloth. "No spare goggles."

"Police are coming up both stairs," Rhyll said to Cat as she passed.

"Shit!" Cat cursed as she continued to cover the downed robbers. "Better hurry then, *chica*."

Covering her mouth and nose with the cloth, Rhyll held her mother's hand and guided her through the darkness. She could sense the bodies on the floor; most were breathing. Two were not.

"Q, I'm sure you know there are people coming up the stairs," she whispered into the commlink. "We're trapped unless you can work out our escape route."

"There are several hoverpods enroute also. I will evaluate."

Rhyll continued to guide her mother, though her eyes stung and started tearing up. She blinked rapidly. Searching in the darkness was going to take too long. "And can we have the lights on in here?"

Instantly, the function room lights came on. The room was chaos. A dozen robbers lay on the floor, some too incapacitated from smoke inhalation to do more than wheeze, some lay unmoving, but breathing, others not at all. There were a couple of men in suits, clearly patrons shot earlier by the robbers.

Several tables had been knocked over, spilling artefacts onto the floor. The buffet table was a complete mess, as was the floor around it. The sound of crunching underfoot came from broken champagne flutes.

She saw an elaborate display cabinet, now smashed, and glass shards littering the floor. Now they could see, she let go her mother's hand. Rhyll stepped past a prone woman, groaning and coughing next to the cabinet. The robber was bleeding from her thigh wound. Beside her lay a bag.

"Help," she croaked as Rhyll picked up the bag.

Rhyll was fleetingly tempted to heal, but with the police closing in she simply couldn't risk it. "Help is on the way," she said to the woman.

Wiping at her stinging eyes with the back of her hand, Rhyll then reached into the bag, wondering why she still felt nothing when she withdrew a diamond.

"Shit!" What she held was cut crystal, but not diamond. Rhyll looked for her mother. Not all the artefacts had been bagged, and she saw her mother trying to shift a table.

"This is one of the pieces your father had with him ..." Imogen blinked several times, her eyes bloodshot and streaming at the smoke.

Rhyll helped her shift the table.

"Yes, I remember him showing me that piece!" Rhyll said when her mother picked it up. "What is it again?"

"It's known as the *emerald tablet*. Or one of them." Imogen handled it reverently.

"Exit via the window in the hallway," Q said in Rhyll's earpiece.

There were gunshots outside and a yell from Cat. The other doors to the function room vibrated as someone pounded on it.

"Is that the diamonds?" Imogen saw the bag she was carrying.

"No. They're fake!"

"Fuck. How?"

"I don't know, but we can't stay!" She helped her mother back to the door they'd come through.

"Wait." Cat held her arm up. She reloaded as Ileana sent a volley of shots down the hall to dissuade any police venturing out.

"Q said to exit via the window at the end of the corridor," Rhyll told her.

"Go!" Cat started shooting to cover their escape.

With her mother in front, they walked quickly to the window Q had mentioned. The ship was outside, the ramp extended through the broken window, but not quite reaching the floor. Nala was already at the base of the ramp, and Dan was standing on the hull.

Nala helped Imogen up, then Dan grabbed her hand and led her inside.

"You next," Nala told Rhyll.

"But—"

"No buts."

Rhyll jogged up the ramp. From the side of the hull, she could see the near end of the balcony. The stranded guests who had been cowering there were both shocked and mesmerised by the UFO hovering alongside the building, only metres from them.

As fate would have it, she recognised Tyrone Stradjek from images her mum had shown her. She flicked a finger at him before entering the ship. "Arsehole," she fumed.

"They're clear," Nala yelled to Cat.

The two soldiers started backing down the hall, randomly shooting at the exit doors.

They ducked as a volley of shots came their way. Cataleya grunted and fell against the wall.

"Cat!" Nala screamed, racing forward to help, firing down the hall.

"You take her, *chica*," Ileana called. "I will cover."

Nala handed Ana her gun so she could better carry Cataleya. "Rhyll! Dan!"

Moments later, her colleagues were there to help. They grabbed an arm each while Nala bent to take Cat's legs. The three carefully carried her up the ramp and inside to safety.

"*Peguem isso, filhos da puta!*" Swearing in her native tongue, Ileana opened fire with both guns as she moved backwards.

8

INSIDE THE SHIP, THE TRIO GENTLY LAID CATALEYA ON A CHAIR. SHE was unconscious and her breathing was shallow. Rhyll ripped open Cat's blood-soaked shirt to examine the wound.

Blood oozed out from a hole below the right side of her torso

"Looks like the bullet's still inside," Rhyll said, after gently feeling her back for an exit wound. "Lucky. I don't sense it has punctured her lungs or vital organs."

"Can you heal her like you did me?" Imogen pleaded.

"This is much worse than anything I've attempted—"

"You have to!" Ileana almost shouted, hearing the last words as she backed into the control room.

Imogen took her hand. "Ileana, you know Rhyll will do whatever she can. We all will." She led her away to the other side of the control room. The door spun closed the second she entered.

"As a Quantum Molecular Assembler, I can assist in this."

"What do you mean, exactly?" Dan asked. "This is a human being: a living entity."

"We are all matter — whether organic or inorganic," Q stated.

"You can heal her?" Rhyll asked.

"Yes, and eradicate the projectile. You need to place me over the wound."

Without hesitation, Rhyll collected the alien blob from the console and placed it over the injury. The bleeding slowed, then stopped, as Q spread over the area briefly, then seemed to shrink.

"How do you remove the bullet?" Dan asked, but Q didn't respond.

"Let it work," Rhyll advised.

With the ramp retracted, the ship was now hovering about ten metres from the building. Bullets peppered the craft.

"It's okay. Those shells are harmless." She watched outside through the screen. Two cops stood at the broken window with high-powered rifles trained on the ship. The guests on the balcony milled about, most staring, pointing and recording the ship with their devices while others tried to force the balcony doors open, to no avail.

Rhyll searched the crowd for Stradjek, spotting him talking earnestly to another man about the same height and with similar hair colour.

Several hoverpods now circled overhead, powerful search-lights trained on the ship and the immediate area.

"This will be on the news for sure," Dan said beside her. He knew there was no use trying his tablet or phone: the UFO's hull cut off all signal. "Is that who I think it is?" He followed her gaze.

Rhyll nodded. "He doesn't like the limelight, but mum sent me some images she'd found. He's a bit older now. He looks like his father."

Ileana was on one of the chairs, head in her hands while Nala and Imogen comforted her. Cat remained, unmoving. Q was doing whatever a sentient, million-year-old alien artefact did.

It was a waiting game. Rhyll let out a huge yawn. She rubbed her face and sat on the floor, leaning against the front of the navigation console.

"You must be buggered after everything that's happened." Dan stifled his yawn and checked his watch. "Shit, it's 1:34am. We should all be buggered. I know I am."

"The diamonds are fake," Rhyll told Dan. "That's why I couldn't sense them. Nothing to do with elaborate security." She handed him the bag.

"What? That bastard!" Dan looked at the coloured crystals, but couldn't tell the difference. "I'll have to take your word for it."

"We have to get Tyrone. He must know where they are."

"That's not going to be easy, considering where he is, surrounded by all these people. The cops will get to the balcony eventually, even if they have to cut open the doors to do it."

"We can't do much while Q is working on saving Cat, and I certainly don't know how to fly this thing." Rhyll yawned again.

Dan looked around. "This is one really weird ship," he said, not for the first time.

"The whole situation's weird: aliens, UFO's, Mother Nature killing the population, and only a bunch of crystals to save it."

"Not to mention these stupid greedy fuckers trying to profit from it."

"It is done." They all heard Q as the dark lump dropped to the floor.

Everyone sat up, energised to hear how the healing had gone.

"How is she?" Rhyll jumped up despite her weariness, and collected Q, placing it in the console. Although it didn't seem to mind, she felt uncomfortable talking to it while it was squirming on the floor.

"She will survive," it replied confidently.

Imogen, Nala and Ileana moved closer to Cat. Ileana wiped her cheeks with her sleeve and knelt beside her friend, reaching for her hand.

"How'd you get the bullet out?" Rhyll asked.

"I did not. It is being broken down to its molecular level and will be excreted in due course."

"How—"

"As a Quantum Molecular Assembler, I can also disassemble."

"You said *being* broken down. You mean it's still happening... inside her?"

"Correct. A miniscule part of me — you may know them as nanites — remains inside her to continue the work."

"What!" Nala said, shocked. "Part of you?"

Rhyll put her hand on Nala's shoulder to calm her. "Thank you very much, Q. What you did is amazing."

"I do what I can. There is much activity outside. Do we need to be somewhere else?"

"We do, but we still need to get what we came here for." She told them all what she'd told Dan. "The man that can help is on that balcony, but we can't get to him. It would be too dangerous."

"We could bring him here."

"We can? How?" Dan asked, turning to Q.

"Tractor beam. It is complicated to explain, but an intense force field — an attenuated linear graviton beam to be more precise — that manipulates gravitational forces to push or pull objects."

"Right ... it *is* complicated," Dan said in awe.

"Who is the target?" Q asked.

Rhyll stood by the console. "Him." She pointed to a fair-haired, middle-aged man.

The angle on the screen changed as the ship moved slightly.

A dull beam of green light stabbed the darkness, roving over the balcony. The people below tried to move away in fear when they saw it, but they were hard up against either the wall or the railing, with nowhere left to go. When Tyrone realised it was hunting him, he tried to run but the moment the light found him it intensified and he began to float, legs moving uselessly. He started flailing his arms wildly.

They heard no sound, but his open mouth indicated his dread.

"'Beam me up, Scotty'," Imogen quoted.

Rhyll laughed, but the others looked puzzled.

The man Stradjek had been talking to minutes earlier grabbed him and attempted to pull him down. Tyrone latched on to him with the desperation of someone drowning. Seeing them both being lifted, everyone else panicked and moved out of reach. One unlucky guest fell over the balcony, but grabbed the railing and was pulled to safety by others.

Within a minute, the pair in the beam disappeared from view.

"Where are they now?" Rhyll asked.

"Behind that bulkhead lies living quarters and the tractor room, among other things."

"But there's no door," Dan said.

"It functions like the exit door." A faint outline now appeared, indicating the area.

Ileana stood and faced the back door, drawing her gun.

"Steady, Ileana. We need him alive," Rhyll warned. "And I wouldn't feel inclined to heal him if he were shot."

Ileana holstered the gun and pulled out the taser. "How about this?"

"Much better."

While Rhyll and Ileana stood either side of the door, Imogen, Nala and Dan gently moved Cat to a seat further away in case there was trouble.

"Open it," Rhyll said.

"There is a short passage. The tractor room is two metres to the right," Q informed them all.

Silently, the door irised open. Rhyll strode in, Ileana on her heels. Nala and Dan waited by the doorway while Imogen stayed with Cat.

Another outline of a door appeared further down the short passage. When it irised open, they heard the fearful shouting of the two men. Williams bolted out. Trying to dodge them in his frantic attempt to escape, he collided with a wall, losing his footing, and Ileana zapped him before he could recover.

Stradjek was panting by the door, his suit ripped, appearing very dishevelled.

Rhyll addressed him in a steady voice. "You're about to get the same if you don't tell me where the diamonds are."

"What? They're on display in the function centre. Or the robbers have them!" Tyrone blurted, looking fearfully at the large female soldier brandishing the crackling taser.

Ileana frisked him, removing his small pistol. She tossed it to Nala, then kept a wary eye on him, though he didn't appear like much of a threat.

Rhyll showed him the replicas. "These are fake. Where are the real ones?"

"I ... I don't know. I thought they *were* the real diamonds. Ask Williams." He pointed to the unconscious man. "I hardly touched them. He dealt with them after we received them."

"After you *stole* them, you mean," Nala fumed from the doorway.

"Yeah! Remember, after you kidnapped us?" Dan said beside her. "Because *we* remember!"

"All's well that ends well." A nervous smile creased his face. "You haven't been harmed—"

"Can you believe this creep?" Dan vented.

"We'll worry about that later." Rhyll picked Q up from the floor and held it in her palm. "We do have *other* methods of getting information." She hoped his fear would send his imagination wild.

The moment Tyrone's eyes latched onto the black, slug-like alien, he blanched. "No, no, please! When he wakes, ask him."

Rhyll winked when the frightened man turned away, desperate to escape.

Nala kept a straight face, but Dan found it too difficult; he had to laugh at Tyrone's discomfort. "I can record it so everyone can see what happens when they cross us," he offered.

Williams groaned, and his leg twitched.

Ileana stepped between the prone man and Rhyll, taser at the ready.

Nala checked the weapon from Tyrone, then casually pointed it at him. "Just give me a reason."

He licked his lips nervously.

Ileana frisked Williams efficiently, but he was unarmed. As he lifted his head, she helped drag him to his feet and held him against the wall.

"What did you do with the real diamonds?" Rhyll asked him once his eyes focused.

Williams looked around quickly, slowly realising his predicament. A well-muscled woman with a taser had him pressed against the wall; he was in some dark cubicle; the young, red-haired girl who'd given them all headaches over the last month was staring at him, as were her two companions.

He tried several times to answer, but his tongue was still numb after the tasering. Finally, he said, "I ... wath ordered tho replathe them with crythtal replicath." He licked his lips apprehensively.

"Ordered by who? Him?" Rhyll pointed to Stradjek.

"No. Not me!" Stradjek yelped, stepping back.

Williams shook his head. "No. Thomeone elth."

"What?" Tyrone screeched. "I'm your boss!"

"Ordered by who?" Rhyll repeated.

Ileana shook him and put the taser close to his temple. "By applying this directly to the skull, one could get permanent brain damage."

"I can't—"

The inactive taser touched his skin. "It just takes one little push; less pressure than a trigger. I could simply bump it by accident ..."

In vain, Williams tried to turn his head away from it. "I don't know hith name! He give me orders, I deliver," he said, his speech less slurred as the numbness of his tongue wore off."

"Where are the real diamonds?" Rhyll repeated, gently pulling Ileana's arm away.

"On their way to Sky City, with a commercial courier so it wouldn't get any undue attention."

"Why Sky City?"

"Just what I was told." Williams shrugged. "Maybe that's where my boss is. I've never met him in person, only via a darkened vid."

"You aren't much of a bodyguard."

"Bodyguard? I'm his PA!"

"Not any more, you're not. You're sacked," Tyrone shouted defiantly from inside the graviton room.

"You and Volaris Corp are small pawns in a much, much larger game," Williams retorted.

"How long have you betrayed me?"

"From before you took over after Viktor. You still don't know, do you, you idiot? My father, Harry Webster, is dead because your stupid father and—"

"You two can have your exit interview another time. How can we get the diamonds? What's the address on them?"

"It's going to a Volaris deposit box."

"Maybe we should take him with us?" Dan suggested. "In case there's a trap or something."

"I can't help you—" Williams said immediately.

Rhyll nodded in agreement with Dan. "It won't hurt to have him along for the ride ... if that's okay with you, Q?"

"I have no plans."

"Wh-what about m-me?" Tyrone stammered.

"Apparently you're useless to us; you serve no purpose and you're definitely no longer a hindrance," Rhyll said in a flat voice, trying not to betray her ire. "You are irrelevant."

"Can we drop him out the door?" Dan asked. "We're only fifty metres up."

"There's always the ocean," Nala suggested.

"No. He and his kind are doomed anyway. Let him suffer longer and see all his plans and dreams perish." Rhyll took the taser from Ileana and zapped him, long and hard.

His body spasmed and contorted with the charge. He dropped to the floor, unmoving.

"That's for trying to kill my mother."

"You are far too lenient," Ileana said when Rhyll handed back the taser.

"I know, but I've killed enough people. Can you beam him down please, Q?"

The door irised closed. "Consider it done."

Dan suggested hopefully, "Maybe drop him just a metre short?"

"What about this one?" Ileana kept a firm hold of Williams.

"Q, is there any way out of that room other than via graviton beam?" Rhyll asked.

"Only this door, which he is incapable of opening."

"And is there anything in there he can damage?"

"Again, no."

"Great. Once Tyrone's dealt with, let's use it as a temporary brig. Ileana, as soon as—" Rhyll stopped when the tractor room opened, empty.

"Cool." Ileana dragged Williams across the narrow hall and pushed him in. It was too small for him to fall, but he hit the far wall with a satisfying thud.

The door irised closed, his cries of protest drowned out completely, but there was very faint thudding.

"I should correct my previous statement," Q said. "There is something in the graviton room that he can damage."

"What's that?" Rhyll asked.

"Himself."

The others chuckled.

"Easily forgiven." Rhyll smiled.

Back in the control room a minute later, they gathered around Cat and Imogen.

Rhyll placed Q on the console before sharing the details of what had happened with her mother. While she sipped water from her flask, everyone was silent. *Waiting to hear the next step from me,* she assumed.

After a few moments to gather her thoughts, she spoke. "You all heard the real diamonds are enroute to Sky City, and you know without them, and without me fulfilling my tasks, everyone on the planet will die. We'll keep Williams with us and retrieve them safely. I feel he's still not telling us everything. There's no telling where they'll end up, or who with if we don't make it a priority to retrieve them before that happens."

She turned to her mother and grasped her hand. "To save time, I think you should go to Giza with Nala and Dan. With all the electrical interference I'm useless there — other than as a battery charger."

Imogen was about to speak, but Rhyll continued: "You know the place far better than I do. It has to be somewhere underground; maybe see if you can locate access to the hidden catacombs ... You've got a copy of dad's notes to work with. With no one to stop you, I'm sure you'll find a way to locate the information to find where I need to be."

"Hidden catacombs?" Ileana asked Rhyll.

"There's much the Egyptian Ministry of Antiquities hasn't disclosed to the public; this has been the way for decades — unless something has changed since ..."

Her mother shook her head. "Other than the new administrative centre, they call it New Cairo."

"Will that be a problem?" Rhyll asked.

"No. I'm certain the information we want will be found in Cairo — the original Cairo."

Rhyll continued: "There are supposed to be catacombs under the Sphinx and corridors joining the pyramids."

"What about Sky City and the space lift?" Dan looked more

disappointed about not seeing it in the real. "You might need my tech skills."

"Nice try, but, if Q is willing ..."

"It will be moderately intriguing."

"Then any tech requirements will be catered for. Cat needs to stay here where we can quicken her healing, and if Ileana feels the inclination, she can keep me safe. Or, if they prefer, I can get them back to the GHO." She looked to Ileana.

"I'll stay with Cat, though our orders were to keep Imogen safe."

"I understand, but there's no one in the death zone to threaten Mum, and she'll have Nala and Dan to help. We need to make progress in Giza and Mum is the best candidate for that, and I have little doubt your expertise will come in handy on the space lift. Who's going to look after Williams while we're retrieving the diamonds on the space lift?" She turned to Ileana.

"I guess I could do that for you," Ileana offered. "But why not go with your mother and we'll take care of the diamonds with Williams. I can make him behave."

"I should be able sense the diamonds, whereas he could lead you on a wild goose-chase, and the longer you're on the space lift, the greater the chance of something going wrong."

"What you say makes sense." Ileana decided. "You and I will stay with Cat until she can hear what the plan is. She is my superior, after all."

"Thank you. Now, I reckon we all need sleep." Rhyll stifled another yawn. "I know I do."

9

By the time Tyrone was seen floating back to the balcony, the police had managed to force open the doors. Some of the crowd backed away, fearing the green beam would take them away as it had the host and his assistant. Many of them had their phones and tablets out recording the whole thing.

Several police hoverpods circled the area as well as many drones from various news services. A couple of the drones strayed too close and were caught within the graviton's influence. Their motors whirred with little effect, and they too began floating towards the balcony, along with Tyrone. When the beam of light disappeared, they shot into the night sky to continue their surveillance.

A couple of the less nervous in the crowd came forward and helped him to his feet. Questions clamoured all around: *Were they real aliens? What did they look like? How many? What colour were they? Did they probe you?*

His head was throbbing, he needed some air and time to get his thoughts in order. *I need a drink!* Stradjek shook free of their helping hands. When he stepped away from them, he backed into others. "Leave me—" He stopped, realising it was the hands of the cops now holding him.

"Mr Stradjek, sir. Are you alright?" one officer asked him. Beside him were several other police, one he recognised from news broadcasts as a senior officer.

"Yes, yes. I'm well, thank you for your concern. Just a bit shaken, as you'd understand." He didn't want to be here talking to these men — cops and his line of work didn't mix well — and he was in no position to be overly rude, not with a high-ranking officer looking on and all these witnesses.

"Where's your assistant? What's happened to him?"

"What?" The question threw him momentarily. The crowd gathered around him, all now eager to hear what he had to say.

"Mr Benjamin Williams. Your PA. All our witnesses say they saw him taken, but he hasn't returned."

"Oh. Yes. I'm not sure. We were separated ... He's not back yet? I do hope he's okay."

"What were they like? How many were there—"

"Easy there, sergeant. I'm sure Mr Stradjek needs a bit of time to calm himself over his ordeal." The senior officer stepped in and spoke to Stradjek. "How about we go inside where it's quieter?"

"Yes. I could do with a drink."

"Understandable." The senior officer led him inside, through the large ballroom where the fundraiser was held. There were people lying all over the place; some were guests he'd seen treated harshly by the robbers, but most were, in fact, the robbers.

"Are they all dead?" Tyrone asked.

"None of the guests." The officer followed his gaze. "And only two of the perps are dead. Did you know any of them?"

"Know them? The robbers?"

"The guests, but this could be an inside job, so if you do recognise any—"

"I've never seen them before in my life; either those unfortunate guests or the robbers."

"I see. This way." He was led into a quiet room across the corridor.

Finding a lounge to sit on, the officer brought him a bourbon, having one himself.

"Pardon my rudeness, Mr Stradjek. I'm Inspector Allen. Stephen Allen."

Tyrone nodded. "Tyrone."

"Can you run through the events this evening?"

Tyrone told him all he knew: the fundraiser was organised several weeks ago, and he talked about the artefacts, insurances and security.

"And Ben Williams knew all this?"

"He arranged all of it. Do you think he's behind it?" Tyrone knew he wasn't, but let the cop have his suspicions about Williams.

"What can you tell me about these diamonds?" Stephen showed him the brochure. "These aren't the normal items for an exhibition such as this."

"This is true. It was something I decided on in the last week. You see, Volaris is expanding into the off-world mining sector before it gets too difficult. It's a far cry from what we normally do, but my grandfather was the expert on art. I clearly am not, so decided to rebrand the corporation. I decided on the diamonds purely for the financial boost it would provide."

"I see. And the value of these diamonds?"

"Street value for these two diamonds by weight alone would be almost half a billion geecees, but at auction, I believe it would have been far greater. Diamonds of this size and clarity are normally non-existent."

"And they are real?"

"Most certainly." *Until that traitor forged them!*

"How did you come by them? I'm not in the trade, but if they were previously non-existent I think I — or my department — would have heard of them. Your grandfather ... shall we say, had a reputation."

"Nothing was proven." Tyrone took umbrage at the accusation, he had to play the part. "This is harassment!"

"I have to ask." Allen swirled his ice, waiting.

Tyrone sipped his bourbon, wracking his brain for a legitimate excuse to appease the inspector's curiosity. He was also starting to get agitated by these questions. *It shouldn't have happened like this!*

"To be honest, Inspector, I would have to ask my grandfather. He's the art expert in the family. I only became aware of them recently, when I was doing an inventory of the Volaris vault for the fundraiser. He was coy when I asked, but I didn't push it, his health being the way it is. As I said, art is not my thing, so I didn't think much of it at the time. But I will be sure to ask him the next time we speak."

"And where is Mr Viktor Stradjek now?"

"He's on the moon, at *Inspiration*. Out of your jurisdiction, I suspect." Tyrone tried not to smirk.

"Know what? Let me know when he comes back, I would greatly appreciate it."

"Most definitely, Inspector." Tyrone put the now empty glass down and sat back, holding his head. "Can we continue this another time? Maybe a delayed reaction, but I am not feeling too good at the moment."

"Yes, certainly. My apologies for pestering you after your ordeal." The inspector gave him his card. "Let my office know when it's convenient."

"Thank you." Tyrone took the card, putting it in his pocket. "You'll pardon me if I don't get up."

"Off course. Shall I send in a medic?"

"Yes. It might be for the best." Not that he wanted or needed one, but it would be expected for such an event as alien abduction.

Stephen nodded. "Until next time." He turned and left the room.

Stradjek exhaled, waited a minute, then got up and

wandered to the corridor. The inspector was nowhere in sight, but there were gurneys waiting at both lifts, the occupants cuffed to the sides with a medic and police officer as escorts. He stepped across the corridor to take another look at the function room. There were two body bags, a myriad of officers in paired groups interviewing the guests one at a time, taking notes; another officer was taking pictures of the scene.

This most important night had turned into a complete shambles! *Was Williams responsible for any of this? If not, who?*

He decided to place a call to his grandfather as soon as he could. *After all, he's the one with all the criminal connections.*

"I HAVE TO SAY, TY, I'M VERY DISAPPOINTED. YOUR FATHER WAS overly ambitious and not one to think ahead — didn't take into account the consequen—"

Tyrone paced across the carpet in his penthouse, quickly regretting calling his grandfather. "But Opa—"

"Quiet. I've not finished and don't interrupt! I've given you every opportunity to succeed, even when I had my doubts. In fact, one or two of your ideas had a hint of merit — but it was not to be. From here it's hard to tell if it's the incompetent men you're employing or if it's you ... though there does seem to be one common denominator. It's obvious this fundraiser was a complete debacle. I've already got communications from lawyers that want to sue Volaris for injuries and trauma because of it! This is a catastrophe and it lies at your feet. It's even on the newscasts! If I were you, I'd cash in those diamonds. It's probably the only assets we'll have left."

"But Opa, Williams forged them. Surely you have an idea who did this robbery."

At that moment, the static pixelated the screen.

"Ty? W-what t t wassss th aa tt tt?" The audio became distorted and garbled.

This time, Tyrone sighed in relief and cut the feed.

"Let the old fool think there was an electrical fault," he muttered. "After all I've done for him!" He paced back and forth in his apartment, racking his memory to recall what assets remained at his disposal here and now.

In a fit of light-headedness he half fell, half sat on the lounge as the mixture of alcohol and the shock of recent events took hold.

I was in a real UFO!

Tyrone clutched his head, deciding he needed another bourbon after the events of the night. An idle thought came to mind: *how did the inspector know he liked bourbon?* He poured a drink from the bottle on the table, not worrying about ice, and sat back, eyes closed, and felt the sweet burn as he swallowed the liquor. *Stop being paranoid, it was probably the first bottle he found.*

Stradjek pulled out the cop's card and tossed it on the table. There was no way he was going to help the police with their inquiries. Volaris had connections, but not enough to thwart an ongoing investigation from the Major Crimes Unit.

"Zera, play the latest local news."

He watched the monitor come to life, seeing various aspects of the Carlton-Ritz from drone vids, seeing the crowd, the UFO, and the two of them floating into it in that green light. Then the UFO virtually disappeared, suddenly travelling at lightning speed. Other channels played similar scenes, as well as some images of the function room interior.

At no stage did the redhead or her thug helpers come on screen. *Did the cops even know about them?*

Tyrone considered the happenings of the night. For the robbers to be as successful as they were indicated an inside man, whether from Volaris or maybe the Ritz. But how did the girl get a UFO, and what was that *thing* she had crawling on her arm? It was obvious now her bodyguards with their Brazilian accents brought the mother along.

The girl would probably soon have everything. She had her mother, protection, and soon would have her diamonds back. *And she has a damn UFO!*

I'm in a worse position than when I started! All for what? Volaris Corp was not what he wanted — it was what his father had craved, and it was his grandfather's pet project.

The fundraiser was supposed to be the last phase of the old Volaris Corp, to raise enough funds for the rebranding.

When he heard about the breakthroughs with off-world mining, he knew it was the next place to move into: the sooner the better. Yes, it cost a lot to start, but in nearly all cases, the pioneers reaped the biggest rewards in these ventures.

He wanted in! But to do so would come at a high cost; that was when he'd started to divest all the assets he could. Slowly at first, so others wouldn't get in on it. There were some already doing it — ICON for starters, and they were much bigger fish. Then that redhead came on the scene! Yes, he knew from the GoPro vid *she* personally didn't do it, but she was somehow responsible for his father's death. *Death by piranhas!*

Once he had destroyed the livelihoods of the savages that helped play a part, he needed something else to wreak his vengeance — and the mine *had* paid for itself initially. The last couple years it was only his determination to ruin their lives that kept it going, even at a slight loss.

And it was all worth it! He sculled his glass and poured another as the liquor's sweet tingle warmed his throat.

The troublesome girl gave him a new avenue to vent ... when he saw the diamonds. It was like the culmination of all his dreams: get those responsible for his father's death *and* make a load of credits with the gemstones, enough to get a decent foothold in off-world mining.

When she thwarted his plans time after time, he suspected a mole; he couldn't have been that unlucky. Or that incompetent.

That was all Williams' doing. "The backstabbing weasel!"

He realised now the similar looks between Williams and his

supposed father, Harry Webster. *Also dead because of their haste to steal the works of Ken and Imogen Ellis.*

Volaris Corp was just starting up back then, but it quickly became quite influential in the art and history circles, partly through the diligence, contacts and art knowledge of his grandfather, Viktor Stradjek, and partly through his dealings with the underworld.

"Opa was a masterful fence" — he savoured his drink again — "and knew a surprising amount of criminals, both renowned and unknown."

Dad wanted to impress Viktor, so when he got wind of a successful archaeologist rumoured to be on the cusp of a history-making find in the depths of the Amazon, he thought he'd get the artefact and present it to Viktor personally.

That was the last he saw of his father ... until the video.

Tyrone recalled hearing Harry Webster also left a kid behind. It never occurred to him to seek out a kindred spirit. *Where was the advantage in that?*

"Did Opa know?" he muttered into his empty glass. "Was the old coot testing me like he was always testing Dad?" Tyrone finished his drink, put the glass down and staggered to his safe, fumbling at the combination for several minutes until it finally opened.

His grandfather was on the moon and no longer calling the shots, leaving him in charge.

"So what if the old codger is disappointed? And once he goes into cryogenics, I won't have to put up with his condescending shit any more. Maybe he can go in earlier," Tyrone mused.

He brought out a few remaining items from the safe. "If that asshole has forged these, I'll kill him myself!" Slumping into the chair at his desk, he studied the Cintamani Stone in the lamplight. He knew little about it, except that the green, translucent stone was called moldavite, apparently from a meteorite. He was also glad he decided not to auction this piece off, mainly because he hadn't received an evaluation on them. It would come in very handy now, though he couldn't hope to get the market value for it. *Or could he?*

An idea came to him. Now that the cops were questioning him, it dawned on him as the most obvious answer — he would go to Inspiration to join his grandfather. Viktor was the one with the connections; he could be his fence. And there was still no extradition treaty between the Earth and the Moon.

Tyrone made a call. "Simmons?" he responded to the grunt on the other end of the line when Simmons finally answered.

"Err ... who?"

"Simmons, it's your boss."

"Sir?" came the distant response.

"Book me on the next available space lift. I need to get to Sky City!"

"Book? Sky City? But Willia—"

"I've sacked his lazy ass. Either you're up for this or I'll find someone else more competent!"

"I ... I'll do my best—"

"Excellent. I'm packing now. Don't disappoint me." He hung up and stumbled to his bedroom.

10

———

THE LIVING QUARTERS IN THE BACK PORTION OF THE SPACECRAFT WAS compact and equally as eerie as the rest of the craft, but everyone was too tired to give it much thought. Simple tasks like washing and going to the toilet would have been extremely messy, if not impossible, but for the amazing capability of the craft's furnishings to morph into various shapes to suit.

Imogen wouldn't admit it, but her age had its limitations.

Like mother like daughter, the strain on Rhyll's face over the last couple of hours, and being used as an R&D lab rat for several days had been demanding, both physically and mentally. And as her "ailment" was weariness, healing — which only served to make her more weary — was of little benefit.

Once Cat had been carried through and made comfortable in the sleeping quarters, Imogen and Ileana used the two other beds which sprouted from the floor. Nala, Dan and Rhyll remained in the control room, stretched out on chairs which also moulded into beds.

While they slept, Q monitored the ship, ensuring Williams was securely housed within the tractor room. It also monitored the life signs of the guests. Part of its inherent function was to maintain life. While some of the events it had witnessed were grey areas, no long term physical harm had come to anyone under its charge. Q determined everyone required several hours' sleep to recover from the recent events.

Rising to eighty kilometres, the craft slowed and maintained position above Cairo.

RHYLLIEN WOKE AND STRETCHED, THEN THE CHAIR ADJUSTED TO accommodate her sitting position. She stood and yawned, stretching again, deciding sleeping in the chair was like sleeping in a hammock: okay for a snooze, but not for hours at a time. Turning to the viewscreen, she saw the tableau of the Nile delta spread out below. The craft was motionless in space, high above the city.

"Hi, Q. What have you been up to?"

"This and that; monitoring everyone's health status. There are drones to the south, where we landed before, near the pyramids."

"Damn. Have they spotted us?" Rhyll looked carefully to a separate monitor displaying a blown-up panorama of the southern area, where small black dots were whizzing around the Giza plateau.

"There is no indication. I doubt they have the capability of detecting this craft."

Nala and Dan stirred.

"Are we there yet?" Dan mumbled.

"Sorry to wake you," she said to them both.

"Good morning, I think." Nala nodded in response, taking time to wake up as Rhyll filled them in on their location. "I'll go and see to the others." She rose and stretched. As she walked towards the rear door, it opened. Imogen was on the threshold, about to enter.

"Hey, boss," Nala said as she passed.

Imogen gave her a smile and friendly nod, halfway through a yawn.

"Hi, Mum. Good timing. Q's just told me there are drones."
She pointed to them on the monitor as her mother came closer to
the console and the screen.

"Is that a problem?" Imogen asked.

"Morning, Mrs E." Dan climbed off the bed. "They can't
descend too low or they'll get caught in the interference, but we
don't know how low that is."

"Can you pinpoint where you need to be dropped off?" Rhyll
asked her.

"There." She pointed after a brief look at the urban sprawl
displayed on the main screen.

"You can remember it so easily," Rhyll marvelled.

"Your father and I did spend a bit of time there, but the location — an island in the Nile — is hard to forget. Other than the
agricultural regions on the outskirts, it's also one of the more
greener areas in Cairo."

"I gather most of the government buildings are nearby?"
Rhyll asked.

Imogen nodded. "Including the university and many
embassies."

"You'll need to get out of sight quickly once we drop you off.
If the drones detect us, we'll lead them away."

Nala returned a few minutes later with Ileana.

"How's Cat?" Rhyll asked her.

"She snores very loudly," Ileana answered. "I think she's
much better." The Brazilian surveyed the arid terrain with
distaste, clearly unimpressed by the drab, uniform colour of the
city. "I've never seen land so ... horrible."

Rhyll told her about the drones, but assured her they weren't
going to be a problem.

Ileana cleared her throat. "All the more reason why you
should have a soldier down there, but I understand the situation,
as much as I hate it." She turned to Imogen and gave her a brief
hug. "You stay safe."

"I will, Ana. Thank you. And you."

"Cat will be pissed off if anything happens to you, so you'd better be safe and well next time we meet."

"She's my mother." Rhyll took the soldier's hand briefly. "I'd never put her in harm's way."

"What daughter would?" Ileana nodded, and after farewelling the others, moved to the rear wall where the back door had remained open. After the soldier strode through it closed immediately, putting another barrier between them and the effects of the death zone outside.

They grabbed their packs in preparation for a quick departure.

"What about your *other* bag?" Nala teased Dan.

"Somehow I don't think it will be needed here."

"I thought it was important. What's in it?" Rhyll asked curiously.

"Dan borrowed stolen money from some bank robbers back in Reading."

"What?" Rhyll asked, aghast.

"You never know when you'll need cash," Dan shrugged. "It helped get us to Sedona, didn't it?" he asked defensively. "Can't it be counted as survival foraging?"

"Pfft." Nala rolled her eyes.

He stepped away before Nala could hit him.

"Take us down, Q." Rhyll punched Dan in the shoulder instead.

THE SPEED THE CRAFT DROPPED TO THE DESIGNATED AREA WAS staggering. Feeling dizzy, everyone had to grab the console to steady themselves, but it was purely a visual effect — no one actually felt anything physical.

The ship was suddenly hovering a metre above the old Egyptian Ministry of Antiquities. Surrounding it, Cairo spread out like a yellow and tan tapestry of buildings crisscrossed by straight, narrow roads, some lined with palm trees. The Nile stretched north and south like an exotic blue glistening snake in the afternoon sun.

"Let me know if those drones spot us," Rhyll requested from Q.

"Affirmative."

She quickly hugged her mother tightly. "See what you can dig up concerning entries to the catacombs — assuming they really exist."

Imogen squeezed her in response. "I'll be fine. It's you who should stay safe."

When she released her mother, she hugged Nala and Dan briefly. "We'll be back as soon as we can and come find you," she said to them all.

The exit door irised opened moments later. As before, an invisible force kept the outside and interior air separate.

The trio exited the craft. Dan went to assist Imogen down the ramp, but she slapped his hand away.

"I'm not an invalid yet," she jokingly scolded.

Part of the area had been converted into a roof garden. They headed straight for a gazebo and waved from the shadows.

Rhyll waved back, and the door spun closed.

"Let's go to the sky lift," Rhyll said softly to Q as she took her seat.

"As you wish." The UFO rose swiftly.

They were arcing through the stratosphere by the time Ileana joined her in the control room. She got comfortable in one of the other seats.

"I just checked on Williams. I thought he might need to use the toilet. At first he didn't want to, but when I gave him the option of tasering him in the nethers, he changed his mind."

"Very prudent of him."

"I meant it as a favour. A slight shock and he'd not even feel like going for hours."

"Good idea. I won't tell Cat. She'll think you're getting soft."

"Hardly. I'm getting smart. If there's a mess in there, who do you think is going to have to clean it up?

"I see your point."

"What are the plans now?" Ileana glanced outside, partly stunned, partly uncomfortable with the emptiness.

"The priority is to heal Cat. No doubt we'll need her help on the lift. Q estimates we can be there in four hours."

"Is that good?"

Q said, "I have been able to check the space lift timetable. There are four lifts working at any time. The duration of the journey is approximately thirty-eight hours. Without questioning our passenger more thoroughly, and gauging the possible time-frame from forgery to dispatch, I have ascertained the space lift with the highest probability of having what you seek launched thirty hours ago."

"Can we catch it easily?"

"Definitely, but if you require your friend to be fully healed before boarding, then our velocity is irrelevant."

"As long as we have enough time to find them."

"You will."

"Now, tell me about these nanites."

ONCE THE NANITES WERE ADMINISTERED, THEY ALL SNOOZED FOR A couple of hours, trusting the alien to ensure their journey was safe. When they woke, Rhyll checked on Cataleya's progress; it was impressive. There was hardly any scarring, and her vitals were almost back to normal, as was her colour.

They made small-talk and snacked on ration packs while waiting. The scene outside was fascinating at first, seeing the tether dwindle in both directions. But a fascinating view can lose its appeal after a short period without any discernible change. Even when a descending lift was spotted, it passed so quickly that they barely caught a glimpse before it was gone.

Rhyll laughed at the stories of their many and varied exploits in Brazil, especially regarding a couple of tours when they first worked with Benigno and Felipe.

"When was the last you heard from those two?" she asked.

"I had a call from Beni two days prior to receiving orders to go to São Paulo to protect your mother. They were assisting refugees getting out of Manaus."

"Nothing more?"

Ileana shook her head.

Rhyll was considering asking if Q could contact Benigno once the healing finished.

Q spoke up: "We are shadowing the spacelift from a distance of two thousand metres and travelling at one thousand and two kilometres an hour. Your friend is also awakening."

Rhyll stretched cramped muscles and grabbed another drink of water from the flask. "Thank you. How long before the lift arrives at Sky City?"

"The speed has varied the last couple of hours, but the estimated time of arrival is 16:45 — in one hour and three minutes."

"What time zone are we in now?"

"This is OST — Orbital Space Time. It is the same time zone as the Galapagos."

They stood and wandered back to check on Cataleya's progress. As Q said, Cataleya was awake and sitting up inspecting her abdomen where the bullet had struck her.

"Fantástico." She felt the area and looked to Rhyll in wonder. "You did this?" she said in a soft voice.

"Hardly. It was all thanks to Q and his nanites."

Ileana explained when Cat looked confused at the word.

"Amazing." Shaking her head she started to stand slowly, but feeling absolutely no pain or discomfort, she moved faster. The three of them returned to the control room and she polished off one of the ration packs, with two remaining. They brought her up to speed on what had transpired while she was unconscious.

Surprisingly, she agreed straight away.

Rhyll relaxed. "Thank you for not arguing."

"No problemo; it is either this, or go back to HQ." Cat turned to Ileana. "Anything would be a better gig than back at GHO HQ."

Ileana laughed. "You just don't want to have to tell Benigno you caught a slug."

"He would be most aggrieved." Cat nodded.

"Aggrieved? He'd be teasing you for weeks."

Seeing the space lift climbing the cable in the viewscreen, Cat asked: "Are we ready to go, then?"

"Almost. We were waiting for you to join us," Rhyll said.

"I was happy to go alone, but you know me, boss, I would have shot everything."

"Firing projectile weapons in a pressurised capsule could be problematic," Q informed them.

"And how is our new friend, Williams?" Cat asked.

"He's a pain in the ass," Ileana grouched. "Next time, I'll take the slug and you can deal with the *merde*."

Cat nodded, turning back to business. "Have we got a plan of the lift to work with?"

A schematic of the space lift interior appeared on a smaller screen on the console.

"I am unfamiliar with the lift design," Q continued. "This ship's sensors can identify the various compartments and functions: power, life-support, passenger area and commercial cargo." Each time Q spoke, a section of the diagram highlighted temporarily, then faded. "The lift works by electromagnetic drive along the cables. As you can see, there is the main tether, winch and four cables. Each lift carries forty five passengers — I believe some of them are staff, going by the configuration."

Rhyll looked closely at the details on the schematic. "If the diamonds were sent by commercial courier, I'm guessing the package is in the commercial cargo section. Umm ... How do we get inside?"

"There is an emergency access hatch near the base." A small

section lit up on the screen. "It is out of view of the viewing platform."

"What? You mean we need to be outside? In space?"

"Yes. Is this a problem?"

"We can't breathe in a vacuum, for starters."

"Obviously. You'd be wearing a suit."

"One that fits us?"

"While one is feasible, it would have its limitations. Greater functionality is possible if you don't share." A thin, tall door slid open in the back wall on the opposite side of the door. It was a rack with five dark, one-piece ensembles.

"Like the chairs, these will conform to your specific physical requirements."

"And we can breathe?"

"The previous occupants were of the same physiology and breathed a similar atmosphere to humans. The air supply will last an hour under normal operating conditions, far more than it will require to transit to and from the space lift. The control pad on your sleeve also has an option of camouflage for emergency situations. It is the round tab in the top righthand corner. Use it sparingly, as it will reduce the suit's battery power."

"Surely we can't open the hatch ourselves? What about passcodes? AI security?" Ileana asked, checking out the controls.

"It would be prudent to take me with you to circumvent AI and other security protocols."

"How do we get back? Only you can activate the beam," Rhyll assumed.

"I can program this craft to track the lift, as well as set a timeframe for the beam to reactivate."

"Can't it just stay on until we're back?" Rhyll asked.

"Continuous use is beyond its design parameters. Components would lose functionality." There was a momentary pause before Q continued, "At precisely thirty minutes after our arrival, the graviton beam will reactivate. It will remain on for five minutes. If no one is detected, it will repeat for five minutes out of every ten."

"That should give us enough time," Rhyll considered.

"We will need to be outside the structure for the beam to draw us back in," it added.

Rhyll nodded while watching Ileana and Cat. "You two up for this?"

"Neither of us have had any training in zero-g, but we are prepared to do what we must," Ileana replied.

"I'm feeling very good." Cataleya nodded.

"I wouldn't ask if we didn—"

"I understand. Let it go." Cat walked over to the rack, pulling one of the suits out. "One size fits all, you say?" She held it against her body; the suit had four squat legs, two long arms and looked far too thin. "Even Ileana?"

Her companion's answer was a mutter too soft to hear.

"As you get in it will adjust accordingly," Q explained. "This is the configuration of the previous occupants."

There were enough suits for all of them. Williams wasn't too happy about being pushed into space, and refused to get into any alien suit.

Ileana held the taser against his groin. "Put it this way: you're going. Your choice to go in a suit conscious or unconscious. I will not be gentle, I promise. In fact, I suspect your fertility might be in doubt afterwards."

"You need me!"

"All the more reason why we will ensure your cooperation." Cat said, moving to his other side. "Mind you ... we have our alien friend here, who can override any security measures. We have this *chica* who can sense her diamonds. You know, Ileana, I don't think we need him after all. Once Q slithers inside his head through his ear, it can pull the information out of his brain."

"I thought it went in through the eye-socket? Either way, sounds good to me. Then we can simply jettison his corpse."

"You wouldn't!" he cried, uncertain.

"She *might,* but I have no qualms about it." Ileana shrugged.

"Why wouldn't I?" Rhyll chose to play the game the Brazilians had started. "Many have died already for less, and you're hindering my task. You know exactly what's at stake. We can do this with or without you." She pointed to his groin. "Ileana—"

"No! Wait—" Williams pleaded.

"Maybe there's something he's not telling us?" Ileana pushed the taser harder.

"He *does* seem very upset about something," Cat said.

"P-poison," Williams stammered.

"Where?"

"Contact poison. O-on the diamonds."

"Now you *are* definitely coming along."

With only the slightest of zaps to encourage speed, Williams finally donned the suit. The others quickly climbed into theirs while Q programmed the ship to maintain its distance to the lift and targeted the emergency hatch with the graviton beam.

The suits were similar to a wetsuit or a pair of overalls, though of a completely unknown material. You stepped inside, then pushed your arms in as you shrugged it over your shoulders. Cat and Ileana removed their watches to strap on their wrists after dressing. Once the front sealed shut seamlessly, the suit compressed until it was snug in all areas, yet flexible enough to not hinder movement, though the back, shoulder and neck area seemed bulkier. The extra legs melded into the suit, and the arms contracted to accommodate the wearer.

"What about the face? Is there a helmet?" Rhyll asked. "And how do we breathe?"

"Tap the tab on your left shoulder." Q wrapped himself around her arm to enable communications. Its voice sounded muted, coming from the small inbuilt speakers along the neck.

She did as the alien instructed. A clear cowling grew from the neck and shoulders, with the same flexibility as the rest of the suit. The others did the same.

"The air is from a built-in bladder within the back lining. A readout on the inside of your helmet will show vital signs, suit integrity, and air level."

Similar to the viewscreen, glyphs and symbols appeared in front of their faces on the visor.

"I can't read any of them," Rhyll pointed out.

"An oversight. As long as the glyphs aren't flashing, everything is functioning correctly. The air level is the column you see on the bottom right."

Cat walked around all of them, checking everything was in order. Rhyll gave her the thumbs up. Once all four were ready they moved to the tractor room. Williams struggled futilely, but had a change of perspective when his arm was twisted behind his back.

"It slithers into your brain," Ileana reminded him menacingly.

He complied immediately, but with soft mutterings of resentment.

She spoke quietly but forcefully to Williams. "I will give you this warning only once: if you try anything out there, I will break you and leave your body in space. No one will ever find your remains."

"I u-understand."

"I don't care. You've been warned." Ileana moved him to the side by the wall.

Q's voice was heard in all their helmets.

The tractor room was square and of sufficient size to accommodate the four of them. Like everywhere else on the strange craft, the walls and floor were a uniform black, while the ceiling glowed violet.

"We are now depressurising. Very soon, the outer door will open at the termination of the visual warning."

A small faint circle of light appeared on the far wall. The brightness of the light increased and began pulsating. As the circle expanded the frequency of the pulsations increased, with individual, thrumming lights moving around both clockwise and counterclockwise, crossing each other, glowing intense spots that blinded them temporarily. Suddenly, without warning, they stopped. Like the main entrance, a section of the wall spun open silently.

"I could watch that again," Rhyll mumbled, entranced.

Outside, the UFO had moved within fifty metres of the space lift, which now filled their view.

Everyone stood there, transfixed, gasping at the site, the clarity was breathtaking.

Cataleya was closest to the door. "Everything looks so crisp and clear ..." She took a tentative step outside onto the hull faring and slowly looked around. A section of the surface became textured to allow traction.

Rhyll witnessed the look of awe on Cat's face as she stepped out and joined her observing the wonder of the inky blackness.

"Words cannot ..." Cat's voice trailed.

"No. No. You can't make me!" Williams pleaded loudly over their headsets.

"Get out here, puta!" Over the internal comms they heard Ileana as she dragged Williams outside, forcing his arm behind him again. The look on his face was the opposite of Cat's — he looked terrified, then he started to convulse.

The face plate suddenly became partially obscured by vomit. It was clear he had enjoyed the many and varied dishes at the fundraiser.

"Urgh," he moaned as he brought a hand up in a futile effort to wipe at it. Slowly the muck dripped down inside his suit, leaving discoloured streaks of vomit on the once clear cowling.

Cat shook her head, part in amusement, part distaste.

"I'm just glad I don't have to breathe it," Ileana added.

He coughed several times until his throat was clear.

"If you require water for refreshment or to clear your throat, there is a tube near your mouth," Q advised.

Rhyll strained her eyes and glanced down her cheek to see it, almost flush with the seal. Feeling stupid and awkward, she used her lips and tongue to grope for the tube, sucking in a small quantity of the cool fluid.

All at once everyone began to float and move beyond the edge of the disc, propelled by an unseen force.

"The graviton beam is now activated," Q said unnecessarily as they were smoothly pushed towards the space elevator, which loomed large in front of them.

It was like moving off a cliff: the solid surface was now behind them and the Earth was 35,000kms below. In seconds, everyone's visors became misty with their sudden rapid breathing. The suits compensated, and a few heartbeats later the visors cleared as an unknown device moved the air around inside the suits.

"To conserve your air, it will be prudent to relax."

They all heard Q and tried to take its advice. No one wanted to suffocate, but the sensation of zero-g and being surrounded by the vastness of space was a completely new, if somewhat exhilarating, experience for all of them.

There was a very unsettling moment when all Rhyll wanted to do was flail her arms, but she reached out and put her hand on the shoulders of her friend, partly for reassurance, and partly to prevent any possibility of drifting away, though in her mind she knew that wasn't likely to happen. She realised now why astronauts' movements were so slow: every action, every movement had a reaction to offset the energy expended.

Williams made half-hearted attempts to struggle. Even though Ileana held him firmly, in the weak gravity the applied pressure simply caused him to move in the direction of force. When she relaxed her grip, he struggled more. They tumbled in slow motion like two uncoordinated dancers, the internal comms transmitting his whimpering grunts and her wide range of Portuguese swear-words.

In frustration, Ileana pushed him forward and away. They both separated — he tumbled, marginally faster towards the lift; she drifted backwards but the graviton beam slowed her momentum. She reverted to gliding in the right direction, but several metres behind the group.

The space elevator in front of them was a massive cylinder about fifty metres tall and twenty wide. From their study of the diagram they knew the passengers were kept on the top two decks, which included a viewing deck. Directly below were the passenger facilities, including small offices, luggage and dining. Below was engineering, electronics and commercial cargo. The bottom level was dedicated to power generation and the electro-magnetic drives.

Stretching above and below, the thick tether disappeared into obscurity. Although hard to distinguish against the vast black-ness, there were four cables used for the lifts themselves. The four cable system provided the capability to use several lifts at any time; this was both convenient and functional, as it provided the ability to enable assistance should a lift require it.

The UFO shadowed the lift, matching its speed so precisely it was nigh impossible to believe they were all travelling over a thousand kilometres an hour.

"No green light?" Rhyll wondered, looking around, belatedly seeing a lime-coloured tint on the back of Cataleya's suit.

"Not in a vacuum, unless there is something for the light particles to strike," Q explained.

The unforgettable transit to the lift took a few minutes. Just when she thought they were about to hit the wall, they all slowed simultaneously. Williams, in front, flailed his arms, hit and bounced back in a slow spin.

Reflexively, Cataleya grabbed his leg to stop him, only to slow her progress until Ileana caught up, her mass providing sufficient impetus to push them close enough to grab hold of the lift.

"Ensure you do not venture too close to the base. High inten-sity lasers feed power to the receptor panels," Q warned.

"What's that mean?" Rhyll asked.

"I'm pretty sure it means we'll be fried." Cataleya reached

out to grab the edge of a panel and position herself adjacent to the hatch.

Ileana did the same on the other side. "You better grab something, *cabrão*," she advised Williams.

He grabbed an edge of the structure and hugged it tightly, putting his face against the hull to blot out the view.

Rhyll found a section to hang on to. Below them, the cable stretched down to the Earth. They were directly above the ocean, with the west South American coastline directly below.

"That should be the Galapagos Archipelago," Rhyll said distractedly.

11

"I'VE OVERRIDDEN THE SECURITY. THERE IS AN INTERNAL AIRLOCK large enough for two. Once inside, I will bring in the next two after we've cycled through," Q explained as the emergency access hatch swung silently outwards.

Cat and Rhyll climbed inside one after the other. There was little room to move with both of them crammed inside, and the cycling routine was slow. Once it finally finished, they crawled out and then had to wait for it to depressurise for the next cycle.

This area was mainly a utility crawlspace — not for paying passengers. It was dim, constrained and ugly. Conduits and wiring ran along the bulkheads, and even Rhyll had trouble walking without having to stoop or turn slightly sideways to squeeze past a cluster of pipes.

"I can feel the diamonds now," Rhyll said, a touch of excitement in her voice. She moved back to make room as the airlock finally cycled open.

Minutes ticked by before Ileana emerged, dragging Williams out of the airlock. She exhausted her extensive repertoire of swearing as he had to be cajoled like a child.

"You can remove your helmets," Q informed them all.

With relief, they each tapped the same tabs as before and the clear cowling retracted.

"Not you. You'll stink the place out!" Ileana hissed at Williams.

Too late: he managed to tap the tab before she could slap his hand away. Very quickly, the stench of bile permeated the cramped area.

Williams wiped his face with his gloved hands and flicked the remnants of puke away while gasping in the cleaner air.

"Do we really need this puta? I cannot guarantee he will make it back to the ship safely." The Brazilian crawled away, gagging.

"As long as he helps us with the diamonds," Cataleya said from further up the confined corridor. She had used the time they took to cycle through to explore the short passage.

"And what if I don't?" Williams now showed some bravado, being in a human environment, though the remnants of partly digested crackers and cheese in his hair did little to make him look threatening in any way.

"Then as Ileana said, you might not make it back to the ship," Cataleya said ominously.

"The commercial storage compartment is one level up," Q said, the voice emanating from the inbuilt speakers when the cowling had retracted.

Rhyllien nodded. "Up is where I'm sensing them." She joined Cat by a ladder, putting distance between herself and the smell.

"I need to find a toilet," Williams complained.

"You smell like a toilet," Ileana retorted, pushing him forwards.

He turned awkwardly to confront her, but she met his audacity with the taser, the low-charged stun numbing his leg. Williams hobbled away, grumbling as he caught up with the others.

Cat motioned for Rhyll to climb up first. "In case the hatch needs to be overridden."

Rhyllien nodded and ascended the few rungs to the next hatch. She touched the edge of the structure so Q could manipulate any alarm system.

The hatch hissed slightly as it opened.

Climbing another rung, Rhyll checked it was clear, though Q and her own senses would have alerted her to any presence. This passage was marginally larger and brighter. There were several rungs continuing up the bulkhead to a hatch above labelled *Emergency Exit.*

"All clear," she whispered down to the others before she emerged to the next deck.

Rhyll cautiously approached the door leading into the storage unit. Once Q opened it, she realised there was little room inside.

"We might have to drag some of this stuff out," she said as Cat stepped up behind her and peered in. "I'm the smallest. I'll see what I can do." Rhyll squeezed inside.

There were several stacks of shelves packed high, with thin tracks in the floor and ceiling which guided a mechanical arm to retrieve and place items. Space between the shelves only needed to be wide enough to accommodate the parcels for that section. Rhyllien's lithe frame would fit, as long as she moved sideways. The smooth material of the suit prevented any snagging.

After a few steps, she called back. "I see now why there is so little room. It looks like it's all automated." She continued to inch to the section where she detected the diamonds. She vented in frustration, realising the time it was taking.

They were towards the back, near the floor. With no room to bend, she'd have to lie down to reach it. Struggling to get low, she had a thought.

"Q, are you able to get the parcel with this machine?"

"Indeed. Which parcel?"

"Umm ..." She looked down, trying to determine the exact slot by counting the shelves and rows. "Third shelf from the floor, second row in. B3, I guess, unless they start their count from the door and the ceiling ..."

"I need to be in contact." Q oozed off her hand to the floor, and slid onto the track.

She backed towards the door and waited, careful not to tread on the alien.

"I'm an idiot," she said to Cat, explaining Q could have retrieved the parcel when she first entered if she'd thought about it.

Cat chuckled with her. "You can't think of everything."

"I really need the toilet," Williams moaned, scrubbing at his face and hair.

"You'll tell us about the poison on these diamonds first. If that means you piss your pants, so be it." Cataleya turned to him. Before she could continue, the lights flashed orange and there was a faint beeping. "What's that?" She looked around.

"Maybe we've been spotted?"

"I thought the alien took care of that," Cat answered, checking the other end of the passage. "What does Q say?"

"I don't know. It's overriding the machine in here," Rhyll said apprehensively as she waited. "We're not on the ship now, and I don't think Q can communicate to us without being physically in contact."

There was a faint whirring sound. A tall, thin beam with a four-pronged claw sped smoothly along the track, stopping within arm's reach of Rhyll.

"Thanks, Q." She grasped the small box as Q stretched onto her hand. The prongs snapped open and the device sped back to its enclosure. "Can you tell us what that alarm is?" she asked, putting her hand on the bulkhead as she stepped back into the passage.

There was a heartbeat of silence. "Fumes detected in this section." As it said this, a loud hiss issued from the ceiling. Q warned them immediately: "Fire retardant. Facemasks immediately."

Everyone tapped their tabs and the helmets formed. A whitish vapour dispersed at pressure from overhead pipes, causing the corridor to become misty.

"More technically," Q continued, "bromochlorodifluromethane, a combination of halon and freon often used on your planet to smother fire."

"What fire?" Cat looked around.

"I can only deduce the fumes from Williams' emesis was misdiagnosed as the result of a conflagration," Q answered.

"Puta! You and your vomit stench!" Ileana spat, shoving Williams against the wall. His helmet struck one of the rungs behind him.

Rhyll held her breath until she saw the steady lights appear on her faceplate. She started to breathe calmly.

"Time to make your presence worthwhile," Cat said as Rhyll passed the parcel to him.

"I don't want it!" He tried to avoid them.

Ileana pulled him forward and shoved the taser points against his spine. "If you're lucky, this might only paralyse you," she threatened.

Nervously, Williams took the box, gloved hand shaking.

"What do you need to counteract the poison?" Rhyll asked him.

"S-soaking in a strong alkali will neutralise it."

"Like what?"

"Sodium hydroxide would be good, m-mayb-be bleach," he stammered.

"Bleach? I saw a maintenance compartment back by the ladder we used to climb up," Rhyll said, pointing to the small door in the bulkhead.

Ileana pulled him around and shoved him towards the maintenance hatch. He staggered, but caught himself before he tripped.

The small door to the compartment wasn't locked. Williams

pulled the handle. The door swung up unexpectedly on gas struts, hitting his faceplate. He yelped and dropped the box to clutch at his nose; a reflex action as he must have assumed it was broken, or at least bleeding, from the impact. Of course it was neither, and he couldn't touch his nose through the clear cowling.

At the same time a door behind them hissed open.

Cataleya spun at the noise, drawing her gun as two security droids entered.

Rhyll ducked behind a vertical pipe a second later. It only provided marginal protection.

Ileana remained standing, but flattened herself against the opposite bulkhead as she unholstered her gun. She heard the hatch to the ladder slam shut. "Puta!" she muttered as Williams disappeared to the lower level.

She heard a distant grunt, followed by laughter. "Try tasering me now, bitch!"

The two squat droids glided in on rollers. They had several mechanical arms, each different but nonetheless menacing, including a claw, lasers and cutters.

"Unauthorised intruders, remain where you are." The droids stopped several metres away. "Kneel on the floor."

"What do we do?" Rhyll asked, frozen to the spot by the formidable-looking devices.

"I'm thinking." Cataleya stood still, flicking a glance back. "Ana, where's Williams?"

"That puta has gone below." Ileana tried to open the hatch one-handed. "And he's jammed the handle."

"Shit. And the diamonds?"

"On the floor." She pointed to the package.

"Can Q cut his comms?"

There was piercing feedback over all the headsets, and no way to block it.

"Done. If it is any consolation, it was worse for this Williams."

"Unauthorised intruders, remain where you are," the droid repeated, edging closer. "Kneel on the floor."

Rhyll had an idea. "Q, can you override these droids, too?"

"Of course."

The alien slithering across the floor would take too long, and there was no way Rhyll was going to get closer to the droids. She bent a knee, pretending she was going to kneel in submission, but used the movement as a feint to hurl the slug-like creature on her hand towards the droids. "Do your thing, Q," she said as the alien sailed down the hall.

A burst of energy from one of the droid's weapons hit her in the shoulder, spinning her back and causing her to tumble to the deck with a cry of pain.

Instantly Cataleya returned fire, hitting one of the armoured droids several times, but to little effect. A bolt of energy zapped along the bulkhead where Cat had stood a second earlier, leaving a dark area where the paint had seared.

With the droid's return of fire and Rhyll's rushed throw slightly off, Q was going to miss, but it stretched like a tentacle. Only a small section needed to contact the droid's surface. The moment it did, the alien gathered itself, adhering to the droid's smooth metallic skin and went to work.

A heartbeat later, the droid turned and fired on the other droid behind. While doing so, it closed the short gap and began using its claw and cutters to good effect. The other droid reacted in self-defence.

Cataleya and Ileana dropped to the deck as bursts of energy zapped and dissipated along the bulkheads around them. A pipe hissed; small tendrils of electricity crackled fleetingly when the tube lighting was struck. The corridor dimmed marginally.

It didn't take long for both droids to be smoking chunks of metal, hydraulic fluid leaking to the deck from severed tubes.

Q dripped off the now defunct droid and slid across the floor to Rhyll, leaving a trail of the viscous fluid behind it.

Cataleya was already there, kneeling beside her. "It was a stun shot only," she informed Ileana with relief.

Her partner nodded, then holstered her gun and turned to open the hatch. "He's definitely jammed the handle on the other side."

Cataleya checked her watch. "We have ten minutes to get outside if we are to make the graviton beam."

"Do you think he will use it?"

"No." Cat shook her head. "Unless he's an award-winning stuntman, he'd be too scared. Besides, I don't think he could cycle out the airlock." Cataleya checked Rhyll's vitals.

Q wrapped over Rhyll's arm and slid to her shoulder.

"Q, is there any other way outside?" Cataleya asked.

"The only other exit is up in the passenger area."

"And there will be people wandering about up there ..." Cataleya considered any alternatives not requiring being seen or risking passengers.

Ileana bent down and rummaged through the maintenance cupboard, pulling out a small bucket and a bottle of bleach. "May as well deal with this while we can." Sitting on the hatch, she dropped the parcel into the bucket, undid the lid of the bleach and began pouring the fluid over it. Soon the box was sitting in several inches of bleach. Ileana was then about to undo the packaging. "These gloves will be safe in the bleach?" she asked.

"Of course," Q replied.

The soldier continued and after a few minutes of fiddling, removed the wrapping and pulled the box apart. She kept the gemstones immersed in the liquid, while scrubbing them vigorously between her gloved fingers. "Did Williams say to soak them?"

"He did."

Holding the gemstones in one gloved hand, Ileana emptied the contents of the bucket in a corner; she then replaced the stones and poured more bleach in. She sat back while she waited. "Now what?"

Around them, they heard a sudden rush of air. The misty cloud could be seen rushing out as it expelled into space through exhaust vents.

"It is safe to remove the cowling now," Q informed them as the readouts in the faceplates flashed green.

They pressed their tabs and the cowlings retracted.

Cat tried Rhyll's but it didn't work.

"I have modified her air for a higher concentration of oxygen. She will revive presently."

Rhyll's eyes fluttered open. There was the merest look of confusion in them before it all came back. Her cowling retracted, presumably by Q's activation.

"Hey there, chica." Cat smiled with relief.

"We have your diamonds," Ileana pointed as Cat helped Rhyll sit up. "I thought there were more."

"Are they safe to touch now?" Rhyll peered into the bucket, seeing the violet, red and yellow diamonds. "Hey! The red diamond was supposed to be going to someone named Hart." She held her hand over them and closed her eyes.

"Depends on whether you trust Stradjek or Williams," Ileana replied.

"These feel safe now." Rhyll reached in and examined each one. "No forgeries here."

"So this Hart has got one of the fake diamonds?"

"Probably. Not my concern now. Where's Williams?" Rhyll asked, looking around. "You didn't ..."

"No. When the droids arrived, he bolted and is now hiding below. He's wedged the handle." Ileana gave the handle another twist. It still didn't budge.

"So we can't return to the ship?"

Cat shook her head. "Not that way, and before you ask, we doubt Williams would be willing to return to the ship all by himself."

"He couldn't do anything without Q, nor could he cycle through the airlock."

"That is our thinking."

"So then ..."

"Q says the only other exit is in the passenger section."

"Oh. And we can get there?"

"We were waiting for sleeping beauty, but now that Q revived you, we can depart."

"Thank you, Q," she said to the alien wrapped on her right hand. "Sorry for what I did."

"Not required, it was a necessity. The lift will be arriving at the Sky City terminus in twenty-seven minutes, and we have missed the window of opportunity for the graviton beam."

"That's it, then. Time for us to move." Cataleya stood and stretched, then helped Rhyll to stand.

Ileana grabbed the diamonds, wrapped them in a cloth from the maintenance compartment, and handed them to Rhyll. There were other cleaning utensils inside, but nothing to adequately wedge the door handle.

Cataleya led them past the ruined droids, squeezing between the bulkhead and the appendages of metal struts, servos and braided conduit. Rhyll had less of a problem with her slighter build.

Ileana had to breathe out, but still had trouble. She backed off, bent down and covered her gloved hands in the hydraulic fluid, then smeared it over her suit where she thought it was going to rub against the droids. The soldier tried again.

"I've been working out," she muttered, glad her idea worked and that the suit's smooth material didn't snag and compound her difficulties.

"I didn't say anything." Cat chuckled as she moved to the doorway the droids had arrived through.

When it hissed open, they saw it was a tiny elevator. The three of them squeezed in as the door hissed closed.

"What floor?" Ileana asked.

"Exit is on the third level," Q replied.

"Are there people up there now?" She pushed the button.

"Not at this time, but passengers have access to offices, luggage and dining."

Cat clicked her tongue in irritation. "Very well, we'll assume there are some people readying themselves for the arrival, with more venturing down when the lift docks."

"I can't taser everyone," Ileana said.

"When I was in a hoverpod," Rhyll spoke up, "it was hacked. They said they modified the oxygen level so I'd faint and remain unconscious until I arrived."

"And Q did modify your suit's oxygen to revive you," Cat pointed out.

Q spoke up. "I can do this, but it will be best if I am at the main console. If I err, lives could be lost, a risk I will not take."

The elevator stopped and the doors hissed open on the third floor.

"Isn't engineering on the fourth floor?" Cat asked.

"Correct."

Swearing, Ileana hit a button on the console. Two of the staff turned just in time to catch sight of the group, but their cry of alarm was cut off as the doors closed and the lift descended.

———

WHEN WILLIAMS SAW THE DOORS AT THE END OF THE CORRIDOR open and the two security droids roll out of the lift, he'd hoped the distraction would provide a slim chance to escape. The moment the big woman's attention was diverted, he'd dropped down the hatch and reached up to pull it closed, spinning the locking mechanism.

In desperation, he pulled at some wires from the nearest conduit. There was a zap and crackling. Even though suited, he was careful not to touch the exposed wires, and he quickly wrapped them around the handle. *Just in time.* He laughed at his success when they tried to open it.

Williams felt the handle shift, but the impromptu restraint did its job, preventing the hatch from opening. "Try tasering me now, bitch!"

He had no idea what the wire's purpose was — and no doubt a light somewhere in the control room would illuminate indicating some failure — but he was glad the airlock didn't suddenly cycle open.

There was an ear-piercing screech inside his helmet. He doubled over in pain, futilely clutching at his head to stop the noise. After several agonising seconds the sound abruptly ceased, but he felt something warm trickle from his throbbing eardrums.

Williams sat heavily, and was rocking back and forth waiting for the aching to stop when he heard muffled gunfire and unfamiliar noises. There was a momentary hope Rhyll and her friends had tried to resist and were killed in the process. He could barely hear anything, and wondered if it would be permanent. In a futile attempt to relieve the pressure, yawning only adding to his discomfort.

He eventually became aware of the flashing green glyphs in his faceplate. They were solid red when the chemical mist came down. Holding his breath, he tapped his shoulder near his neck like the others had done; the cowling retracted and he tentatively sniffed. *Clean air!*

Feeling around his ears, his fingertips came away wet and sticky from the blood, and there were red drops staining his shirt.

He took a few deeper breaths as he began moving along the narrow passage, searching for anything of use; perhaps a comms unit or a monitor and keypad. It soon became apparent that there was little he could do here except wait. The airlock control panel was in front of him, and while the instructions were as plain as day, the idea of cycling through the airlock by himself and jumping to the UFO across the void filled him with dread.

There was no way he was willing to undergo that again. He used his hands to wipe at his face and scrub more of the filth out of his hair. Returning to the ladder area below the hatch, he sat down in the tight space and considered his options, based on the memories of his previous Sky City visits. Admittedly, he hadn't been sitting in a maintenance crawlspace but up in the passenger lounge with Stradjek on one of their business trips.

With him locking the hatch to the emergency airlock, there was only one other exit for all the passengers and crew, which would mean his three female abductors would need to leave their current level and get up to the higher levels if they wanted to get off the lift.

He waited and listened, ears straining. He tenderly felt his jaw, and ran his tongue over his teeth. He worked his jaw experimentally, deciding it wasn't broken. His fingers came away smeared with the congealing blood from a cut under his chin.

Williams heard some noise. He silently climbed to the hatch and heard the Brazilian leader say faintly , "that's it ... time for ... move."

He was unsure of the next sounds, but considering what they had to do, assumed it meant they were heading for the lift the droids arrived in.

"And that means they've moved away from the hatch." He reached up, pausing and listening intently in case it was a trap.

Silence. Unwinding the wire, he very slowly turned the handle with two hands, hoping that his firm grip was sufficient to keep hold of the hatch in the off-chance it was still a trick and they were lying in wait.

Cracking the seal and peering through, he sighed with relief seeing the passage empty except for the inert droids. The smell of bleach was strong as he pushed the hatch all the way and climbed, noticing the puddle of bleach and the discarded bucket. He looked up; as he suspected, the rungs in the wall meant there was another hatch to the next deck: an emergency access in case of a lift malfunction or a power failure.

Ignoring the 'Authorised access only' sign, Williams continued climbing and tried the handle. After an initial snag, turning the wheel became easy. The hatch swung up on spring hinges before he had the chance to stop it. Fortunately, there was no one up here to witness his appearance, and he wondered belated if any of the hatches had been alarmed. *Would they send more droids down? Surely they haven't got that many.*

Not willing to risk the elevator, he continued climbing to the next manual hatch, leading to what he believed was the lower passenger deck. From here he could use the main exit. He was undoing the hatch when he heard someone above cry out.

"Shit," Ana said, hitting the elevator button several times.

"Chill, sister. They'll be unconscious soon enough."

"Assuming they don't call Security, or alert Sky City first!"

"We can handle any human security, and I can't see them having more droids."

"Our chica here can simply toss Q at them if they do." Ileana winked.

The lift stopped and the doors hissed open again. In front of them was a short empty passage to the outer hull.

"So far, so good. No alarms." Rhyll exhaled, realising she was holding her breath, not relishing having to throw the alien around all the time.

"Which way?" Cat stepped out, Ileana on her heels, taser now in hand.

"Turn left at the next intersection," Q said through the headsets.

The trio swiftly moved, following Q's directions. At the intersection, the passage going left and right curved out of sight.

"Stands to reason," Rhyll said when she noticed. "The lift really is a cylinder, after all."

"I hate not seeing what's ahead." Ileana moved to the outer wall to glimpse as far ahead as she could.

"We are here," Q informed them after several minutes. The door next to Rhyll had a label, *Environmental Control*, stencilled on it.

All the lights started flashing.

Opening the door silently, they saw there was one technician at the console checking monitors. He was in the motion of standing when Ileana tasered him. He slumped, unconscious, back into his chair.

Rhyll put her hand to the console automatically. Q peeled off and flattened against the surface.

Checking the monitors, they could see the temperatures, air quality and air pressure on the various decks. Other statistics indicated water temperature, pressure and quantity. Slowly, the air quality dropped from green to amber in the upper floors.

"I have reduced the oxygen levels and marginally increased the carbon dioxide sufficient to cause unconsciousness. Understand though, to err on the side of safety, some people may not be entirely unconscious, depending on their fitness and physiology."

"I see. As long as they don't pose a threat to us." Cat didn't look too concerned. "Is it done?"

"Optimal effect will be in four minutes. I have also taken the initiative to deactivate their communications ability."

"Good. And we've got ... nine minutes before we dock?" Cat checked her watch.

"Eight minutes, thirty-six seconds."

"Let's go. We need to be ready to leave immediately." She tapped her tab to bring the helmet up. The other two followed suit.

"Any idea of the docking procedure?" Rhyll asked.

"No doubt there'll be customs and security, much like an airport," Cat guessed.

"That would be true for the passengers. What about the commercial cargo bay? It's lower down so wouldn't that mean a different entrance on a different level?"

Cat considered this as they made their way along the passage. "It is a worthy idea. There will still be officials ..."

"But probably not security? It might be as simple as worker droids."

"I like your thinking, chica." Ileana slapped her on the back.

"We have to go back down below. And it will be a tight squeeze moving through the stacks of cargo."

"Maybe for some," Cat joked.

"What was that? All I'm hearing is static," Ileana commented, tapping her cowling.

Now arriving back on the lower level, they retraced their path to the commercial cargo bay. Rhyll stepped inside and once again started moving sideways to squeeze past the neatly stacked parcel racks. As there were a few rows, the other two could have one for themselves, thereby saving time.

Ileana, being the last to enter, was waiting in the passage. Rhyll was in and had started down her row; Cat was just moving in. The big fighter casually glanced down the passage and noticed the hatch was now open.

"Fuck!"

"What is it?" Cat called back.

"That puta is up here somewhere."

"Well, he's not in here and will more than likely be unconscious in a few minutes. Let's go."

"Couldn't we have used this before?" Rhyll asked, thinking of the precious time wasted going up and down the levels in the lift when they could have been gone by now. She continued edging sideways.

"There is no airlock here; as such it is not a designated exit."

"Q, this cargo bay is airtight?" she asked again.

"Obviously."

"No, I mean the door we just came through from the passage. When we open the cargo door to space, what will happen?"

"I estimate the internal door should sustain a controlled depressurisation only."

"You hearing this, Cat?"

"I am; you want this cargo bay to be an airlock," Cat stated.

"And we can get back to the ship. No one needs to be hurt at all, and we can avoid any security."

"As long as we can get out before we dock. Do it."

"Q?" Rhyll had been getting closer to the hull. She reached out as she approached.

Q stretched the remaining inches and coagulated on the wall.

"As it is not designed to be an airlock, the only way to depressurise is to open the door slightly. Ensure you are all secure. There will be great air pressure differential for several minutes." A couple of seconds later, the door lifted, revealing a two-centimetre gap at the base.

Instantly the lights changed to flashing red and there was an audible alarm. Rhyll felt the drag on her feet as the air was sucked out. She held on tight.

"Docking is imminent. I will need to proceed at a faster rate."

"Do what you need to do. Hang on, everyone."

The door rose incrementally. There was a sudden pulling of air. By the time it rose a metre, the air pressure had virtually disappeared and the force of the expelling air reduced dramatically.

"Docking in fifty-two seconds."

"Everyone get out now!" Cataleya ordered.

12

RHYLL PUSHED AND PULLED AS HARD AS SHE DARED, TRUSTING THE integrity of the alien suit as it scraped across the metal struts of the shelves. Slipping free with the last push she nearly spiralled out into the void, but she managed to grab one of the struts. She twisted and pulled herself back, now standing on the lip of the cargo bay entrance at the end of a row of shelving.

Looking to the next aisle, Cat also emerged.

"You can do it, sister," she heard Cat encouraging Ileana.

Rhyll turned her gaze upwards, speechless at the massive structure now looming above them. Sky City was almost two kilometres in diameter, with the lift dock at its centre. Though much reduced, the speed was still significant and they'd be arriving very soon. Too soon!

Rhyll looked worried as they continued to approach the docking bay. "Umm ... Q?"

"I'm stuck!" Ileana called out.

Cat jumped the short distance to the next aisle. "Use those muscles, sister," she urged, bracing herself and pulling Ileana's arm at the same time.

Rhyll felt herself sweating with the tension as more of the lift disappeared. Over her comm she could hear Ileana and Cataleya swearing and grunting with the effort.

"Q?" Rhyll called again, apprehensive at the lack of response from the alien. She lost her footing as the lift suddenly braked hard. The jolt was so unexpected her body swung around, and she continued to fall upwards with the impetus. Her hand slipped. In a fit of panic, she snatched wildly at the lip of the cargo door as she floated past. She missed, and the gesture only served to cause her to spin. The hull of the lift, then the underbelly of Sky City, swept into view. Something grabbed her ankle.

"Got you, chica." Looking down in surprised relief, Rhyll saw Cat stretched out from the lip of the doorway to reach her, her other hand gripped by Ileana, who in turn was holding onto a rack strut.

Rhyll was too stunned to respond. She was pulled down until they were all firmly standing on the cargo deck again.

Looking up, she saw that half the lift had entered the space dock before it ground to a stop. The internal lighting was still flashing red.

They heard Q suddenly. "The lift drives are quite a distance. It took most of my functionality to reach it. I'm detecting rapid heartbeat and breathing, along with high blood pressure. Are you not well, Rhyll?"

Rhyll breathed in pent-up relief. "I'm fine, and thanks for stopping the lift."

"It is only temporary, lest the drives burn out."

With the threat of imminent doom over for the moment, they took a few minutes to breathe. As they let themselves relax a little, they looked about and noticed, with alarm, that the alien vessel was nowhere in sight.

"Where's the ship?" Rhyll asked anxiously.

"This doorway is not on the facing side of the ship."

"How far is it?" Ileana looked around. She saw the imposing bulk of the city above, the lift protruding from the docking facility, and the mostly smooth surface of the lift curving away left and right. In front of them was wide open emptiness.

"The craft is seventy-eight degrees to your right," Q informed them.

"Okay then ..." Cataleya leant out, craning her head to see, but the craft was lost beyond the curve of the lift.

"How did you stop the ship?" Rhyll asked. "I thought you had to be onboard to control it."

"Part of the initial programming was to shadow the lift at fifty metres," Q responded immediately. "The lift stopped; the ship stopped."

"Nice." Cat looked to Ileana. "You okay?"

Her companion nodded, remaining silent. Cat gripped her shoulder briefly, then said, "It will be a challenging climb to the other side."

Ileana nodded, looking apprehensively at the streamlined hull. "There is not much surface to grip."

One at a time, they turned around so they were facing the lift. Cataleya led. She reached out to grip the barest edge of one of the panels, looking for the slightest protrusion to gain a better purchase. When she thought she was secure, she attempted to pull with her fingers, but immediately slipped, gaining little traction.

Ileana grabbed her to prevent her friend drifting, and pulled her back to safety.

"This could take quite a while." Cat flexed her fingers and started again.

"What about up there?" Rhyll pointed.

The two Brazilians stopped and looked where Rhyll indicated.

"Sky City?" Ileana stared.

"Just the base of it. It's not so smooth, and it looks like there are plenty of handholds. We could use it easily to work our way around the lift."

"And the UFO?"

"Q, you said the ship was programmed to maintain fifty metres?"

"Affirmative."

"And it was more or less adjacent to the emergency hatch." Rhyll turned back to her companions. "The UFO should be close to the city's base, just in a different direction."

"So instead of jumping from the lift, we jump from the city. Seems more feasible." Cat nodded approval.

"You will have to be quick before you run out of air. I estimate Rhyll has approximately twenty-five minutes left. Your larger masses will require more air; you will have less time."

"Is it saying I'm fat?" Ileana scowled.

"No—"

"Joking, chica. Let's go."

As they prepared to kick themselves up, the lift lurched into motion and started rising again, resuming its insertion into the bay, but it was slow.

"I guess that'll make it a bit easier," Rhyll suggested hopefully.

"It's not as if we can miss it," Ileana stated, eyeing the large structure above.

"As long as we time it right. I don't want to get smeared between the lift and that dock."

Looking up, they saw the lift disappeared within the maw of the city dock.

"See that receiver dish? Let's all aim for that," Rhyll suggested.

To reduce movement whilst adrift, they put their arms out, ready to grab the dish, or anything else that presented itself should they overshoot their intended mark.

"Ready?" Cat tapped them and they crouched. "Nice and easy, people. Jump."

Gently, they used their legs to push themselves up and away.

Moving slightly faster relative to the lift, they drifted upwards.

The three figures gracefully rose closer and closer to the satellite dish, outstretched fingers gripping the structure with ease. Their bodies slowly arced around until the momentum was spent. The mass of the three women moved the dish a few degrees.

By the time they were stationary, the tail of the lift disappeared inside the dock . The massive underbelly of the space terminal stretched as far as they could see in all directions, the only significant difference being the glow from the docking bay where the massive length of the tether stretched almost thirty-six thousand kilometres down to the base tower between Ecuador and the Galapagos islands.

With the lift now completely inside the bay, they could see the UFO maintaining its programmed distance, hovering on the other side of the tether. It was clearly visible, with a portion of its black surface contrasting with the opal planet below.

The entire structure was anchored to the ground by a massive nano-fibre tether which passed up through the docking bay and beyond. The four lightweight yet super-strong cables used for the individual lifts were placed equidistant around it.

"Do you see what I see?" Rhyll asked, pointing.

"Those other cables?" Cat responded.

"Yes. If we move closer to the tether it will only be a short jump to them. We could use them to climb down to the craft which will be closer."

"I think our little chica is starting to enjoy herself," Cataleya quipped to Ileana.

"I always thought there was something not quite right about that girl."

"Hey, I can hear you!"

Cataleya got back to the business at hand. "We should do something before they investigate what happened on the lift." With that, Cataleya started pulling herself hand-over-hand along the surface of Sky City's base. The underside had plenty of areas, panels, antennas to use as handholds, and they covered the thirty metres in a few minutes.

With no gravity to hinder them, it was a disconcerting time: there was no up or down. When they stopped, the rest of their body wanted to continue, and they had to remember to counteract the momentum.

This became more important when they neared the edge of the dock. They could see the underside of the lift about twenty metres inside. The dock itself was about fifty metres in diameter — wide enough for a lift each side of the massive tether.

"They keep the dock open all the time?" Ileana asked, peering up.

"That must be an internal airlock," Rhyllien pointed to the large, concertina-like tube now between the lift and the city superstructure.

"Let's move around the perimeter." Cat forged ahead after a brief look into the dock. "I don't want to find ourselves sucking vacuum."

"It does not work that way," Q said.

In steady, stop-start glides, the trio made their way around the dock to the cable nearest the UFO, now almost directly below them. Once there, they paused to judge the distance to the cable.

"You have approximately fifteen minutes of air remaining," Q informed Rhyll.

"Did you hear that?" Rhyll asked the others.

"Roger," they both replied.

"I'll go first," Cat said. With that, she gently pushed off, sailing slowly towards the cable. It seemed to take a long time, but twenty seconds later her outstretched hand wrapped around the cable; it was as thick as her forearm.

"After you, Ana." Rhyll rested her left hand briefly on Ileana's shoulder.

"Right. Yes," Ana replied, but still hesitated.

"How about we go together? That will increase our chances of getting hold of the cable," Rhyll suggested calmly.

Ileana nodded.

"And I'm here to catch anyone drifting away." Cat waved at them in encouragement.

"On three?" Rhyll suggested to her.

Ileana nodded.

"One ... two ... three."

They both jumped; Ileana was a split second after the young girl. With her hesitation, she jumped harder to counter her delay. The pair started rotating like two dancers in a slow-motion pirouette.

"Fuck!" Ileana vented her irritation.

"It's okay." Rhyll kept her eyes riveted on the cable and on Cataleya, who was waiting for them. "We're still heading in the right direction."

"I've got you." Cat had climbed a few arm-lengths along the cable. When they got closer, she scissored her ankles around the cable and stretched both arms out, catching the approaching pair and slowing them down.

The combined momentum sent the trio into a slow arc around the cable, held in place by Cat's interlocked boots until Rhyll was also able to grab hold.

"See? Easy."

"Si. Easy." Ileana nodded. "Thank you."

"Just imagine the trouble we would have had if we had Williams," Rhyll joked.

"He would have been zapped into unconsciousness before we left the lift." Ileana's reply was a sign she had recovered her brief bout of nervousness.

"Time to go." Again, Cat took the lead and started pulling herself hand-over-hand down the cable. Once she had sufficient speed, it was simply a matter of using the cable as a guide until she was close to the UFO.

Rhyll followed, but as the cable was too thick for her small hands to get a good grip, she made a circle with her arms and simply glided down the cable while Ileana pushed her by the boots. She tightened her arms, using the suit as a brake before colliding with Cat.

Ileana was right behind her, now back to her normal gruffness.

"Are we all good?" Cat asked, looking at Ileana.

She gave the thumbs-up to her friend and commander.

The trio turned towards the craft drifting fifteen metres away. As they judged the distance, the cable vibrated.

"Can you feel that?" Rhyll asked.

As one, the three of them looked down the length of cable to the planet's surface but nothing could be seen.

"What's happening?" Ileana asked, confused. "Is that another elevator coming?"

"No," Q informed them calmly, then added, "but another lift is departing."

"Look!" Rhyll said.

Ileana swung her gaze up. "Fuck. It's on this cable!"

"Quiet! Everyone crouch and get ready to jump. Like before, a gentle push is all we need. On three, people. One ... two ... three ..."

As the trio launched, they reached out for each other. The slight disparity with their jumping effort only caused the slightest of tumbling. Seconds later, the bulk of the downward-travelling lift skimmed by their boots silently and smoothly.

Cataleya, Rhyll and Ileana glided towards the craft, on track at a slightly oblique angle. There was no telling what part of the craft faced them, as it was completely devoid of any feature that would distinguish front, back or sides.

"Nice and easy," Cat murmured. "We got this." Her cowling had misted slightly with the recent tension and exertion. A quick glance at Ileana showed the same.

Cat was the first to make contact. Her outstretched hand and splayed fingers brushed the hull ... and kept sliding, with little reduction in momentum. "Fuck!"

"Shit!" Rhyll remembered too late. "It's frictionless!"

Cat slid off the surface, her arms floundering in vain.

"You need to release me," Q's voice came over the headset as they continued to slide across the hull's surface.

"Can you grip the surface? You won't slide off as well? We'll all be dead if that happens." *And so will the world's population.*

"If can override the frictionless aspect, I should then be able to cycle th—"

"I can't see!" Ileana let go of Rhyll's hand. At first she made futile attempts to wipe at her cowling, then scrabbled at the featureless hull.

"Q will keep us safe," Rhyll said, trying to calm her. The tumbling, combined with Cat's and Ileana's sudden release of her hand, had accentuated her spin. As she slowly spun away from the craft, she tried to keep calm as the crystal-clear, starry sky swept by, until she was facing the craft again.

"There you go." She gently pushed the alien toward the hull.

It was only a couple of metres, but with the three of them now slipping to the far side of the craft and nothing to stop them drifting into the void, their lives relied on the slug-shaped thing.

———

Q's FIRST TASK WAS TO FORM A TIGHT BALL, THEREBY REDUCING THE centre of gravity and preventing any wobble which could push it off target. Once that was achieved, it then stretched its form along the axis of trajectory, creating as much surface area as possible. At the current velocity and angular momentum, it calculated there was 3.73 seconds to interface with the ship's hull before it, too, would slide off the edge and drift into space. This wasn't a concern, it having survived over a century in deep space previously.

To a device which measured time in eons, drifting into space was nothing — especially this close to a planetary body; the gravity would draw it in inexorably. Q would modify its shape to reduce speed and therefore remove the possibility of damage

caused by friction, perhaps even glide close enough to civilisation — primitive as it was — and eventually find another host to
utilise in another bid to get off-world. Not that this would help
the three human females currently adrift in the void: the human
female who had provided an avenue for his freedom had less
than eight minutes of air left.

It briefly contemplated how and why it came to be in this
predicament in the first place.

The entity known as Rhyllien Ellis possessed traits not
dissimilar to others it had encountered — and, though a rarity
even after a million years' existence, spanning two galaxies — it
was intriguing.

The intrigue had been so great, Q had done a very rare thing
— almost as rare as Rhyllien's abilities. Q had inserted a minute
portion of itself inside her, programmed to modify specific parts
of her brain to create a neuralink. It was a step only a million-
year-old intelligence could comprehend, but it felt the potential
outcome here would far surpass the fleeting sense of impropriety
at having invaded another entity.

Fascinating as she was, her mind — like every other one of
her species — was still far too primitive to comprehend what
could be achieved by the modification, which would allow her
interstellar communication.

Only if humankind survived long enough to develop their
brains to full potential would they realise there was a galactic
consciousness. Not a god, but a network of awareness, a recogni-
tion that they were anything but alone in the universe. Equally
advanced races had already achieved this, and contact had been
made over vast distances.

Q was simply making a subtle advancement in this natural
development and determined the Rhyllien entity would not be
informed of the change, thereby not being able to take advantage
of it for personal gain — though from what it could ascertain of
her personality, she was unlikely to be that egocentric.

However, as the small portion was a part of itself, Q would

be aware — and be able to keep in contact, though only one way. She was a rare enough find to warrant such intervention — only three planetary messengers were known, and the last was several million years before Q's existence.

Q had initially sensed her back in what the humans referred to as Area 53, somewhat methodically working her way closer to its location. Extrapolating from the miniscule data it had to work with — that being the harmonic frequency she and the gemstone were radiating — there was a 99.85 per cent probability she'd succeed and reacquaint herself with it. There was a .15 per cent chance the forces between her and her goal would prevail. Q determined to put itself in close proximity and take advantage of the situation — the most promising opportunity to leave this world.

A side consideration was that perhaps it was simply bored ...

After a couple of milliseconds, it was as prepared as it could be for the fleeting contact it would have with the craft's mostly frictionless surface. The crude culture that designed this craft — though not as primitive as the humans currently inhabiting the planet below — had not quite perfected the concept.

"Mostly frictionless" is what it was counting on.

Q's own designers had perfected a truly frictionless capability, and it was the first test flight of that design which inadvertently found itself caught in a temporal vortex, shunted across the intergalactic expanse to emerge within the gravity well of a small G-type star.

A highly improbable scenario, considering the distances between stars, but occurring nonetheless. The concept of *luck* was new, though it seemed humans depended on it far more than on logic and inherent ability.

With its brief and sporadic interactions with humans, Q established they had great regard for many obscure beliefs, one being that there was such a thing as luck, and this manifested into either *good* luck or *bad* luck; the amount of either having influence on any particular subject or venture was incalculable.

And Q found such a dilemma, that something was incalculable — left purely to the vagaries of randomness — scary. Or would have, if its designers had had the foresight to endow it with the concept.

Q was amazed how — even after the many failures witnessed over the decades it had been with them — they still reached the existing low level of technology they showed.

In human parlance, it was a series of fortunate circumstances, both positive and negative, which had brought it here, to this current predicament.

Was it merely bad luck to be involved with the failed ship experiment and good luck it survived? Was it good luck it had been removed from the Area 52 facility just prior to the catastrophic failure of their researching the anti-matter drive?

If only they had asked it; it could have assisted.

And that, it determined, was why it was really in this predicament now. Its programming was to carry out tasks, not make inquiries as to this or that.

In this regard, because of its designers strictures, Q had been slow on the uptake, and determined to remedy that by actually *asking* if assistance was required; it was clear the majority of the humans didn't have the wherewithal to even consider asking ... what was it they referred it as ... a slug?

Even after a million years, it still had things to learn. Primitive cultures had some benefits — though extremely few.

Contact ... 1 second ...

2 seconds ...

3 ...

13

THE UFO DISAPPEARED IN MOMENTS IN THE GLARE OF THE SUN OVER Cairo. Even knowing what it was, the speed of it stunned those left behind on the roof. The various flocks of carrion birds feeding off the carcasses in the plaza below scattered in a flurry of feathers.

The area had been developed as a rooftop garden, though most of the plants had stiff brown fronds since the automated irrigation system stopped; only the larger palms survived for now. Other than the gazebo with its table and chairs, there was a small water feature, lounges, rugs and scattered cushions. Swathes of sand were everywhere, blown in by the almost constant wind.

Other than the susurration of the breeze in the overhead palm leaves and cawing of the birds, the city was silent; there was none of the general hubbub of traffic or of thousands of people going about their everyday life.

"It doesn't smell as bad as I thought it would," Dan sighed in relief.

"Maybe not up here; wait until you get to ground level. I can assure you things will be different when you're surrounded by corpses. But," Imogen added upon seeing their faces, "with the heat and the lack of humidity, we'll probably find they've dehydrated sufficiently over these weeks to not smell too much unless you are really close."

Dan looked below, seeing scattered bodies and inert droids. *Fuck I hope those droids stay dead.*

Imogen abruptly turned towards the northeast. "Can you hear that?"

Luckily, the three of them remained concealed under a gazebo as two jets roared overhead. They banked sharply, doing several tight circles before expanding the circumference.

Dan squinted at the jets as they circled, then dug into his pack and pulled out his camera.

"Does that still work?" Nala asked him.

"Q told me he repaired it while we slept." Dan paused, looking over it. All the digital readouts and screen showed normal functions. "He says it's far superior to what I had before."

"Do you think they saw us?" She attempted to study the jet markings but their speed and the glare made it difficult. "Any idea who they are?"

"I don't recognise the logos. Could be any of the major corporations in the area: MedCorp, the UAL ..." Dan offered, zooming in on the craft, but they were moving too quickly. "It would be really handy to know how high this death wave or the electrical interference goes."

"Egyptian Air Force," Imogen informed them both with conviction. "As soon as they go I think we should get off the roof. I'm sure they'll be calling for some form of support. If their interest is piqued — and I doubt their arrival here and now after the UFO visit is coincidental — they'll strive to do something. So, we should find what we came to find and be ready to go whenever we can."

"Ground troops will die and anything automated like droids will malfunction," Dan said.

"The city is deserted. Only the dead remain. With no more

potential casualties or witnesses, there are other ways to attack unwanted guests."

"You mean aerial attack?"

"If we're lucky — and assuming it came to that — we'd be fortunate if it was only gas ... but if they detected the UFO — that would mean aliens to their military minds, and the possibility of getting their hands on advanced technology. For that, I have no doubt they'd stop at nothing to grab it."

The jets moved off to other parts of the city. As the roar faded with the distance Imogen pointed at a stairway and started walking towards it. Within a few minutes they were under cover. By the time they were down to the next level the jets could no longer be heard.

They passed door after door, Imogen seeming to know where to go down the dim corridors. Where the windows were left open, drifts of sand and leaves were prevalent.

"There are no bodies in here," Nala noted after peeking through the open doors as they passed.

"It's as if the government knew something beforehand," Dan suggested.

"They know much more than they tell, but I doubt even they could foresee this."

"So, you've been here before?" Dan asked as he followed her down long corridors with parquetry flooring.

"Cairo, yes, several times with Ken, and a couple of times since, but the last time was about five years ago as senior curator for the São Paulo University to speak at a conference."

"Not New Cairo, then?"

"No. It is weird, but I believe it's because of the proximity to the necropolis they kept this particular department here." At the end of the corridor she stopped at double doors of solid wood. "And here we are, the office of the minister of Egyptian antiquities. While I doubt the information we need will be found in here, there will be something to point to the next clue." She laughed at their disappointed faces. "There's a reason why it's been a secret for so long. You think they left a map with X on it for everyone to see?"

They spent over an hour going through the old filing cabinets, with little to show for it as the light grew dim. At first they used discarded files to make a fire as a light source. Imogen knew a smattering of Arabic, enough to know they weren't burning anything of value. Eventually they found an oil lamp, which helped a great deal.

"Rub it and see if a genie comes out," Dan joked to Nala.

"You know what, kids? There's little point in this stumbling around in the dark. We have several comfortable lounges here, and the tearoom is just down the hall. I think we should see what's available, have a snack and drink and sleep. We can do so much more in the morning."

There were biscuits and some fruit and nuts. The fruit looked dubious but the nuts were fine. Using some of the wooden utensils, they managed to boil enough water. With no milk, Dan screwed his face up at the thought of black Egyptian coffee and settled for black tea.

Nala drank it in small amounts. "Even black coffee is better than tea," she said eventually.

"It's an acquired taste." Imogen sipped at the hot brew. She pulled out Ken's notes, and by the lamplight they worked though his notebook to see what they could glean from his writings and doodling.

———

WILLIAMS HEARD HIMSELF GROAN. IT TOOK A FEW MINUTES FOR HIS drowsy mind to remember what had happened. He waited, listening to the activity on the deck above. The voices were muffled and distant, but it sounded like someone panicking. *Did they see the intruders in the elevator?* With utmost care he cracked the seal to the third level, keeping hold of the hatch so it wouldn't spring open.

Now that the voices had gone, he risked a peek. The passageway here was much wider, well-lit and less austere; all the pipes and conduits were behind the thin cladding made to look like wooden panelling.

He knew he was as much an intruder as those women were, and would be treated no differently when the security team found him. As he was wearing the same alien space suit, they'd assume he was with them, and he doubted anyone would believe he'd been abducted by the women and arrived here in a UFO.

"They'll probably think I'm crazy and sedate me," Williams muttered, deciding he needed a plan to escape from everyone.

From his previous trips he recalled there were some small cabins on this level. Climbing up the remaining rungs, he closed the hatch and started trying the doors, hoping that at least one person had assumed there were no thieves aboard and wouldn't have bothered locking up. As he moved along the corridor, he found a first aid box on the wall. Williams was looking at its contents, the germ of an idea to hide his identity hatching in his mind, when the door he'd tried a couple of seconds earlier opened behind him.

The thin fellow stepped out unawares and promptly doubled over when Williams spun and punched him in the stomach, then rammed his head into the bulkhead. The passenger dropped to the deck unconscious and bleeding. Williams stepped over him and dragged him back into the cabin by his feet then dashed back to the medical box and grabbed some of the items before he closed and locked the door.

Back in the cabin, the passenger's bags were on the bunk, packed for the arrival. Williams checked the tag: *Walter Green*. Rummaging through the belongings, he found a pair of pants and a long-sleeved shirt to replace his bile- and bloodstained one.

Williams began peeling off the space suit. There were no zips or clasps, but as he grabbed the neck and pulled, the centre unravelled all the way down to his crotch. He shuffled his shoulders free and then it was an easy matter of pushing it down his legs and stepping out.

"Fuck it!" He looked at the damp patch in his pants. "When did I do that?"

Before he tried the shirt, he turned to the basin for a quick wash, gently dabbing at his cut chin before scrubbing his face and hair to remove traces of vomit and blood, then used the damp towel to give himself a quick wipe down. It was the best he could do under the circumstances, but he was sure he still stank.

An idea had formed in his head, and moving back to the bunk, he began to put his plan to work. He unclipped his tie-pin and placed it between his thumb and forefinger, where it would overlay his biochip. It was very basic, but would interfere with a random ID scanner. The next step was to bandage the finger to cover the clip, disguising it as an injury.

As he stood to swap the shirts, he began to feel dizzy and slumped heavily against the vanity unit behind him. Williams held his head, feeling a headache coming on. He quickly splashed more cold water on his face and filled a glass to drink.

After a short time he opened his eyes, still feeling groggy and confused. The headache remained, and massaging his temples had little effect. Breathing was a chore and even when he filled his lungs, it wasn't enough. Time passed as he sat there in a stupor. He eventually noticed a message flashing on the inhouse monitor by the bedside table. Something dropped from the ceiling.

Other than a commlink to staff and the galley, the monitor normally depicted various aspects of the journey: speed, altitude, distance to and from each dock and arrival time, as well as atmospheric controls for each relevant cabin. Williams' vision was blurry and he stumbled closer to read it. The screen was flashing a warning of low oxygen level.

Williams then realised it was an emergency facemask that

was dangling by the bed. He grabbed it and breathed deep, but felt nothing.

"What have those bitches done now?" he mumbled vehemently, trying to suck air from the mask. *Nothing!*

The room spun. He dropped to his knees, then the floor, falling across the discarded space suit. Everything was silent, but he heard a faint hissing. Williams blearily gazed at the carpet as his body reacted to oxygen deprivation. He blinked as his drowsy eyes focused on the suit ... *The suit!*

He struggled to pull it up to his face, feeling the bile-scented cool air on his cheeks. Williams breathed deeply with much relief, disregarding the powerful tang of his vomit. He didn't care and kept breathing deeply; he had to.

In small, deliberate movements, Williams continued to remove his shirt and pulled Walter's on, revisiting the suit when he needed more air.

"You're a skinny prick, Walter," he said as he put his arm into the shirt, then the other arm. Before he buttoned the front, he paused to breathe more from the suit.

Movement was restricted by the tight fit, and it would raise some curious stares, he was sure, but it couldn't be helped and he wouldn't need to wear it for long. There was no way he'd fit into the trousers.

Williams took more breaths as he considered what to do next. Seeing the bleeding cut on Walter's head where it had hit the door jamb, he carefully dabbed his bandaged thumb against it to make his own wound look more authentic.

He lifted off the floor when his surroundings slowed dramatically, landing on the edge of the bunk before tumbling to the floor. The lights blinked momentarily and a faint alarm was heard from outside the cabin.

"Now what?" He used the bed to climb to his feet, briefly wondering why no one was yelling or screaming, before his addled mind worked out everyone else was unconscious with the lack of oxygen.

One of Walter's bags had toppled onto the floor, spilling some of the contents, including a toiletry bag. Williams opened it and emptied the contents on the bed. There was a small bottle of aftershave.

"Yes!" It wasn't a fragrance he'd normally use for himself. "Anything's better than *eau de bile*."

Careful to not splash it on his cut chin, he lathered it on, relishing in not reeking like a drunk. When his breathing laboured again, he stuck his head back into the suit while he got his thoughts together. His current predicament was going to be awkward to explain.

Embarrassing enough to explain why I wet my pants. He cursed the big Brazilian woman under his breath.

Williams assumed some alarm had been raised and was certain that as soon as they docked, security would swarm onboard and search the lift. They'd find everyone unconscious, and then medics would probably take them all to the infirmary. Once recovered, they were all sure to be questioned.

He would have to somehow avoid that. Timing was everything. He couldn't be in this cabin when they docked. If he was near the airlock, he'd be found first. *Maybe I can take advantage of the confusion ...*

Williams was inhaling the suit's air when he felt the lift begin to move again. He rose and stumbled to the small porthole. Looking out and up, he saw the blackness of space and the huge belly of Sky City directly above slowly getting closer.

Realising docking was imminent, he took a last lungful of air before dropping the suit to the floor. Holding his breath, he walked out of the cabin, ensuring the door was locked behind him and made his way towards the airlock, where he found several other passengers and two staff lying on the deck. He checked they were unconscious.

Through the thick window in the airlock, he saw the interior of the dock glide past. Choosing his position, he lowered himself to the floor close to the airlock, exhaled and started breathing the low-oxygen atmosphere.

Once docked, the transition tube stretched out and sealed around the lift airlock. Automatic sequencing took place and within three minutes the airlock door cycled open. There was the slightest hiss of air pressure equalisation.

Medics were ready at the airlock to enter and attend the bodies lying on the deck.

"They're alive, Commander. Just unconscious," one said.

The young commander was going through the computer logs. "Says here the oxygen level dropped, but nothing about any leaks. I'll let the techs go over it. For now, once the preliminaries are done, get them to the infirmary." She looked up at one of the medics, who was cursing. "What's the problem?"

"This one's got an injured hand. I can't get his ID." They were looking at a forty-something male in a shirt two sizes too small. "He's pissed his pants."

"Look, he's got a boarding pass in the shirt pocket," the commander pointed.

"Walter Green," the medic read from the pass.

The commander checked her tablet, scrolling through the passenger manifest. "He checks out here. Walter Green, Cabin 3G. Take him out and we'll deal with them all one at a time to get to the bottom of what happened."

"Yes, ma'am."

Gurneys were already waiting on the city side of the transition tube. They were quickly wheeled in by a line of medical staff, and one at a time the unconscious passengers were taken to the infirmary.

14

THE TRIO GLIDED SAFELY INTO THE SHIP VIA THE GRAVITON BEAM, being deposited gently on the floor as the outer door irised closed.

Ileana was asphyxiating, tapping frantically at her shoulder tab to open her cowling.

"Q? We need air *now!*" Cataleya shouted. Her HUD was flashing red too; it could be any second that she, too, would start gasping like a fish on land. "Ileana, it won't open in a vacuum." She held her friend's hands, trying to calm her, trying to hide the trauma she, too, felt from her face. Ileana was gasping carbon dioxide and not paying attention, and now her eyes were closed. "Stay with me, sister!" Cat shook her to stimulate her enough to remain conscious.

"How long, Q?" Rhyll asked looking around for the alien, noting how the pulse of the lights was slowing.

"Eight seconds," the entity responded over their speakers. The alien was on the wall by the external door. It dropped to the floor and oozed across to the inner door. The lights were almost steady now.

"Ana. Very soon." Cat was worried at the wheezing noises now coming from her comrade.

Ileana dropped to her knees. Cat helped her down gently, but her heavy, listless body made it difficult.

Just as Ana began to slip into unconsciousness, the lights steadied.

"Now," Q informed them all calmly.

Immediately Cat hit the tab on Ana's shoulder, then her own. "Ana?" She shook her as the cowling retracted.

"Check her pulse," Rhyll suggested, her cowling now retracted.

Cat grabbed Ileana's wrist. "Can't in these gloves." She gently slapped Ana's face to revive her. "Breathe, sister."

"Q, is there a medical room, or something you can do?" As soon as she'd said it, Rhyll realised she could help here. She quickly pulled her suit down, extricated her arms and knelt by Ileana, she then placed a palm on her pale forehead and concentrated to heal.

This was different to the other healing, there being no wound, but once she relaxed and concentrated it seemed her body or subconscious knew how to respond.

Shortly, Ileana started coughing, heaving in a lungful of air, and then another.

"Easy," Cat said softly. "You're safe now."

After a few minutes, they helped her up and out of her suit.

"I do not want to do that again," she said. "Ever."

"You won't need to." Rhyll led them out of the tractor room and turned towards the control room.

"I need to hit the head first." Ileana turned to the sleeping quarters, her hand against the wall for support.

"Hit the head?" Rhyll asked.

"She needs the toilet," said Cat. "It's a term from the days of sailboats."

Rhyll nodded. "I'll have to remember that bit of trivia." She hung her suit up.

Cat did as well, along with Ileana's, before slumping into the chair.

"Thanks, Q. Is everything here okay?" Rhyll asked.

"Everything is functioning normally."

She considered their next move. "Well, we have all the diamonds now. I guess we go to Cairo and see how Mum's doing ... but ..." She paused.

"What to do with us?" Cat guessed.

"I ..."

"If I may make an observation?" Q cut in. It had slid back onto the console where it could easily control all the functions of the ship.

"Sure. You don't need anyone's permission to do that." Rhyll shrugged at Cataleya.

"When I first sensed you back in Area 53, I noted the powerful aura surrounding you, resonating with the diamond you were seeking, and I now note the other diamonds do also — though each with a slight variation in frequency.

"Again, when I encountered your friends Nala and Dan, they also exuded an aura resonant to yours, but at a greatly reduced level of power; then too your mother, as well as Cataleya and Ileana. If this is what is concerning you, I can assure you they both have the same ability as the others."

"I wasn't sure ... but that's great to hear!"

"What's great?" Ileana entered, looking much better now that she had freshened up.

"Q says you will both survive when we go to Cairo."

"I'll be happy, as long as there's plenty of gravity and air."

"After that little adventure in space, I think we all will," Cat nodded.

"I quite liked it, though it took some getting used to," Rhyll offered.

"Like I said after we first met her in Brazil," Ileana spoke softly to Cat, "she's not quite right up here." She tapped her skull.

"Be nice." Rhyll pretended to pout.

"That *was* me being nice." Ileana grinned as she flopped into the third chair, which quickly conformed to the sudden weight increase.

"Good to see you back to your usual self."

"Sorry about all—"

"Nonsense. This is beyond anything we were trained for. I don't foresee it being added to our curriculum any time soon."

"Not us, maybe, but if not already, there is bound to be a space military of some description one day."

In the process of Q manoeuvring the ship to collect the three drifting women with the graviton beam, it had moved a bit further away from the Sky City docking area. It still loomed above, filling the majority of the viewport.

"I wonder what happened to Williams," Rhyll said.

"He will have a lot of explaining to do." Ileana chuckled. "And who'll believe he crossed through space from a UFO? They will put him in a cell as a stowaway, for sure."

"I don't know," Cataleya answered. "He strikes me as a wily one."

"Sneaky, weaselly men give me the creeps."

"No arguments from me, sister."

"So, shall we go to Cairo?"

The others nodded.

———

THE GLARE OF THE LIGHTS CAUSED HIM TO BLINK AND TURN HIS head until his eyes adjusted to the brightness. Once they did, he slowly looked around him, already chastising himself for moving his head. He wanted to slip away quietly but if anyone was watching, they'd see he had awoken. Fortunately there was no one present — no one conscious; he counted over a dozen unconscious passengers filling the room on portable bunks similar to the one he was on.

His ad hoc plan had worked. By using the suit's air until the last minute, the oxygen deprivation he suffered was minimal in comparison to the other passengers; therefore, he'd hoped to regain awareness sooner.

It was a gamble that had paid off.

With another glance around, and hearing no alarm, Williams carefully levered himself off the bunk and checked the rest of the area beyond the doorway. Every part of his body part felt like a dead weight, but he had to move. There was no telling how many more passengers still had to be brought in. For all he knew, the medics could be returning now, and then his real identity would surely be discovered.

Breathing deeply, he forced his legs into motion, managing to stagger to the wall by the double swinging doors. There was a square window in each. Peering through, he could see that, apart from several more occupied trolley beds lining the wall, the corridor was empty.

His memory of Sky City was fresh in his mind from his last stay only a month ago, but he didn't recognise this area as he'd had no need to visit the medical facility. All he knew was he was on the same level as the passenger terminal and closer to the centre; that meant he needed to go up and further out in to get to the area he did know. He picked a direction and moved, each step getting easier. The curve of the corridor indicated the rim of the complex was to his left. As luck would have it, he came across a map of the level.

After seeing the *You are Here* label, it was easy to determine he should turn left at the next junction and follow that until he reached another intersection. From there he could access elevators to take him up to the level he required, but it was still quite a distance to where he wanted to be. The longer the walk, the more attention he'd receive in his ill-fitting shirt.

Or is that me being paranoid? he wondered as he quickly moved on.

• • •

"AH, MR WILLIAMS," THE CONCIERGE SAID, RECOGNISING HIM FROM the last visit. She eyed his attire curiously. "Welcome back ... but I don't see a booking ..."

WILLIAMS NOTICED HER NOSE WRINKLE; HE HAD BECOME TOO familiar with the odour of his sickness.

"No booking?" Williams thought quickly. "Damn that new intern. It seems nothing's going right this trip. The passenger beside me got space sick, and then I find my luggage wasn't loaded!"

"I'm sorry to hear that. I'm happy to arrange for any services you need." As she spoke, she was working on her terminal. "We can fit you in, Mr Williams. May I ask how long you'll be staying with us, and will that be on the Volaris account?"

"What? Oh yes, of course. Thank you. I believe this business visit will be several days; book me in for three days with a provision to extension if possible."

"It has been rather hectic, with all the drama currently on the surface." She indicated with her head towards a muted monitor running news footage. "But as Volaris is a valued client, I've blocked off a week for you. Will Mr Stradjek be joining us?"

"No. I don't believe he will be this time."

Within ten minutes, he was showering in is his suite and a new clothes order on its way. He considered his next steps. He needed rest as it was close to midnight, hours since his abduction, with the added trauma of being roughed up and tasered. Other than his Volaris associates, the only people he knew here worked for ICON. Since they seemed to value his information, maybe he could get some work through them.

After putting a call through to Lucas and arranging a meeting, he set the alarm and fell asleep the moment his head hit the pillow.

———

A FEW HOURS LATER THEY RE-ENTERED THE EARTH'S ATMOSPHERE, angling across the equator over the South Atlantic Ocean to cross the southern coastline of West Africa. Below was an expanse of dense jungle. This region was in twilight, suggesting it was early morning and that they were heading into the sunrise.

"I'm not one hundred per cent, but I think we're going over Guinea, or Sierra Leone," Rhyll informed them.

Cataleya watched with interest. "I wonder what they're like at jungle warfare."

"I hear they are mostly disorganised militia — thugs with guns, harassing civilians."

"Possibly true, but even so, there's bound to be those with bush skills. They would be formidable, relying on those skills from a young age to survive — not just as a job."

"Survival is a good incentive," Ileana agreed.

The green faded quickly into the mostly desolate landscape of North Africa. As they moved east, it gradually became lighter.

"I have heard of deserts and seen pictures, but this is like nothing I had imagined." Ileana stared at the empty, yellow-hued vista.

"I recognise this area — we're over Niger now, where I had to go to retrieve the first stolen diamond, then I was kidnapped to Area 53." Rhyll briefly wondered how Niels Franke was going.

The swathes of yellow and tan dunes below soon turned into a more rocky terrain. Far to their left, a blue tinge came into view on the horizon.

"There's the Mediterranean."

The craft descended as it neared the coastline for their approach to the ancient and sprawling metropolis of Cairo, now bathed in the morning sun.

"What's that?" Ileana stood beside her, pointing to a green smudge to the north of the sprawling city they were approaching.

"That's the Nile delta. There's not much left after the sea-level rise."

"Will we be heading back to the same building?" Cataleya asked. "I'd like to get an overview of the immediate area."

"I guess so. It's only reasonable to assume if they aren't there, they won't be far away." Rhyll looked down to Q, in its usual position on the console. "Are you able to make contact with any of them?"

"I am not. The electromagnetic disturbance remains."

"Oh, well. We'll just have to find them ourselves."

"Maybe a couple of shots in the air will alert them to our presence," Ileana suggested.

"Worth a try, I guess."

They watched as the craft turned to follow the river, heading towards the island where they'd dropped off Imogen, Nala and Dan a little over fifteen hours earlier.

"I can't see any drones," Rhyll noted.

"I am not detecting anything within several hundred kilometres," Q said.

"Is that unusual?" Cat wondered.

"Perhaps they found the others ... and somehow worked out how to take them?" Ileana suggested.

Rhyll shook her head. "Nothing works here. Is that still the case, Q?"

"If the electrical interference is capable of stopping my sensors, it is highly unlikely there is any technology here that will work."

"It is suspicious." Cataleya looked carefully, regardless of the result from the ship's sensors. "We need to land, but away from where we think they are, just in case."

"Draw their attention elsewhere if they're watching, you mean?" Rhyll guessed.

"*Exatamente*," Cat nodded. "We'll find your mother, but quietly and with far less danger if we don't have to contend with drones, or worse."

"But not too far," Ileana suggested. "Those bridges will be

difficult to cross undetected; motion detectors, or thermal imaging will pick us up quickly."

"True. We'll land on the island, but as far as possible from where we think they are."

"What about those sporting fields?" Rhyll suggested.

"Again, too open. Can the ship get lower? Maybe near a building with a car park ... or we can use those trees as cover." Cat pointed to a treed parkland.

"I should point out that it is still possible for thermal imaging to detect you. Just because nothing in the vicinity works, it doesn't mean remote surveillance won't be functioning."

"Merda!" Ileana paced the cabin.

"However, the suits will protect you the same as you are currently protected by the advanced technology of this craft. You will need to keep the helmets up until you are indoors."

"And the air?" Cat asked.

"Has been replenished. It is an automatic function when the cowling is down." The rack slid out from the wall.

They descended to what turned out to be the garden at the rear of a mosque where several large trees grew. It was across the road from the ministry building where they'd dropped off the others. It was a simple matter for the ship to get to ground level and move under the canopy, the lower branches being pushed to the side by the almost frictionless hull. The craft had to pivot slightly as one of the branches obstructed the doorway.

Once they'd clambered back into the suits, they grabbed their packs and walked down the ramp and looked back from the base of a tree, waiting.

"I still do not detect anything," they heard Q say in their headsets after a couple of minutes.

"Thanks, Q." Rhyll turned to the soldiers, addressing Cataleya. "What now?"

"First, we cross to the ministry building. If they are not there, then as Ana suggested, we fire a gun. If they are close, they will hear it."

A path between the mosque and another building led them to a low wall separating the grounds from the road. It wasn't high, and they climbed it easily and quickly crossed the street.

"That's the building," Cataleya pointed. Before long they were climbing the stairs, calling out on each floor.

Ileana found a directory. It was mostly in Arabic, but had subtitles in several languages. "Would the Director General be of any use?"

"It's a place to start I guess. If anyone is going to know anything, you'd think it would be the head honcho," Rhyll agreed. She followed them up several more floors and then down a carpeted corridor.

Ileana went to the doors at the far end and entered. "Looks like they were here," she said, stating the obvious.

They found signs of recent habitation: the burnt papers in the metal bins, used cups and biscuit crumbs, and the makeshift beds on the lounges.

"So, they are no longer in the building. We would have heard them, or they us," Rhyll said, sounding disappointed.

"We would have been very lucky if they were still here," Cataleya said, patting her shoulder. "We'll find them."

"I think I know where they are," Rhyll said suddenly as she moved quickly to the desk where an old oil lamp lay. Beside it was a note written in her mother's handwriting. As she picked it up she heard the loud thunder of explosions nearby.

The three of them ran to the window to look out, but the noise was on the other side of the building.

"Upstairs!" Cataleya ordered as she jogged out the office.

15

THE MEETING WITH LUCAS DIDN'T GO EXACTLY AS HE HAD HOPED. Lucas seemed amiable enough when talking via commlink, but in person he was distant and not very communicative.

"You realise this is quite awkward," Lucas said to Williams. "Normally we do the headhunting, not having people turning up unannounced at our doorstep. The best I can do is make a suggestion to my superiors, but I have to be honest, with the recent news, you may not be a good fit."

"Good fit? What recent news?" Williams wondered.

"You haven't heard? If it's not that girl plastered everywhere, or the updates on the deaths, it's you and Stradjek being abducted by a UFO! Have a look." Lucas stood and walked him over to the other side of the lounge where a screen was playing, but muted.

Over the course of several minutes, he saw the tail end of a reel he had seen many times where the redhead girl was walking amongst the druids at Stonehenge. Then he saw what Lucas was talking about: drone footage of a flying saucer hovering over the Carlton-Ritz. There was a faint beam of green light and two men were floundering in the air, being drawn into it.

A drone flew too close and got caught in the graviton beam,

but the vid from it showed brief closeups of his face and that of Tyrone's. He recalled his fear at the time, but seeing it on his face and shown internationally, it was highly embarrassing.

The text below gave the gist of what happened.

'Alien abduction of Tyrone Stradjek, co-founder of Volaris, and his PA, Benjamin Williams.'

"It's not a good look at all, and not a good fit."

To Williams, the little runt sounded condescending. "See how the fuck you handle it, you little prick." Williams stormed off through the busy lounge.

People stopped and gawped, realising who he was. There was a short-lived silence, then a susurration of many subdued voices all gossiping at once.

"Assholes," he muttered, quickening his pace.

When he returned to the apartment, he ignored the concierge in the foyer trying to get his attention. Cute as she was, he wasn't in the mood for chitchat.

Entering his apartment, the commlink was buzzing. He headed for the bar and fixed himself a drink to quell his nerves and to think. After the third glass, he saw the flashing light of a message.

Reluctantly, he strode to the bedside dresser and activated it.

"Benjamin?" He recognised the mysterious voice immediately. "Hail the Light. What an interesting time you've had of late. I hope this doesn't affect our arrangement. Be in the viewing lounge at 21:00." The message ended.

"Fuck!" He stumbled back to the bar and poured himself another drink.

When there was a knock at the door, he jumped, dropping the glass on the thick carpet. It didn't break. He breathed in and out several times to get his thoughts together.

Surely the Illuminati wouldn't come doorknocking?

Propped up by the alcohol — and armed with a knife from the kitchenette — he summoned the nerve to go to the door and open it.

He sighed with relief, seeing the concierge. "Maria, isn't it?" He forced a smile and tucked the knife into his pocket, unseen.

"Mr Williams ... this is not policy but I should warn you the SCS are looking for someone. I thought I should warn you."

"Sky City Security? Me? Why?" He knew he was blabbering — also from the effects of the alcohol. "Do they know I'm here?" *How do they know who I am? Did they scan my ID while I was unconscious?*

"I was on a break when my colleague spoke to them. He gave them a list of the recent arrivals. They didn't know your name, and he hadn't seen you—"

"Then why would they want to see me? Did they say anything?"

"Everyone else had been booked in for weeks. You're the only one who was a walk-in — which is highly unusual."

"Okay ..." His mind raced. "Oh ... thank you for telling me, Maria." He closed the door. *What to do? What to do?* There was a knock again. Maria was still there.

"You should go now, but by the back way — through the service area." She showed him a security pass.

"Oh, shit. Yes. I'll just grab my gear. Better come in."

Maria entered, but waited close by the door.

Williams turned on the inhouse monitor. He packed while a string of ads scrolled on, before the screen changed to a talking head.

"An alert has been put out by Sky City Security. All citizens are to be on the lookout for a Caucasian male, dark hair, in his mid-thirties. He is believed dangerous and involved with an end-of-life event."

No picture? "So they didn't scan my ID; they don't know who I am yet," he muttered, checking his watch. *19:43.* He still had over an hour before the meeting. His other predicament kept bobbing to the surface from his subconscious. The Illuminati were awaiting a delivery of rare diamonds — his ticket to joining them. Now that the diamonds were lost, he'd have to appease them another way.

Maybe I can pin the blame on Stradjek, he considered.

"Hart!" He snapped his fingers. "Joseph Hart has the red diamond." Now all he had to do was convince the Illuminati all wasn't lost. "The red was worth almost as much as the others combined." He smiled at how upset those bitches would be when they found out there were only two real diamonds in that box. He had reluctantly swapped the red one out with the possibility Hart would get it valued before the auction. *Unlucky for them; lucky for me.*

There was something else bothering him. *Damn alcohol!*

"Maria, what's this 'end-of-life' event they go on about?"

"They say someone died on the lift."

"Died?" *Did those bitches kill someone?*

"A man named Walter Green."

Fuck!

"It's what they say. Did you know him?"

"Me? No. I wasn't feeling good and kept to myself." Williams quickly hefted his pack and turned to her. "I'm just surprised. We should go." He followed her closely out into the hallway.

She led him to a service area and down one flight, though the stairs continued for several levels. "On the other side of this door is a corridor. To the left is the mall and the right goes to offices."

"Can you tell me how to get to the viewing lounge?"

"Head left. There's a bank of elevators in the mall. Take it to the top." She swiped the card and opened the door.

Williams stepped through and turned to say thanks, but she was gone. Unsure of her reasons, he wasn't about to waste this opportunity. Head down and cap pulled tight, he walked to the mall. It wasn't late, and there were still quite a few people milling about, following their own mundane routines. He wondered how anyone could consider living here long term.

· · ·

WITH HIS CAP PULLED DOWN TO COVER AS MUCH OF HIS FACE AS possible, Williams reached the viewing lounge without incident. There were several other people gathered about in the darkened area, some sitting in the relaxing chairs, others standing closer to the large domed window, their attention directed to the Earth.

He sat as far away from them as he could and snacked from the stash in his bag. Above him a large, clear dome exposed everyone to the sight of empty space. The seats had inbuilt headsets and vid goggles allowing visitors to go through an in-depth discourse of the visible stars, the birth of the solar system, the planets and even the universe.

Looking at his watch, he saw that he still had thirty minutes before the meeting and was tempted to having a listen—

"Hail the Light."

Williams jolted upright, knocking his pack to the floor when he heard a different voice close behind him. A female voice, but it was strangely familiar.

"Don't turn around, Benjamin."

"Let the Light be your Guide," Williams stammered after a breath.

"Tell me about Walter Green."

"Green? I didn't kill him. He was breathing when I left him."

"Why were you with him in the first place?"

"An accident." Williams bumbled through his explanation of the spacelift events. "The oxygen deprivation must have killed him!" Williams sat up again, stopping himself from turning. *Who owns that voice?* "Those Brazilian bitches were responsible for that!"

"What can you tell me about the UFO and the aliens?"

"Not much. Everything was dark and black. The only *alien* I saw was a slug-like creature, but Rhyllien carried it like a pet."

"And was Nala Xaschoal on the ship?"

The moment he heard the name, he recognised the voice. Despite his orders, he leapt up and faced the speaker.

"You!" he spat, seeing Nala sitting there.

"Sit down, Benjamin, you're making a scene," she said in a voice of steel.

He sat, but at an angle so he could watch her. "What the hell are you playing at? Where are the other Brazilian bitches? Wait until I get my hands on them—"

"You had plenty of opportunity, yet you chose to run."

Williams inhaled, a rebuke on his lips.

"I'd watch what you say, Benjamin. I'm not who you think I am, and it would be foolish of you to try anything. And fatal." She showed him the muzzle of the gun under the papers she was carrying.

He sat, glaring at the woman. *Who else could it be? Same hair, height, complexion. Even the voice.* Williams reached down to collect his pack as his mind raced. His hand reached into his pocket, feeling for the forgotten knife.

"Are those grey cells sparking yet?" She smiled.

Even her teeth are identical. "You're Nala's twin sister?"

"That wasn't too hard now, was it?" She paused as if listening to another voice. "Okay," she muttered. "Ben, time for us to go. We wanted to make sure you weren't being followed, but it seems SCS spotted you on a cam." She stood and walked towards the rear emergency exit. "Coming?"

Releasing the knife, Williams shouldered his pack and negotiated the seats in the dark, following her into a dim passage. The door sealed behind him.

He was escorted down a flight of stairs, following Nala's twin sister into the next passage. There was a flash of movement and a momentary glimpse of two waiting figures before his mind went blank.

————

"BLOODY SIMMONS!" TYRONE STRADJEK ROLLED OVER ON THE lumpy, narrow bed. At such short notice, it was the only accommodation available. Private bathroom facilities were the only redeeming features. Tyrone checked his watch again and tried to snooze the remaining hours away.

It was only a short time later that he woke again. There was no point in trying to sleep. His mind was in too much turmoil. Deciding to refresh himself with a quick shower, he grumbled as he climbed off the bunk and stripped.

The hot water was nice, but too brief. It went lukewarm, then cold, after only three minutes.

Simmons is cactus when I get back! he thought.

Once he'd towelled himself dry, he put fresh clothes on and left the cabin to go to the bar. On arrival, he estimated half the passengers were there in the lounge, talking, smiling and chatting.

"Don't they realise their world is dying?" He glowered at them. "Bourbon," he said to the barman.

"Your cabin number, sir?"

"4F."

"Ah. That's twenty credits, sir."

"What? Put it on the cabin account."

"Sir, level four cabins have no account."

Bloody Simmons. Tyrone waved his credchip by the scanner.

"Thank you, sir. Would you like ice?"

"Will that cost too?"

"Oh no, sir." The barman smiled.

Not trusting himself to speak, Stradjek nodded. He moved away to a corner table and watched the crowd. Those that weren't amiably chatting were watching the newscast.

The sound was too soft for him to hear, but he recognised some of the snippets of news he saw on the screen.

That damned girl again. Can't I have a moment's peace without her interfering in my life? He stood and sauntered closer when the vid changed.

Now it was showing groups marching in the streets. Tyrone was about to turn, but he saw their placards. "Is this some joke?" he muttered.

"Oh, no. That girl's a hero," one of the viewers said.

Tyrone realised, belatedly, that he'd spoken louder than he meant to.

"Saving all those lives ... These are her devotees. They're cheering her on and urging the governments and corporations to do something to help."

"Fat chance," Tyrone replied. "They're all too busy lining their pockets. Where's the profit?"

"No profit in a dead world."

Tyrone heard the words, but the vid now changed. It looked all too familiar. He was caught like a wild animal in headlights, gesticulating like a madman as he was taken into the spaceship.

"Astounding news earlier today in Miami when Volaris Corporation CEO Tyrone Stradjek and his PA were drawn into a UFO."

A closeup from a drone caught in the beam showed a view of Williams' face contorted in fear.

Tyrone burst out laughing, much to the ire of some of the viewers, who glared at him.

"Mr Stradjek and his colleague were within the alien craft for several minutes before Mr Stradjek returned alone."

The vid showed Tyrone now emerging from the UFO. "There is no sign of his PA, Mr Benjamin Williams, and Mr Stradjek was unable to provide any clues to the reasons or goings on within the alien craft, and it appears he is now missing. The police are unable to locate him to answer any questions and to undergo medical examination. They fear he may be contaminated with a number of unknown viruses or diseases. Medical authorities warn to keep clear of him and contact their nearest enforcement agency as a matter of urgency to prevent any possible contagion. Viewers are reminded this is merely a remote possibility, but all precautions must be taken."

People started looking at the screen, then glancing at the stranger standing among them. They backed away, pointing and murmuring.

He gulped his bourbon down too quickly, a partially melted ice cube temporarily choking him. "I'm not contaminated!" He coughed loudly.

Pandemonium broke loose as everyone rushed to the elevators and frantically pushed buttons to close the doors against him.

"Idiots. I am *not* contaminated." Stradjek turned to the barman, but he'd ducked out the side door, carrying a communicator with him.

"Damn you all!" He stomped towards his cabin, then pivoted back to the bar and grabbed a full bottle of bourbon before continuing to his room and locking himself in.

Several minutes later, after his second glass, the loud knocking started.

Tyrone was drunk when the hammering on the door finally stopped.

He heard someone talking, too soft to understand. Stumbling closer to the door to listen, he knocked his head sharply, but the pain didn't register. One of the voices stopped.

"Stay where you are, Mr Stradjek," another called out.

"Ha! "Think I've got the plague, do you?" He demanded again: "Do you?" Tyrone tried the door handle, but it was locked from the other side. "Hey, what is this?"

"Better stay inside your cabin, otherwise there'll be serious consequences. You'll be taken care of the moment we dock."

"Cabin? This is a shoebox!" He stumbled back to his bunk and collapsed onto it. "Bloody Simmons."

16

A DISTANT RUMBLE TO THE NORTH DREW THEIR ATTENTION. HALF A dozen hoverpods had appeared in the sky near the centre of the ancient city, and white clouds rose from somewhere on the ground below them.

"Hey boss, look." Nala pointed to the north. "Do you think Rhyll's back?"

"Maybe a hoverpod crashed?" Dan suggested. "It's been known to happen," he said seeing Nala roll her eyes.

A hoverpod? Seriously? Nala didn't trust herself to respond kindly. Dan had been out of sorts all morning. They all had frayed tempers; the heat, the lack of food and sleep, and the hike had worn them down. "Should we go back?" She didn't want to, but if Rhyll was there ...

"No. If Rhyll has returned, I'm sure she'll either find my message, or failing that, come this way. And, while you may not have noticed, I'm not quite as young as I used to be. This hike has tired me more than I'd like to admit. Have I thanked you for carrying all my gear?"

"Only a dozen times." Dan smiled, realising it probably sounded trite. "Mrs. E, you've done amazingly well."

"For an old biddy," Imogen chuckled. "Thanks, Daniel."

"It was Nala who suggested we use the boat. It must have shaved at least eight or nine kilometres off our trip."

"And you thought of the bikes," Imogen added. "I'm lucky to have two astute and worthy companions. Now, let's get out of this sun; we might even find some breakfast."

Their morning started at dawn when they were awoken by the growling of animals. No one could sleep after that, so with only a few things to grab, they'd warily made their way downstairs and moved slowly south and west.

The fresh air was comforting, though the walk through the dark streets with the threat of carnivores close by made it less so.

Dan's voiced concern about not being top of the food chain prompted the idea to go by boat. The river was close and it seemed obvious to Nala that a boat would be a good idea.

"The water will be cooler, and there'll be less of a chance that something will decide to add us to the menu," she said.

"Except those crocodiles," Dan pointed out.

"I said 'less of a chance', not 'no chance'. And I do have a couple of guns if need be."

"Where from?"

Nala shrugged. "I got that one you found in Reading from the kidnappers, then Ileana handed me one when she frisked Stradjek."

It was mid-morning by the time they had rowed as far south as they needed. After mooring the boat to a wharf near the Abbas Bridge, they found plenty of unused bikes lying around or leaning up against stone walls. After a bit of a search they even found one with a trailer; it would be handy to carry their gear. They followed the Al Haram, a main road leading more or less directly to the plateau.

The bikes weren't in the best condition, with low tyre pressure or crappy gears and brakes, but fortunately the nine kilometre ride was relatively flat. They changed with other bikes a couple of times, but there was always some mechanical fault.

They finally reached the base of the plateau. Even though the incline wasn't much, they decided to walk the remaining distance.

"Before we go further, let's rest in comfort. We might even get some brunch," Nala said to them as she veered to her right into the driveway of a large car park surrounded by garden.

The building Nala had chosen to stop at was the Marriott, conveniently located at the base of the plateau.

"Hey, Daniel, luxury."

"No warm baths or aircon here," Dan grouched, recalling the luxuries of English hotels he and Nala had stayed in.

Leaving their bikes by the door they went inside, where the foyer was moderately cooler.

Dan wiped the sweat from his face with a sleeve. His tyre had gone flat a kilometre back, making it that little bit harder. He smiled in sympathy when he saw the other two walking tenderly, just like him; no doubt their bums were also sore from the hard seats. He hefted his pack and followed.

The bar had mostly packet food, nuts and dried fruits.

"I found these." Dan returned from the kitchen with cans of beans and soups. "A banquet fit for a pharaoh." With his meagre selection, he joined Imogen by the table as she was flicking through some scrunched and tattered papers.

"Water, beer or wine?" Nala offered when she returned.

"Warm beer?" He grimaced. "I wouldn't be an Aussie if I accepted warm beer."

She handed him a bottle anyway. "What about you, boss?"

Imogen looked up and reached for the water. "Though I might try the wine later."

"Did you find anything new?" Dan asked Imogen, looking at some of the sheets she had spread around.

"Since last night, you mean? Not really, but I was tired ... My thoughts are more refined now, if that helps."

"And where exactly are we going, or what are we looking for?"

"The references — and some are still unclear — mention the Temple of Osiris."

"Osiris?" Dan queried.

"The Egyptian goddess of agriculture and fertility," Imogen answered. "But there are records of it below a shaft in Campbell's tomb."

"Campbell doesn't sound very Egyptian." Nala sat down with some bowls and cutlery and began opening some of the cans.

"It isn't. He was a sponsor for some of the explorations back in the late eighteen hundreds by Vyse and Caviglia. He was also the British Consul at the time, so he had a bit of influence."

"Vyse? Rhyll mentioned Vyse's entrance into the pyramid," Dan told her.

"One of the more disreputable explorers, he used dynamite to bludgeon his way in. Probably destroyed more than he found."

"And is the temple under the Sphinx?"

"It's behind it, but there's a possibility there are tunnels leading to it as well as to the pyramids." Imogen twisted the lid off her water bottle and had a sip. "Why don't we have a look tomorrow morning?" she suggested.

"So the catacombs are real?"

"It would appear likely. We shall see."

"Wait. How can this be? How come no one has heard of it before?"

Imogen took a longer drink and sat back, thinking. "I could talk for hours on the subject — I have, in fact. So I'm also able to cut it down to a few sentences. There have been many surveys carried out of the years. The results of most have been quashed as they don't fit with the current ancient Egyptian beliefs.

"The Giza plateau is comprised of limestone, a geological feature which creates natural crevices and pockets in the stone like Swiss cheese. Rumours of underground tunnels and cavities have been circulating for thousands of years. Even Herodotus,

the ancient Greek author and historian, wrote of a temple dedicated to Osiris centuries before the Ministry of Antiquities tried
to quash the rumours. Another discovery reported from the
Osiris tomb was the hieroglyphic word *pr*, meaning *house*. It is
known that the Giza plateau was called *pr wsir nb rsta*, or *the
house of Osiris, Lord of Rastaw*. *Rastaw*, or *rostau*, means the *mouth
of the passages*.

"Other than money, pride is another reason secrets are kept.
Many egotistical scholars would prefer the world remain igno-
rant than for them to be proven wrong. What do you think
would happen if we learnt that the Egyptians didn't really build
the Sphinx, or the pyramids for that matter?"

"They didn't? Who did?"

"That news would cause chaos," Nala answered. "It would
change our whole way of thinking, and ruin many reputations."

"Exactly. The reputations of many Egyptologists for one, and
it would necessitate our relearning of our true origins."

"My weird-shit-o-meter is cranking up," Dan said.

"When surveys showed anomalies conflicting with current
knowledge, they were shut down, the scientist deported and any
released results were publicly ridiculed by a plethora of
'experts'."

"All saving their skins."

"And at the behest of the Ministry of Antiquities, even
though there are several tunnels and cavities they won't talk
about. For instance, this 'Tomb of Osiris' is one of the most
incredible discoveries, located thirty metres below the surface
behind the back of the Sphinx. Under the paws of the Sphinx,
seismic surveyors found two rectangular chambers at least eight
metres deep."

"So, in short, there are plenty of things we don't fully know
about because of politics and greed," Nala stated.

"If the Egyptians were such advanced engineers and archi-
tects, why did they suddenly stop? This is something Ken had
researched before I met him." She waved her arm towards the

window facing the plateau. "After so many centuries, you'd think there would be thousands of pyramids like these.

"Finally, there are those who theorise the Sphinx is many thousands of years older and the pharaohs basically called it as their own, modifying it to suit. Herodotus aside, who do you reckon writes history?"

"The survivors?"

"Close; the winners."

"I see where Rhyll gets her cynicism."

17

"THEY'RE BOMBING THE UFO!" RHYLL EXCLAIMED, RACING TO THE window, but the mosque where the UFO had landed was out of site.

The trio ascended the stairs, arriving on the roof to stare at the white smoke clouds wafting a short distance away.

"Not bombs. I think they're gas grenades." Cat pointed to several hoverpods circling the area. She moved under the gazebo for cover, the others close behind.

"Lethal gas, or sleeping gas?" Rhyll asked.

Cataleya shrugged. "Cowlings up," she ordered, hitting her tab, as the breeze was blowing the cloud in their general direction.

"Q, can you hear me?" Rhyll spoke into the commlink, trying not to sound as scared as she was.

"I can. As I suspected, it appears they have a surveillance satellite and are now aware of my presence."

"Are you in any danger?" She ducked reflexively as more loud explosions reached her ears.

"Hardly, but my fear is this attention will only escalate and I cannot risk endangering you."

They saw the craft rise, still partially obscured by the trees, but then something unusual happened: it tilted, slowly, ninety degrees.

"All of your remaining property is now on the grass," Q said.

"The concept probably means nothing, but thank you and ... good luck in regenerating. I hope you gain full functionality. Maybe we'll meet again. I'm sure you'll know where to find me if you do."

Q considered the neuralink he had established within her brain, ensuring a connection; communications within the galactic consciousness was not affected by the electrical interference as it was on another plane — a plane humans still considered myth. "Our meeting was mutually beneficial. The future is obscure, though perhaps a reunion is not overly improbable."

"Wait, what about these space suits?"

"You need them and I do not foresee gaining any passengers where I am going. I assure you the tech is sufficient for your needs." The craft began to right itself. As it moved away, many of the hoverpods followed, but a few remained to continue scouring the area.

"Where are you going?"

"There is a reference in the navigational data for the home-world of the previous occupants. Perhaps they have advanced somewhat and will provide a more suitable vessel for my needs." After several minutes of slowly cruising south to draw the attention away from the area, the UFO gained speed, then shot up into the sky and disappeared in seconds. The majority of the pods attempted pursuit, with futile results.

"Not much for goodbyes," Cataleya said softly.

"That's that, then." Ileana put her arm across the younger girl's shoulders.

"Somehow I don't think that was a farewell." Rhyll considered the sky.

"You find the weirdest friends in the most unlikely places."

"You can say that again." Rhyll hugged her back. "We can use this gas cloud as cover when it gets closer to get out of here.

If they were surveying the UFO, they may have seen us, or at least assume someone or something is here."

As she said this, they became aware of many drones issuing from the bowels of larger hoverpods that had just arrived.

"Merde! Where did they come from?"

Cat's voice was steady, as was her gaze, at what was unfolding before them. "We'll need to move before the place is surrounded."

They raced back to the stairwell before the drones got too close, but there was no guarantee they hadn't been spotted. Back downstairs in the office where they found the last evidence of their friends, Rhyll flattened the forgotten piece of paper on the coffee table. She'd crumpled it tightly in her hands when she first heard the explosions?

"Like I said, I think I know where they are," she informed them.

"And that is?"

"Campbell's tomb."

As they feared, there were hundreds of pods scouring the skies; a dozen were focusing on the UFO landing site and the nearby areas, the rest could be heard buzzing across the city.

"It is maybe fifteen kilometres to the Giza Plateau. No cars work, and the temperature is already in the low forties." Ileana considered their options.

Cat agreed. "I guess we'll have to walk. Stay in the shade when and wherever we can and drink plenty of water."

"And keep out of sight of the drones. Easy," Rhyll added.

"We will need to get food along the way, since they left no snacks for us." Ileana had searched offices on the way down.

"That was probably Dan," Rhyll commented, smiling.

"Not forgetting the other gear Q dumped."

"And these suits?"

"We keep them. If we are spotted — and that is very likely with so many drones — they may drop gas." She stood and paced the room, looking at their packs. "With what Q has dropped, we will have much to carry. Walking will be slow, tedious and made more difficult with the drones."

"We have our suits. I'm thinking the advanced alien tech will keep us safe ... Does it matter if they do see us?"

"Our air only lasts an hour or so, and if the gas grenades aren't working, they may decide to drop something other than gas grenades."

"Oh. Well ... we'll just have to do our best."

"That's what I like about you, young chica: always being positive." Ileana slapped her shoulder. Rhyll's cowling popped up unexpectedly, which made them all laugh.

"Okay then. Saddle up and let's go before we are surrounded." Cat hefted her pack and strode to the door.

RHYLL BROODED IN HER THOUGHTS, HALF-NOTING THE WAY THE TWO professionals moved from shadow to shadow as they zigzagged their way towards the river.

In the street, the closer proximity to the bodies was gruesome, even to the hardened soldiers. Rhyll saw them as well — it was hard not to — and as in Brazil when walking the streets of São Lucas, part of her mind acknowledged the deaths, but her empathy was chillingly lacking.

It made her feel uncomfortable — inhumane even. Not getting visions was also disturbing. Getting them was one thing; not getting them — not hearing the voices and chanting — was also getting her down. *Was it a sign of failure?*

She heard Ileana's voice asking whether she was okay.

"Hmm?" Rhyll didn't realise she had stopped walking. "Sorry. Lost in thought."

"We'll be lost if you don't tell us where to go."

"You mean to tell me Cataleya hasn't mapped the city in her head? I am shocked," she joked as she caught up with them.

"South and west is what I've got. Do we take the river?"

Rhyll noticed they were now overlooking the bank, a bridge

to their left providing cover when they moved under it. "Won't the drones see us?"

"We have the cam option on the suits," Cat reminded them.

"What about the moving boat? Surely that will grab their attention."

"Boats go adrift all the time," Ileana replied.

"But they rarely, if ever, float up stream." Rhyll chuckled and punched her arm.

Cat scanned the area. There was a row of bikes further along near a waterfront eatery. "Unless you all want to hike the distance carrying all this gear, how about these bikes?" She moved over to examine them more closely.

"Great idea, boss." Ileana started searching for a suitable bike, but the selection was poor. "Hey, chica. What about you?"

"If I have to ..."

"You prefer walking?"

"I don't know how ... I've never ridden a bike before."

"You're kidding! Never?" Ileana said in surprise.

"Nope." She shook her head, eyeing the bikes dubiously. "There was never a need, especially in the jungle."

"But it's so easy!" Ileana got on the bike and rode around in a circle.

"Easier if you've had the training," Cataleya said in Rhyll's defence. "We'll work something out. How about we take them to that undercover car park and have a lesson where we aren't dodging drones?"

Some of the bikes were locked, but there were enough left unsecured to choose from. They each selected a bike to suit their sizes. Cat walked with Rhyll while Ileana rode ahead to the indicated car park. The lesson went relatively smoothly; Rhyll only ran into the wall twice before Cat was satisfied with her progress.

Since the car park was below a mall, they went upstairs to search for food. Most of the fresh food had already deteriorated, as had anything that required refrigeration. All that remained was in packets and cans. While none were overly enthused with the selection, it was better than starving.

Rhyll compared what they were doing to the survival foraging they did in England, including the various accommodation venues they found.

Loading up what they could reasonably carry in shopping baskets, they returned to the car park and the bikes. Using wire and rope, the baskets were tied to the handle bars and Ileana had a parcel rack as well. Cat made sure everyone had a couple of bottles of water.

"We'll take the bulk of the load," Ileana offered as they finished loading all the other gear. "I was unfair before, and riding with a load throws one off the balance."

"Sure, but once I get the hang of it, I expect to carry my share."

Checking all were prepared, Cat led them out with Rhyll in the middle and Ileana following.

"We'll go slow and steady. Keep an eye and ear out for the drones. Head for cover straight away if you can; if not, hit the camouflage button. It should cover our heat signature, but we'll try to conserve the battery as much as we can."

They stopped and waited beneath the canopy of a tree on one of the ramps to the bridge. Crossing would expose them to view more than they'd been during any other part of their journey.

"It is pointless waiting for the area to be clear of drones," Cat said, venting her frustration after ten minutes. "The moment one moves away, two more are moving in. I suggest we activate the camouflage and get across as best we can." She pressed the button Q had indicated.

"Merde." Ileana watched in amazement. "Other than your head, you sort of faded away."

"Did I? I can still see me." She waved her arm. "I guess the cowling should be up as well." Cat's voice could be heard, but her head disappeared. "Now?"

"Gone." Ileana activated her suit's stealth option and tabbed her cowling.

"Wow! I see what you mean."

Rhyll did the same. "If we can't see each other, how can we ... oh, our bikes are still visible."

"It's the best we can do. If we go one at a time, perhaps it'll reduce the chances of being seen." Cat's voice was heard in their speakers. "See that mosque with the bronze roof on the far side to the south side of the road? We will all meet there in front, on the path. I'll go first. After a minute Rhyll goes, then Ileana. Okay?"

Cat moved off as soon as they acknowledged their understanding. They watched and waited.

"Your turn, chica."

"See you on the other side." The squeaking of her brakes could be heard and the clicking when she changed gears.

Rhyll concentrated on keeping a straight line. It wasn't as hard as she thought it would be, and she had always excelled in physical activities. Her heart raced when a drone flew overhead, but it continued unabated.

"I guess the camouflage works well enough," she heard Ileana mutter.

"You doubted the alien technology?"

"I'm sure even aliens make mistakes," Ileana replied.

"Rhyll, what's your progress?" Cat asked.

"Halfway," Rhyll replied.

"And I'm starting now," Ileana stated.

Once everyone met as planned, it was decided to follow the more circuitous route instead of the main thoroughfare. "The open roads will be faster, but more chance of exposure and the camouflage won't last the distance. All these narrow side streets give us ample opportunity for cover."

With their cowlings down and camouflage off to conserve energy, they hugged the side streets and used whatever cover they could. The streets were like a maze, making the trip tedious and slow. The decay was so bad that a couple of times they had to don the cowling and breath from the suit, or risk throwing up.

Every now and then they passed numerous droids, which tended to be in groups of four or six, but they were all immobile, as were the Reaper vans they saw. Other encounters were of the wild animal kind, but with Rhyll's presence, the animals either wandered off after a cursory sniff or continued devouring the bodies.

As soon as they heard the buzz of a drone they rode to the nearest shelter — whether that be a tree, a carport or the doorway of a building. When this happened they used the opportunity to eat, drink and stretch their legs while they waited. Being fit didn't prevent the stiffness on the buttocks and legs from gruelling bike riding. The further they moved away from the UFO landing area the fewer the drones. Not to say there were none, just a lot less.

"I can see it now," Cat called back over her shoulder.

The unpleasant journey had taken most of the day, and even the two experienced warriors sighed in relief seeing the end in sight.

"If we're riding up that slope, I'll need to rest first." Rhyll scowled at the road going up the plateau. "And I don't know about you, but I could also use the toilet. There's the Marriott."

"Good idea. We can walk the remainder of the way up the plateau if you prefer."

"That would be better, and the drones here are few and far between."

"There are other bikes here," Cat noted as they rode the last few metres through the car park.

With groans, they dismounted the bikes and walked them into the foyer of the hotel.

"Do you think they were left by Imogen and the others?"

"Three people, three bikes." Rhyll looked around the area for any sign her mother had been here. "Chances are they would have had to come this way, and it's reasonable to think they, like us, needed a break and refresh before hiking up the plateau. Let's hope they aren't too far away."

"We left them for what, less than a day? Your mother is spritely for her age, but I'm sure even she has limits," Ileana said.

Rhyll considered this. "They'd have to be very lucky to have come across information so quickly."

"So, we rest after a quick search. If need be, as Ana suggested before, we can fire a shot to let them know we are here."

"Surely they would've heard the explosions," Rhyll suggested.

"Perhaps. The bikes suggest if they did, they didn't try to head back."

"Assuming the bikes are theirs."

"We'll find out soon enough."

SEARCHING THE GROUND FLOOR, THEY SOON FOUND A TABLE WITH three sets of plates, glasses and empty beer bottles.

"It's looking promising. These biscuit crumbs aren't all that stale."

The split up, going to different floors and calling out, but in less than twenty minutes they met on the rooftop with no sightings. Before they stepped out into the open air they were careful to check for drones, but nothing was heard.

Cat was already there beside a large vent, scanning the plateau with her binoculars. The height of the rooftop was about the same height as the plateau. "Ileana, want to fire a couple of rounds off and get their attention?"

"You don't have to ask me twice." Ileana unholstered her gun and fired a couple of rounds, with a few seconds between shots.

Cat continued to play the binoculars across the landscape. "Any idea where I should be looking?"

Rhyll squinted into the low sun. "Campbell's Tomb is somewhere behind the Sphinx. My guess is … from this angle, they should be to the left of the Khufu pyramid."

"Which is …?"

"That big one."

"Wait … I see someone. Two … three someones."

"How will they know where to look?" Rhyll asked, waving.

"I could fire again," Ileana suggested.

"Drone!" Cat barked, waving them down.

The three girls activated the suits' stealth ability and dropped to the floor, keeping still until the sound faded.

"I'm glad we didn't remove the suits just yet," Ileana sighed. She deactivated the camouflage to conserve the battery. As she sat up the sun glinted off the smooth alien material.

"That gives me an idea." Rhyll stood up and activated her cowling. She then started twisting and turning, bending back and forth.

"Is that a new dance routine?" Ileana sniggered.

"I'm hoping the sun will glint off the cowling. Luckily it's setting. I'm trying to get the right angle, aiming it at them, but I can't tell if it's working or not."

Cat smiled at the antics, then continued watching the plateau.

Ileana moved around between Rhyll and where they had seen the figures and gave directions. "Bend back, turn … a bit more … there." She squinted at the bright reflection. "Now just do very slight twists. Good." Ileana nodded as the sun intermittently glinted off the glassy surface. "Now, left foot in, left foot out—"

"I can see them. They must have taken cover from the drone as well."

"Do we know if they've seen us?" Rhyll asked, twisting back and forth.

"I'm … I just saw a camera flash twice. I think Dan's answering."

"Now, do we go to them, or they to us?"

"Considering it will be dark in an hour or so, I'm hoping they come down." Ileana chuckled. "And you can probably stop dancing now."

"Oh." Rhyll stopped twisting and tapped her shoulder to retract the cowling. "And you can stop laughing. It appears my idea worked."

18

WHEN STRADJEK WOKE, HIS HEAD THROBBED AND HIS MOUTH FELT like he'd swallowed the contents of a cremation urn. Rubbing his eyes, then his mouth, he squinted at the surroundings. It was barely an improvement of the dogbox Simmons had booked for him, but it was most certainly not the same cabin.

When he tried to get up, he felt the tug on his ankle.

Chained to the bed!

"Hey! What the fuck's going on?" he called out. He noticed a cam in the corner. He waved at it. "Hey. Get me outta here!"

Tyrone gripped the chain and tugged at it for a few seconds. It held tight, and the bed was also bolted to the floor. He continued to yell and struggle against his leash for close to an hour, with occasional breaks to sit on the edge of the bed, before he heard the door unlock.

"It's about time!" he growled, then stopped at what he saw. "You!" He sat up.

"I'm not the *you* you're thinking of, not that I give a shit either way. Take him," she called over her shoulder at the two thugs.

"Wha ... what are you doing to me? Where am I?" Stradjek yelled as the two men approached. One pulled a hood over his head while the other bound his wrists tightly, before undoing his shackles.

They dragged him out the room. When he couldn't keep up he stumbled painfully to his knees. He was pulled up by his cuffs, causing them to pinch his skin. He made sure he kept apace after that.

Eventually the area they entered was brightly lit, there was carpet on the floor and soft music nearby.

They pushed him. As he flailed his arms vainly to keep his balance, he landed in a cushioned chair. His wrists were unbound and the hood removed.

He was in a well-lit and nicely furnished office. Glancing around quickly, he jumped at who he saw in an identical cushioned chair beside him.

"Williams! You little traitorous shit. What the fuck's going on?" he croaked.

"Where did you get this?" the girl asked before Williams could answer. She held the Cintamani Stone.

Tyrone's jaw worked, but little came out this time.

The woman ordered a glass of water to be brought to him. One of the large men obliged.

Stradjek drank it quickly, dribbling onto his shirt. He wiped his chin irritably.

"No doubt you're disappointed it isn't bourbon, but that will have to wait. Answer my questions, stop being a pain in the ass, and things might go well for you. Where did you get this?" she repeated.

"I don't know. My grandfather has had it for decades. It was in the Volaris vault, and I held it back from the auction."

"Why?"

"I ... I don't know." He shrugged, unable to furnish the words.

"I'll assume you have no idea it's true value?"

"That's my grandfather's purview." He shook his head, hating the fact that three times in a row he'd had no idea of the answer. "Is there a finder's fee?" As irritating as this girl ordering him about. "If you aren't that Brazilian companion of that redhaired brat, who are you?"

"I'm Aitana. Nala is my twin, but in looks only. In everything else, we're poles apart." She put the stone back into a wooden box with velvet padding and placed the lot in a drawer of the desk.

"What do you want with me?" Tyrone looked dubiously at her, then sideways at Williams. "And what's *he* doing here?"

"Benjamin has been working for us for quite a while. We were thinking you might also join us, considering your time in Volaris seems to be coming to an end."

"End? It's just beginning anew."

"You seriously think you'll be getting into the off-world mining business?"

"I have a chance ..." He stopped at the woman's grin.

"You'll have a far greater chance if you join us."

"Join? Who are you?"

"Benjamin, why don't you tell him."

"Tyrone, this organisation is far-reaching, and has been for centuries. They are the Illuminati."

"Is this some sort of joke? The *Illuminati* isn't real, man!"

Williams nodded in understanding. "I know exactly how it sounds, and how you feel. I thought that when I first met them."

"When was that?"

"Before Viktor recruited me to join Volaris. After your father got my father killed."

Dismissing the accusation as nothing, Tyrone sat back, thinking. "If this is true, then why me? What do you want from me?"

Aitana pulled open another drawer to withdraw a folder, and walked around the desk. Her physical looks were identical to her sister's, but her choice of clothing was vastly different. From what he had seen of Nala, she wore loose-fitting, practical clothing for the rugged outdoors; what he was seeing here was far from loose-fitting, and more suitable for the sumptuous indoors ... or the catwalk.

"— are called *emerald tablets*," she was saying.

He saw her smirking at him, realising he had been staring.

"Tyrone, focus on this, not me." She dropped the folder into his lap. "It's taken our organisation several centuries to unearth four of them." She pulled out a familiar brochure. "And you had one in your auction. Where did you find it?"

The brochure showed the green tablet his father had stolen before his death. Tyrone told her everything he knew.

"And so it appears you and Benjamin here are linked; both your fathers died getting this very thing. Surely that's enough to get you to work together. Ben was simply doing his job — he wasn't backstabbing anyone, simply following his true loyalties. If anything, Tyrone, perhaps one might consider your gullibility in this. It isn't as if you haven't personally betrayed people yourself, going back on your words. What about those men you got to do your bidding in Reading? They risked their lives, assured you would keep your word and look after their families. And did you?"

"I ..." It was true, though it grated his ego when it was told to his face.

"However, we aren't casting judgement, just making an observation. These are the same traits we have relied upon over the ages, much to our success. Wouldn't you prefer to work with us — to guarantee your progression into off-world mining — than to fight us and fail miserably?"

"What do you need me to do?"

"Initially, we want the other tablet."

"Initially?"

"This Rhyllien has several other artefacts in her possession we desire. She has the sun-disc of Amaru Maru and also a crystal prism of great import. We are of the belief that with these items, we could find the other tablets."

"How do I do this? As you know, people that go up against her die. *I might die!*"

"I'm going to make it easy for you: if you don't, you *will* definitely die."

While he mulled this over, he felt a cold glass put in his hands. He sipped, thinking it was more water and coughed in surprise at the tingling of one of the finest bourbons he had ever tasted. He savoured every drop, almost crestfallen at the drops he had wasted in his coughing fit.

Tyrone still had no idea what was so special about these green slate tablets. He asked.

"If the legends are true, the tablets — once deciphered — can teach us how to have unlimited power, and unlimited life; they are the words of Thoth, the last Atlantean."

"Atlantean?" Tyrone looked quizzically at her, deciding although she was stunning, she was also insane. "You mean ... from Atlantis, the fabled city?"

"I certainly don't mean Atlanta, Georgia.."

———

AFTER A FINE MEAL AND SEVERAL GLASSES OF THE EXQUISITE bourbon, Tyrone had a bath and a very comfortable sleep.

When he awoke, he enjoyed a full breakfast, sipping his coffee when Aitana entered without knocking. Williams was behind her like a lapdog, but no henchmen could be seen.

"Ah, good morning," he acknowledged, unaccustomed to people wandering in on him.

"All refreshed, I see. I hope you've you given serious consideration to our request?"

"I'm in favour of it. Despite the imminent threat to my life if we fail or refuse, what exactly would I be looking at if we were successful?"

"A guaranteed foothold in the off-world mining boom, for starters."

"And there's more?"

"We'd get a percentage of the profits, obviously — it costs a substantial amount of credits to keep an organisation as vast as the Illuminati going over the centuries. And no doubt, over time, we may require a favour or two."

"I see. Well, I guess I cannot argue with your case. I accept. Do I need to sign in blood or something?"

"We've progressed since those days. We don't even need the heart of your first-born." She smiled.

Stradjek wasn't certain if she was joking or not.

"Later today, you and Benjamin will be taken through the plans we have for retrieving the items."

"For an organisation that's been around for centuries, you appear to be in a bit of a rush."

"We *are* very keen to get this, the impending destruction of the world's population being in point; also, the benefit of knowing where Rhyllien is at any moment would outweigh the costs or difficulties we might encounter."

Aitana went on to explain: "There's an intense electrical disturbance surrounding Cairo. If Rhyll is successful — and so far she has managed to be so — we believe her next target will be Tibet."

"Why Tibet?"

"Do you know about chakra points?"

"Superstitious mumbo-jumbo Rhyllien rambled on about." Tyrone shrugged.

"Myth, like the Illuminati? I can assure you, chakra points, like us, most definitely exist."

"The next closest chakra point is Mount Kailash. Rhyllien needs to get each one as quickly as possible to save as many lives as she can. We'll make it easy for her to get there, and easier for you to grab what we need and get out."

"How exactly?"

"More will be detailed at the briefing, suffice to say the Illuminati has much sway with many governments, including China."

Tyrone nodded. "Does this require her death?"

Williams interjected. "In my dealings with ICON, they know where Rhyllien is as well. My understanding is they are keen to wipe her off the face of the Earth."

"We may have to intervene if that is the case." She made a note in her tablet. "If we can get the emerald tablets — their locations, or those artefacts — we may not need her at all, or the earth's population. Best to let her continue with the remaining diamonds and finish her task. You *can* however bring my sister to me. We haven't seen each other for such a long time."

19

THEY ALL MET IN THE DINING HALL AS THE SUN SET.

While waiting, the trio scrounged around for more supplies; Cat and Ileana did a more thorough job of investigating the kitchen and storage areas, while Rhyll raided the rooms — there were so many of them. In time, a larger selection of food and drinks was available and several baskets were placed on a nearby table for anyone to grab what they wanted.

Although it had been less than a day, it was a relief for all to find themselves together again and catching up on the recent events.

"What do you mean 'Q is gone'?" Dan questioned. "You mean *gone* gone?"

"As gone as much as a flying saucer with interstellar capabilities can be." Rhyll patted his shoulder in commiseration.

"I thought Q was going to help us." He slumped in obvious disappointment.

"Q helped quite a lot already. This isn't Q's fight, and it had its own agenda. The reason was its appearance was a risk to us. I assume you saw and heard the grenades earlier?"

Nala and Imogen nodded.

"So it seems whoever is controlling the drones and these

hoverpods are overly keen to try to capture the 'aliens'. The obvious drawback for us is we will need to find transport later, though I am not relishing a bike ride all the way to the boundary of the death zone."

"We had a sweet ride back in Sedona. I've still got the codes, so I reckon I can call it in if we can get a signal. I reckon if I get above this interference I can call it, but it will take close to fifteen hours to get here."

"Assuming Thurston hasn't reneged," Nala added.

"Thurston? The English reporter? What's he got to do with any of this?" Rhyll queried.

"It's part of that bank robbery story we touched on earlier."

"I gather there was no sage advice from a million-year-old intelligence?" Dan probed, changing the subject. "Maybe it thought we were too primitive."

"No, but he left the suits and had the courtesy of dropping all of our gear before he left." She pointed to the pile of packs by the door.

"Dan's just happy to see his loot's safe," Nala joked. "It might make up for him missing the internet."

"Oh, I see how it is," Dan grumped good-naturedly, going over to the bags. "New continent, new jokes."

"We don't need a new continent for that," Nala insisted.

"Poor Daniel." Rhyll laughed in sympathy.

"Nothing *poor* about Dan." Nala winked. "What's left, Daniel? Eighty thousand pounds?"

"Something like that," he said."

"Eighty thousand? I'd like to hear that story." Ileana strode in from the kitchen. "Imagine our Dan, a bank robber."

"How about we eat?" Cat said, carrying a tray, walking beside her companion. She placed the steaming food in the centre of the table and the two of them grabbed a seat each.

"You bet, I'm famished." Dan strolled over, happy to move away from the subject of the robbery. "How did you cook that?" he asked, sitting at the table.

"There was a deep freezer out back, full. The stuff on top had gone off, but at the bottom there was some stuff still frozen ... more or less."

"And there's a barbecue out back," Ileana added. "They are now minus some deckchairs."

"I'm not going to complain." Dan helped himself to a steak.

"You realise that's camel?" Imogen asked him.

Dan paused briefly, then shrugged. "Meat's meat."

"Rhyll, they had frozen veggies as well, so we made up a sort of stew," Cat offered.

Rhyll nodded her appreciation.

"Would you ever eat meat?" Ileana asked her.

"If it meant not dying from starvation, yes. I'm not against meat-eating completely, it depends on the culture; those cultures where agriculture is extremely difficult like the Inuit or Bedouins, I can understand, but western society can produce so many crops they don't need to kill any animals to get sustenance. There's ample nutrients in a vegetarian diet. Sorry. I'll get off my soapbox." She dug into her vegetable stew.

"What about now?"

"I don't have to. There's still plenty of other food to eat first." She turned back to her mother. "Were you at Campbell's Tomb?"

"I gather you saw my note. There were some extra notes about it in your dad's sketches. I'm sure it's the right place."

"How so?" Rhyll leant closer to her as the others glanced at the discoloured and creased sheets of paper Imogen laid out between the plates.

"If this information is correct, it's got all the hallmarks of what you are looking for: tunnels and chambers beneath the Sphinx, and there are shafts going quite deep. Then there is this titbit of info about a columned chamber beneath the Tomb of Osiris."

Rhyll swallowed her food before replying. "That's incredible. It would save us so much time if it was what we were looking for."

"There is one slight drawback," Imogen added.

"And that is?"

"It's supposed to be underwater."

"Ah. That could be trouble."

"Don't tell me you can't swim." Ileana stopped, food hallway to her mouth.

"I can swim fine. How deep is this water, though? The other times I placed the diamonds I had to lay down on the slab for a while."

"You have the suit. It has air for an hour," Ileana reminded her.

"I had to be naked each time. Even cotton clothes caused too much interference."

"See, Dan, we could have used those pictures after all." Nala chuckled at his blush.

———

MUCH DISCUSSION WAS HAD DURING THE EVENING ABOUT THE BEST way to progress. The empty plates were taken away, and the bar provided a variety of drinks, both alcoholic and non-alcoholic.

"First off, the notes refer to shafts up to fourteen metres deep."

Dan looked dubious. "That's a pretty big extension ladder."

"We can always use ropes," Cat suggested. "If we find a harness, I can rig it up for abseiling."

"What do we do about the water issue if Rhyll can't wear the suit?"

"I can wear scuba gear," Rhyll offered.

"Have you done that before?" Ileana asked.

"Plenty of times. When sailing on our yacht I had more opportunity to dive than to ride a bike."

Dan looked puzzled. "How is scuba gear any different to a space suit?"

"All I really need is a facemask and air. I don't need to wear the whole thing."

"Fair enough." He nodded.

Cat summed it up. "So tomorrow we need to go and find ropes, and scuba gear."

"Ha! A dive shop in Cairo?" Dan giggled and rolled his eyes. He was on his third gin. "I'm sure that will be easy-peasy."

"So glad you volunteered," Cat laughed. "Ileana and I will be organising the ropes and harnesses."

"Ha!" Nala chortled.

"I'm sure to need some help. I volunteer Nala, too." Dan's grin was ear to ear.

"Rhyll, can't you just ... drop it somewhere?" Ileana asked. "Like Nala said you did in that place in the UK?"

"If that were the case, I would have felt the effects the moment I came near a chakra point, but I'm not getting any sensation at all here. And unless I know for certain, I don't want to risk wasting time, or the diamond."

"Those visions aren't helping?" Cat asked her.

"I've not had any since I was at Area 53."

"What did they do to you?" Dan asked.

"I was treated like a lab rat. They were draining my blood — apparently it's now a rare type—"

"I didn't know it could change."

"It can't — well, it's not supposed to." She shrugged, deciding not to mention her crystalline bones and increased mass.

"I have no doubt it was traumatic, but we're here together now." Her mother squeezed Rhyll's hand for a moment. "Can we see everything you've got with you? Ken was gifted at many things, but drawing really wasn't one of them. Maybe we'll recognise one of your artefacts from his doodling. And there is *a lot* of doodling." Imogen flicked through the sheaf of papers, then laid them out on another table while Rhyll grabbed her bag and spread out what items she had.

There were the three remaining diamonds, the prism, the ankh, and the emerald tablet. The Brazilians were with her when she discovered the prism, as well as the tablet, but had no knowledge of the ankh.

Imogen picked it up. "This is made of orichalcum, like the sun-disc." She laid the items side by side. They had the identical colouring and sheen.

"Weird how I never noticed that." Rhyll shook her head.

"Do you think this druid queen was here?" Ileana asked once she heard the story of how Rhyll found the ankh near Stonehenge.

"Boadicea? No. I doubt she travelled out of England, but the Romans were everywhere, as were the druids. Druids played a very important role, especially back in those days; they had the ear of many noblemen and leaders. And with the Romans controlling a lot of the areas, the ankh getting from Egypt to a wife of a Roman nobleman as a gift isn't too far-fetched when you think about it. Sometimes people just liked shiny things." She shrugged.

There was a moment of silence as they examined the artefacts, so Rhyll continued, "Besides, it may have absolutely nothing to do with what we're doing — I can't expect every trinket I find to have relevance to my next task, otherwise I would have brought her sword and torc." A momentary memory flashed through her mind of the battlefield. It left as soon as it arrived. "This isn't a jigsaw puzzle or one of those quest stories you read about in a novel."

"And what is this green slab? Is that like a Rosetta stone?"

"That's the emerald tablet ... or one of them. There's supposed to be thirteen of them."

"Wasn't that the artefact you and your mum picked up from the Volaris auction?" Dan asked.

"It is," Rhyll nodded.

"And what does it do?"

"It would turn the archaeological world upside down,"

Imogen said, opting into the conversation. "Ken found this with the sun-disc near where the Erdany mine is. Neither of the artefacts should ever have been there." Imogen then went on with a brief talk on the history of the area. "Needless to say," she continued, "the sun-disc proves the legend of Amaru Maru has truth to it — and you've seen the sun-disc work. The emerald tablets are supposed to be hidden elsewhere; the legend says the other priests of the Temple of the Seven Rays took them, scattered across the globe, and the sun-disc can access those areas. If the Amaru legend is true — and it's said he was a Seven Ray priest — then there must be an element of truth to what they say."

"What's the Temple of the Seven Rays?" Dan asked.

"A religious order of the time ... rumour is it's still in existence."

"And what are these tablets supposed to say?" Nala picked it up carefully.

Imogen sipped the last of her wine. "It starts getting weird now—"

"Weird *now*?" Dan coughed. "UFO's, people disappearing in a blue flash of light, diamonds that save those attuned to Gaia ... Mrs E, how much weirder can it get?"

"Atlantis." Imogen poured more wine.

———

RHYLLIEN, CATALEYA AND ILEANA WALKED UP THE WINDING PATH. The two soldiers took a short detour via the El Haram police station as it was only across the road, before ascending the plateau to Campbell's Tomb.

"It's always handy to have weapons and ammo," Ileana said as they raided the armoury. Extra clips of suitable ammunition were tucked into the pouches on their utility belts before they continued their journey.

The sun rose as they neared the top and walked into the

shadow of the Great Pyramid. A breeze started, sending drifts of sand across the paved causeway that stretched between the pyramids and swirling around their legs.

Ileana gazed at the massive structure to their left, while Cat scanned the area on the opposite side of the road. "What's that area?" she asked.

"Mastaba tombs — underground burial places. Each one of those structures is the room on top of the tomb to store gifts and offerings. It's generally for the nobility and rich merchants, friends and relatives of the monarch."

Over the wind, the buzz of a drone reached them. It was an automatic response now to stand still and hit the camouflage button. They weren't concerned moving would make them visible, but they could lose sight of one another and possibly knock someone over.

"Done," Cat said, and they all reappeared. "That is a really unsettling look."

They moved on. Between the Great Pyramid and the Pyramid of Khafre, the road branched east and west.

"Campbell's Tomb is over there," Rhyll pointed as she turned east. The three of them walked of for a few hundred metres, then climbed over a small, weathered stone wall.

"What are those other holes?"

Rhyll looked where Cat was pointing. "Exploratory digs, perhaps. Maybe airholes to the underground catacombs. Without going into each one, I can't be sure. What I do know is this is the one we're interested in." She stopped at the edge of a deep, square-cut hole, measuring roughly four metres each side.

With the sun still low, it was deep in shadow and would remain so until noon.

Ileana picked up a rock and dropped it over the edge. The crack of it hitting another surface came almost instantly.

"Did Imogen say this one was about ten metres?"

Rhyll nodded. "It turns a bit, then a fourteen metre shaft. There are three levels, apparently." They walked around the edge, looking down. "I guess we'll need torches as well as ropes," she pointed out.

"I think we should get camping gear," Cat suggested. "It would save time going back and forth, as well as being much safer than risking the drones spotting us. Not everyone has a suit to use."

"That's a bit of work. I hope it's the right place and not a waste of time."

"It is what it is, and all we have to go by at the moment," Cat said, sounding annoyed at her friend voicing doubt.

"I trust my parent's judgement in this. If they had an inkling this is important, then I'm sure it's what we're after. And, as Cat said, it's all we have to go by. Nothing else even comes close."

It was a quiet return trip, with two more drones passing by overhead.

"How did it go?" Imogen greeted them as they traipsed inside the hotel lobby.

They discussed the idea of camping, raising the dangers of a drone spotting them if they kept walking back and forth.

"Good idea," Imogen nodded in approval. "While it sounds straightforward, these things can become slow and tedious, especially in the dark and using only ropes."

"If it comes to it, one of us can use a suit to go and find more food and water, but I'm hoping it won't take more than a day or two."

"Where's Nala and Dan?"

"Off to find some breathing gear. Dan was of the opinion it would take a hell of a long time to find anything of use on foot."

"That man is lost without the internet." Ileana shook her head.

"I reckon most of society is," Rhyll said. "Who's for breakfast?" She wandered with her into the dining room to find food.

––––––

AFTER A QUICK BREAKFAST, NALA AND DAN MOUNTED THE BIKES after the others had departed to check out the entrance to the tomb.

"I don't know about you, but my thighs are killing me." Dan winced.

"You don't really think I'm going to answer that, do you?"

"Why not?"

"I'll say my ass is sore, and then you'll come up with some sad joke."

"Your arse is no joking matter."

"See what I mean!" She rode off down the drive, not looking back.

"What did I say?" Dan muttered as he followed in her wake. *Mind you,* he thought as he watched her pedalling away, *I've seen a lot worse.* He had the trailer, and the wonky wheel made the bike vibrate if he got up too much speed.

Nala picked a random direction, keeping an eye out for anything that suited their needs. Scuba gear was best, but she also thought dive shops in Cairo would be few and far between.

"I'm sure there's more than one place to find breathing apparatus." She was still fuming over Dan's joke, and huffing and rolling her eyes, rode off.

Dan's shout behind her brought her thoughts back into focus.

"Nala! Drone!"

She hadn't been concentrating, and now a drone was cruising above the road, following her. She veered sharply under the high canopy of a service station, but it offered little shelter from view and before she could dismount and run into the building, the drone had angled its position for a clear line of sight. The buzzing stopped suddenly, though, and it fell out of the sky.

"Bugger," she said, as she looked back from the doorway.

Dan raced under the canopy and jumped off the bike. "You

okay?" he asked when he caught up with her. "What were you thinking?"

"Why did it fall?" she asked instead. "And don't say *gravity*."

Dan looked back at the smashed drone, forty metres down the road. "I think it dropped too low and fell from about the thirty-metre mark."

"So, above that height should be good for signal?"

He shrugged. "I hope so. We won't know until I try it." He scanned outside, looking for a building above that height. "There." He pointed to a tall building several blocks away.

"I wonder how long it will take before more drones arrive?"

"Let's not be here when that happens."

The pair checked it was clear before they jumped on their bikes. Their route was more circumspect, keeping to narrow streets and under as much cover as they could find. Other drones began appearing within five minutes of the first one going down.

"That's going to make things more interesting."

As they moved around the area, one section had them both on edge when passing very close to a couple of droids. There was a Reaper van around the corner. Logic told them it should be fine, but their experience in Barton Stacey played on their minds and had their nerves tingling.

Slowly but surely they made it successfully to the building in question.

"We could have done this earlier."

"True, but now we know for sure the height the interference goes. Before this, it was guesswork."

Leaving the bikes at the entrance, they began searching for stairs, which were located beyond the elevators. As they passed, a strong, unpleasant smell assailed them.

"I reckon there's a bunch of bodies in there," Dan gagged as he walked briskly through the area.

Nala was in front and pushed open the stairwell door, but it was hard.

She waited for Dan to come over to help. The two of them managed to push it ajar, but an even stronger smell hit them like a wall as the putrid air rushed out.

Nala turned and threw up, almost splattering Dan, who stepped back at the last second.

He fetched a water bottle from his pack and handed it to her when she had emptied her stomach. She wiped her mouth with the back of her hand before accepting the bottle.

Nodding her thanks, she swilled the water in her mouth and rinsed it out a couple of times before taking a drink. "Those space suits would be nice about now." She handed the bottle back.

"Want to look for another set of stairs?"

"I think they'll all be similar. It was more the shock to the nostrils than anything else." Nala walked a few paces away and took a few deep breaths, holding the last one. She indicated with her head she was ready to go.

Dan repeated the process and they gingerly stepped around the gruesome mass of bodies cluttering the lower stairs. At the beginning of the second floor he started breathing again, as did Nala.

The odour wasn't too bad in this area, though they still saw a body here and there; it wasn't a sight they thought they'd get used to ... or forget.

"And I thought São Lucas was bad."

"It was, but those were fresh and the droids took care of most of them already. These poor souls will be here until they're dust."

They continued the arduous climb to the top floor in silence, partly because there was little to say, and partly because they needed to save their breath.

By the time they reached the tenth floor, their legs felt like lead. Exhausted, they put the handrail to good use to ease themselves to the floor, breathing deeply as the air was much clearer up here.

While they rested, Dan unslung his pack and retrieved his phone, but it was flat; he'd had no use for it when they arrived and hadn't thought to get Rhyll to recharge it. He popped it back in and pulled out his camera.

"How will that help?" Nala asked.

"It uploads to the cloud automatically if the signal is strong enough." Dan turned it on and waited for the icon which would show the presence and strength of signal. "Yep, we have four bars!" He whooped, the yell echoing loudly inside the concrete enclosure. "Sorry."

"I wish it took longer," she sighed.

"What? Why?" Dan looked at her as if she were crazy.

"Now we have to climb back down."

20

"THAT'S NOT SCUBA GEAR," ILEANA POINTED OUT WHEN DAN RODE up with his trailer. They'd heard the rattle for several minutes with the deterioration of the wonky wheel due to the extra weight of the gear he and Nala had uncovered.

"Other than air pressure, the concept of breathing apparatus is the same whether it's for underwater or firefighting. We found this at a fire station." Nala rode up, breathing hard. Her tyre had gone flat. "The drones are aware of us, too."

"We thought there was more activity. What happened?"

"I was too slow in finding cover." She let the bike fall against the wall.

"But there's good news. Now we know the interference is about thirty to forty metres high."

Rhyll and Imogen came outside to greet them. "You two took so long. We were worried."

"We had to divert the drones away."

"You mean you let them see you again?" Cat was clearly annoyed.

"Not *see* us exactly, but we distracted them by flashing broken mirrors at them from hiding positions, then ducking away and leading them closer to the river."

"And we checked the signal. It's good above the eighth floor."

"So you called your hoverpod?"

Dan explained he only had his camera to work with. "I'll have to go back with my tablet for that, bearing in mind it will take hours for the pod to get here from Sedona. And we need to work out where you want it to land, right?"

"True." Cat agreed. "It'd be shot down before it gets close ... or failing that, they'll either follow us when we leave, or force us out of the sky."

"Can you at least call it closer, so when it's time to move, we won't have hours to wait?" Rhyll suggested.

"Sure, but where?" Dan asked.

"Use your internet, Daniel," Nala suggested. "Check out on the newsvids where the death wave has spread."

"Maybe the pod can go to New Cairo—"

"New Cairo?" Rhyll echoed.

"It's the new administrative centre about forty kilometres east of here. They even built the tallest tower in Africa there. The *Oblisco Capitale* is a kilometre high."

"That's a lot of stairs to climb." Dan baulked at the thought of it.

"We wouldn't be climbing it. And you can't land the pod on top: the roof is conical and made of glass. But the area is far enough to not gain their attention, and close enough to come back here at short notice. I'm sure you'll find a suitable building where we can land for the time being."

"Okay. Nala, ready for another run up those stairs?"

"I'm not running, and I'll be taking breathing apparatus for myself." She told them of the pile of bodies in the stairwell.

KNOWING THAT A SIGNAL WAS NOW POSSIBLE, SHE HAD SPENT SOME time charging everyone's phones.

They made plans to split up after the midday meal. Dan and

Nala would go to the tower and arrange for the pod, if possible, to fly to New Cairo; Cataleya and Ileana would find ropes and abseiling harnesses, while Rhyllien and Imogen would look for camping gear.

"Let's be back here before nightfall, and don't forget to be alert for drones. Even if their attention has been diverted, they'll be watching; before they only suspected there were intruders here, now they're certain. If you get stuck, go high and send a message. We'll check regularly and see what can be done."

"Sorry, everyone." Nala sounded contrite.

"Hey, it could have been anyone. We're just lucky we've got these space suits," Rhyll replied in her defence.

They all parted company, heading in different directions.

Rhyll and her mother went last. "I have an idea to try. It's something Q said when he first showed us the spacesuits. You were here at that time. They were still in the shape of the previous occupants ... they had four legs, long arms ... well, it was really weird."

She climbed out of her suit and experimented with it by pulling it gently. It took a few seconds before it stretched in different directions. She widened it to accommodate the both of them.

Imogen looked unsure. "It's okay, darling—"

"Bear with me, I'm not crazy." She pushed her hand to create a divot. "Put your foot in there."

Feeling silly, Imogen braced herself on Rhyll's shoulder and stepped inside. The pocket expanded to fit around her leg.

"Now do the same thing here." She created another divot. Once her mother had both legs in, Rhyll climbed into her original leggings, now standing with her back to her mother. "Just lean back a bit to give me some room." Reaching down, she pulled up on the sides. Her mother watched and helped.

"It goes on like a wet suit. Shrug into it and it will seal around us."

"What about our heads?"

"I'll show you." The suit expanded and contorted to fit the extra mass. The neck was much wider.

"We must look silly ... like when two people are in a horse costume."

"That's what I was hoping would happen." Rhyll grinned. "But a horse with four arms"

"And the air?"

"It was good for one for an hour, so I can guess we'd be okay for half that as long as we don't overly exert ourselves."

It took a few minutes of experimenting to be able to walk around without tripping.

Rhyll laughed at their antics. "Just walk in-step like Cat and Ileana, they're always doing it."

"Do you think they know it?"

"Nope."

Finding a tandem bike was out of the question, so they walked.

"We have a camouflage option." Rhyll showed her mother the button on the one controller. "And if we need to put the helmet up, we tap the shoulder." She demonstrated to her mother. "See our reflection in that window?"

"Yes."

Rhyll activated the stealth ability. Imogen gasped, now just seeing two disembodied heads. They were completely hidden when the cowling came up.

"I'm glad that cowling worked," she said in relief. They moved off in search of camping gear.

WHEN NALA AND DAN DIDN'T TURN UP BY LATE AFTERNOON THE two soldiers, who had only just returned themselves, rode to the nearest tall building with all the phones, not knowing which number Dan would be messaging.

They returned just before nightfall, which was fortunate as there was a new moon.

"Has anything happened to them?" Rhyll asked the moment they brought the bikes into the foyer.

Cat handed the phones back to their respective owners, showing her the text messages.

"Lucky everyone had each other's contact details." Ileana slumped into a lounge chair.

"They're alright. Dan needs to keep tabs on the pod. They're comfortable and have food and water. In the morning we'll head back up and get an update."

Relieved, Rhyll showed them the shopping trolley full of camping gear and the dehydrated food. "Just add water and a bit of heat. I'm glad I'm not paying for it, though, it's very expensive."

"And as you can see, we've enough rope to climb that Oblisco Capitale building you mentioned." The trailer was certainly full with coils of rope, harnesses, and topped with a large canvas bag. "Hard hats, head torches and gloves," Cat explained.

"Rhyll has something else to show you, too," Imogen said proudly.

"Oh ... yes." Rhyll collected the suit which had been draped over a table to one side of the dining room, and they made their way into the nearby bar and lounge area. It was sumptuously furnished. The two Brazilians sunk into the deep chairs with sighs and relaxed.

"Four legs?" Ileana noticed. "Did it change back to its original shape?"

"Nope." Rhyll turned to her mother. "You're in this, too."

Laughing, Imogen climbed into the back of the suit behind Rhyllien.

"Remember what it looked like back on the ship."

Cat laughed. "I was joking when I said 'one size fits all'."

Mother and daughter climbed out of the suit. Rhyll handed it to Cat and Ileana to examine, then they briefly experimented with their own pushing and prodding.

"That means, with six of us and three suits, we can all double up," Cat assumed.

"As long as we're not riding bikes," Rhyll said.

Imogen came back from the bar with glasses, beers and wines. "I think we deserve a celebratory drink."

"Poor Nala," Ileana said, a sparkle in her eye as she reached for a beer.

"Why?" Rhyll asked.

"Who do you think is going to have to share a suit with Dan?"

They ate dinner and relaxed for a while in the comfortable chairs.

Later in the evening, Cat took Imogen and Rhyll through basic abseiling techniques, then Rhyll reciprocated by assisting in getting the suit fitted for the pair of them as well as the spare suit for Dan and Nala.

Like she thought, the two of them were well-matched, walking in step like it was in their blood. "Just be aware, the air will only last half as long."

Ileana's face clouded over at the memory of almost suffocating.

"Will it fit them?" Ileana questioned, when Rhyll was modifying the other suit.

"Just like it contorted to fit each of us when we first wore it. Sure, we all have different physiques to Dan or Nala, but once they climb in, it will adjust. I just wish I could see how they cope initially when they realise they have to share."

THE FOLLOWING MORNING THEY ALL TESTED THEIR ABILITIES IN THE suit by heading to the nearest tall building to speak to the others.

"I had an interesting message last night," Dan was saying. Cat had him on speaker phone. "Did you know there are desert druids?"

"Rhyll paused to consider. "I'm sure there are those in every culture who care for their environment more than others, even deserts ... I didn't know they thought of themselves as druids."

"They sound the same to me except they don't party as much ... anyway, there's a couple of Bedouins following my blog—"

"Dan has a blog?" Ileana asked in surprise.

"— and they messaged me," Dan continued. "They want to help."

"How do they know we are even here?"

"I may have mentioned it in last night's blog ... I didn't know it was a secret. And Rhyll has a following now. Check the news if you can, they're everywhere and growing stronger and larger by the day. You can thank me later."

"About these Bedouins ..." Cat prompted.

"They suggested a place to land the pod. They want to come in and help."

"They'll die," Rhyll spoke up, concern in her voice. "It's too early. I haven't placed the diamond yet."

"They know. A couple of them are sort of sensitive to the change, a bit like you can sense things, I guess. They'll know when you've succeeded and I'll fly them in shortly after. They reckon the electricity interference will also go."

"It's a big risk!" Rhyll didn't want more people dying unnecessarily.

"Don't worry. Nala will go down a few floors below the current interference level and check. We won't fly in until we know it's gone."

"So you guys will wait up there to confirm?"

"Sure. You don't need our help, do you?" Dan asked.

Cat rolled her eyes at Ileana's smirk. "I'm sure we'll cope. We'll let you know once we've completed the mission."

"Roger that. Out," Dan signed off in an official voice.

"Like I said, poor Nala." Ileana shook her head in sympathy. She saw Rhyllien pouting. "And what's got into your knickers?"

"I was thinking how much fun it would have been watching them both in the suit."

"And here I was thinking you liked Nala." Cat put the phone back in her pocket.

SHARING THE SUITS MADE THE TRIP TO CAMPBELL'S TOMB MUCH less risky, though it was hard work pushing the shopping trolleys up the gradual incline. Since Dan and Nala weren't coming back for now, the two Brazilians reverted to individual suits. The tomb was about fifty metres from the road at its nearest point.

Now they were less conspicuous, Rhyll and her mother climbed out of their shared suit so Imogen could rest in the shade of a low retaining wall.

"I'm not used to going on digs anymore." She panted as she sat in the cooler area.

Rhyll handed her a water bottle. "You take care. I'll need you down there."

"You've coped well enough so far without me," her mother said after sipping the water.

"Maybe, but I reckon I was lucky. I think I'm out of my depth here. I need you." Rhyll began working the suit back in the single user configuration.

"Pfft. Like your father, you're more resourceful than you give yourself credit for. I'm slowing you down more than anything."

"Mum, I don't want to hear you talk like that!" She climbed back into the suit as she spoke. "We wouldn't be exploring Campbell's Tomb if not for you. Drink more and rest. We'll get the remainder of the equipment and have the camp set up shortly."

"I'll be here." Imogen waved her off gently.

Rhyll joined the others bringing the gear over bit by bit, and within the hour everything was placed in an orderly pile around them. They only had to make use of the stealth option once while a drone came closer, but its attention was elsewhere.

"I'll be glad to get down there. Cooler, and we can relax a

bit." Cat started taking her suit off. "These suits might be great for space, but are still restrictive down here."

The others also removed their suits while she set out the various ropes they needed, and fitted a harness to herself. Afterwards, she fitted a harness to Ileana and Rhyll. They then checked each other's fitting.

"I'll go down first and see what it looks like," Cat said. "Then we'll get you down and help Ileana when she lowers the gear with the other rope."

Rhyll nodded, starting to feel apprehensive.

"You'll be right, chica," Ileana encouraged. "Watch what we do and how we do it. It's pretty straight forward. The one thing you have to keep in your head is to trust your equipment. These ropes and harnesses have a breaking strain of over two tonnes. Pretty sure you don't come close."

Not by much. "If it can hold you, I'll feel much better." She grinned.

"Ha!" Ileana clapped her on the shoulder.

"Lucky she likes you, chica." Cat shook her head, her chuckles fading as she descended into the hole. The sun was high, though not directly overhead, so the interior was merely dim, not dark.

Rhyll watched intently, leaning forward as Cat moved lower, seeing how she controlled the device she'd called the *descender*. The woman's head torch played along the roughly chiselled sides and swept across the approaching ground. And then she was down.

"Ten metres is easy," Ileana was saying.

Cat went out of sight temporarily, reappeared a minute later. "There's a metal grid and a gate. I'm going to shoot the lock. How's the drone situation?"

Ileana and Rhyll scanned the sky, both agreeing there was no hint of a drone.

"Fine. This should only take a second."

"Mum, Cat's just going to shoot the lock off a gate."

Imogen smiled and waved. "I bet Ileana would rather be doing the shooting."

"Ha!" Ileana laughed and nodded just as a loud bang echoed out of the darkness, followed by another one. "I would have used only one round."

After the screeching sound of rusty hinges being forced into use, Cat called out, "All good. Give me some more slack."

Cat moved off again as Ileana paid out some rope, ready in case there was a slip.

Rhyll sat on the edge, dangling her feet over the side. There was nothing to do now but wait. According to her father's sketches, the first and second chambers followed an east-west axis, with the connecting shaft of fourteen metres emerging at the west end. The second chamber was where seven sarcophagi had been found originally.

Several metres north of the base of that shaft was the third shaft, which led to the Osiris tomb, the one reported to be under-water. It was also where the sketches indicated corridors joining up between the Sphinx and the pyramids.

Cat returned below and called up. "This chamber is flat and empty, other than sand and some rubbish. I'm going to the next chamber. I'll signal when I'm about to descend." She backed out of sight after Ileana gave her the thumbs-up.

After several minutes there were two distinct tugs on the line, then it went taut, vibrating slightly.

"It's a bit like fishing," Ileana explained. "You get a feel for the line and can tell how the climber is going. Though seeing would be better."

The passing minutes were tense. They had to use the camou-flage once when a drone buzzed past. Then the rope started jiggling.

"She's climbing back up."

After another ten minutes, Cat was helped out of the hole, her trousers saturated.

"The third chamber is underwater," she said unnecessarily.

"There does seem to be something in the centre of the floor, surrounded by a circle of columns."

That was positive news to Rhyll and her mother. By late afternoon, they had everything, safe and out of sight in the first chamber. They set out a campsite, though tents weren't required.

"I hope no one sleepwalks," Cat said, setting a crude rope fence a metre from the lip of the second shaft as a warning of the lethal drop nearby.

Although tentative at first with the new experience, Rhyll loved the small bit of abseiling experience, and couldn't wait to do more. She went down to the second chamber, and the two soldiers lowered Imogen using an elaborate block and tackle. Armed with tablets and torches, they explored the area, looking for anything of interest.

They were aware the place had been looted time and time again over the centuries, long before the recorded explorers rediscovered the area.

"I think it has to be in the blood; only a true archaeologist could appreciate even an empty chamber that dates back several thousand years," Imogen said.

"You would have loved the cavern under Lake Titicaca."

Imogen bent down and crawled into one of the niches where once, the body of an ancient queen must have lain inside a sarcophagus. Both, sadly, were gone, only hieroglyphs giving indication of the former glory that had rested here. "If I died now, I would die happy."

"Mum! Don't say that. You've got so much exploring to do. Once all this is done, you and I can go wherever we want, and explore whatever we want with no red tape, no university time-line or priority."

"I would like to see Atlantis, if it really exists."

"Keep breathing, and we'll visit it together."

"Deal, but it'd better be sooner than later."

They returned to the first chamber to rest and grab a snack, after which Rhyll and Cat climbed out of Campbell's Tomb to get an update from Dan and Nala.

"Are you thinking what I'm thinking?" Rhyll looked up at the tip of the Pyramid of Khafre.

Cat followed her gaze. "It is the tallest structure around here."

"Actually the Great Pyramid is bigger, but it's on a slightly lower section of the Giza plateau, making the Khafre pyramid higher. Not that it matters. We won't have to climb to the top, just high enough to get signal. It shouldn't be too much higher."

Checking no drones were in the area, they walked to the base of the pyramid and started climbing. Less than ten blocks up, their phones pinged.

They both sat on the edge of one of the two-ton blocks, and Rhyll placed a call.

"Dan. How are things?" she asked.

"The pod has landed on the western edge of Qarun Lake. It's a tad under 90 kilometres southwest of us," Dan answered. "There's a dozen of them there, but they'll collect more on the way. Apparently there's a couple of tribes of them waiting near the death wave perimeter."

"Isn't that too close?" *Obviously not if they are breathing, dope.* "Are they safe there with the death wave expanding daily?"

"They say they have some *sensitives* with them — but maybe that was lost in translation. There's someone there who can speak a bit of English. It's not perfect but better than guesswork. The *sensitives* are the ones who can tell where the death wave is, as well as when you do your thing."

"Hopefully that won't be too long from now." She told them about camping inside the tomb.

"How do they expect to be of use to us?" Cat asked.

"They can help deal with the drones. They are well armed."

"And they're willing to do this?" Rhyll asked.

"That's what they say. I keep telling you, you have a following — even in the Sahara."

"How's Nala?"

"I'm well enough. I'm away from the smell; there's a breeze up here—"

"And there's always the internet," Dan spoke over her. "But the battery is almost flat again, so we'll head back in the morning."

Finishing the call, they carefully climbed down the rock wall in the dark and made it back to the tomb before the next drone flew overhead.

21

On their return they shared the news with the others.

Ileana had made a small fire, more for the light and cheer than the warmth, though she used it to warm the water for the dehydrated food packs. They sat and ate their dinner.

Rhyll put her finished container down and looked to Cataleya. "We're so close. Let me try this tonight."

"Are you sure? Can you sense anything?"

"Still nothing ... but I'm not tired, and while everything indicates this is the place, I won't sleep well until I know one way or the other. If it isn't the place, then we'll know soon enough, but if it is, our problem will be over before dawn."

"I will be coming with you."

"Can you scuba dive?"

"No, but we aren't really doing that. We're wearing breathing apparatus in an enclosed stone vault. I've seen it, the water is barely over a metre in depth. I've been in deeper bathtubs."

"I'll be glad for the company. No one's seen me do this before. Don't forget to tell me what happens."

Rhyllien checked the gear while Imogen spoke to her.

"I know you have to do this, but I worry," her mother said.

Rhyll put the gear down and held her mother's hands; the

firm grip of the intrepid explorer was still there. "Mum. I'll be fine. Really." She tried to reassure her with a hug.

When Imogen pulled away there was a tear. "I'm getting too old for these shenanigans."

"Nonsense. You're tired after a long day. Sit back and keep Ileana company. You should tell her the story of how you and Dad met. I'll be back before you finish."

"Liar." Her mother smiled, but sat back on her sleeping bag and leant against the wall.

Ileana had already lowered the gear to the next chamber. She watched silently as Cat, then Rhyll, abseiled down. When they were safely on the ground, she joined Imogen.

THE ONLY WAY THEY COULD VIEW THE CATACOMBS WAS BY USING their head torches. It would have looked spectacular if there was sufficient light. They had to be satisfied with the wondrous view bit by bit, as the circles of light played across the walls. There was a raised ledge around the chamber with shards of pottery and rockfall strewn along it.

"I wonder when was the last time someone came down here," Cat asked.

"I'd be surprised if it was more than a decade. Disappointing, isn't it?"

"I just don't understand why they have this at their doorstep and totally ignore it. Even locking it up."

"I'm sure Mum can talk your ear off about the secrecy, stupidity and sheer stubbornness of the powers that be. Mind you, the Egyptians are as bad as the Americans."

"Or the Chinese," Cat added.

"Or the Russians," Rhyll followed.

"Everyone," they both said together and laughed.

"I'll have to ask your mum where all this water came from." Cat helped Rhyll take off her harness, then removed hers.

"Probably the natural water table. Don't forget we descended close to forty metres or so. And over the millennia, the Nile has moved. It was much closer."

"Want to check it out first?"

"I do, but I don't want to sit around all night in wet clothes." Rhyll took her clothes off and laid them in a neat pile on the ledge and lowered herself over the lip. The cold water lapped around her ribs. There was a momentary shiver, then her body kicked in and the uncomfortable coldness disappeared. "Remember, if this is the place, I'll have to be naked for it to work." She waded towards the centre while Cat shone the torch across the surface.

As Cat had said, there were columns surrounding a circular section. Darker areas to the sides indicated corridors branching east and west. *Connections to the pyramids and the Sphinx, like dad's sketches showed.*

Moving within the circle of columns, she carefully shuffled her bare feet across the sandy floor, sliding them between fallen stonework and nudging aside pottery shards. In the darkness she was near-blind, but for the flashes of light from her head-torch, and the oil-dark waters afforded her little view of her feet. The waters rippled silently around her, and she could imagine she'd also lost her hearing. Her toes stubbed against something large and hard. Wincing briefly with the sharp pain, she numbed it with barely a thought.

At least I've not lost all *my senses.*

She reached out to feel for the large object. Her initial hopes were dashed; what she could feel was smooth, but not the large crystal platform she sought. With more exploration, she determined it was an altar.

When Rhyll turned back to Cat she reported her findings.

"Damn. I'd hoped it was what you were looking for."

"Perhaps it's further in. There are tunnels leading to the pyramids and the Sphinx."

"Are they all underwater?"

Rhyll climbed out and, after quickly drying herself off with her blouse, got dressed. "I can't say. I'd guess there'd be less water near the pyramids as they are higher. The tunnels leading to the Sphinx could be level, or maybe even descend slightly. There's only one way to find out."

"How did I know you'd say that? I assume you'll be wanting to do this now?"

"We do have all the equipment here ..."

Cat sighed and stood. "Ileana? Start lowering the suits. And a spare coil of rope."

"Did you find anything?" Ileana's voice came down from the darkness.

"Heaps, but not what we need," Rhyll called back.

In a couple of minutes, the suits were lowered and before they climbed into them, Rhyll emptied her pockets and put the items in her pack. They only had a narrow shelf to stand on so they helped each other keep balance. The extra coil of rope arrived shortly after.

"Do you remember the sketches?"

Rhyll's head nodded in the torchlight. "We've actually come a little closer to the back end of the Sphinx. If my father's sketches are true, it should be less than ten metres down there."

"Ah, so about thirty metres then," Cat joked.

"Give or take." Rhyll flashed a smile. "I can't access anything if it's inside the suit," she explained as she donned the backpack.

Cat wrapped a length of rope around the girl's waist and knotted it. She paid out another two metres, then wrapped it around her waist. "I'll tie the end to the closest column to the tunnel. If we don't find anything when this line is done, we're calling it quits tonight. Deal?"

"Deal." Rhyll sighed.

"Then I'm ready as well."

Rhyll slipped back into the water; Cat followed, letting Ileana know what they were doing by talking into the suit's commlink. They waded to the circle of columns and turned toward the dark niche at the eastern end.

"Stop there for a moment," Cat said as she paused to tie the end of the line around the chosen column. "Onwards," she commanded on completion.

As they moved off, the rope slowly uncoiled behind them, sinking out of sight beneath the water. The circle of light from the head torches became smaller and more intense on the wall as they neared.

"So far so good, the water level's the same," Rhyll said.

"Your mum wants you to describe what you are seeing," Ileana said.

Rhyll first described the columned chamber and that it was an altar in the centre, not the platform as hoped.

"The walls have murals and hieroglyphs, but they're in bad shape, probably due to the moisture. The ceiling has a slight curve to it. Everything looks like it's been cut out of the limestone bedrock."

As she entered the tunnel, the description was basically the same. "The tunnels are rectangular, slightly shorter than me, so I'm stooping." She activated her cowling when water sloshed into her suit over the lip of the neck and ran down through her clothes.

She turned to look behind her; being taller, Cat was stooped low with her cowling up already. Rhyll continued.

The tunnel went on for another fifteen metres.

"Looks like a large opening ahead," Rhyll said, continuing her description of the area.

There was a rumbling sound behind her.

"Rhyll, look out!" Cat yelled.

Instinctively Rhyll moved forward, but the rope went taught. She was jerked off her feet and pulled underwater. If not for the suit's protection, she would have rope burn, at a minimum.

"Cat—" She floundered for a heartbeat as the water surged over her.

Her commlink was full of all three voices yelling, and it was hard to work out who was saying what.

"Silence!" Cat ordered. "Rhyll, are you okay?"

"I think so ... "

"There is a slab of rock between you and me. It slid down from the ceiling," Cat said on the other side of the blockage.

"A rockfall?" Imogen asked.

"No, it's a well-formed slab. It's pinned us both underwater. Rhyll, you better untie yourself."

"Can you open it that side?" Rhyll started working at her waistband. "Is there a lever? I'll look here, too." The rope was hard to undo with her gloved fingers, and the knot had expanded in the water. The best she could do was wriggle it over her hips and down her legs.

"No lever here," Cataleya said. "I'm free of the rope now, but the water level my side is rising."

Rhyll got to her feet. The water was now halfway up her neck. "That's funny, the water level in here is still rising as well!" She ran her hands down the rock slab now blocking her exit, and along the walls each side, feeling for something, anything that might help the situation.

"I can't see shit!" She tried not to panic. "The water has churned up all the sand; the whole place is murky." Rhyll knew her mum would be worried sick. *Shit, I'm worried sick!* "Mum, I have at least an hour of air. I'm okay, and don't worry."

"I'm not convinced." Her mum's voice came over the comms.

"Too bad Dad's sketches didn't mention 'there be traps here'," she said, trying to make light of the fact she was in a flooding tunnel, forty metres underground, that probably hadn't seen life for decades.

"Darling, it's a secret ancient Egyptian tomb; there's always traps."

"I'm counting on there being ways to get out of them, too. I'm heading down the tunnel. There may be something down that way." Moving forward was hard through the roiling water. The torrent gushing from the ceiling was throwing up a sheet of spray so thick that her torchlight was barely able to penetrate, and she was unable to make out details at the end of the tunnel. The water was now chin-height.

"There's nothing I can do this end," Cat called. "I'll make my way back, and see what we can come up with. I'll try something to use as a lever. Ileana, see what you can find up there, maybe go to the police station for search-and-rescue equipment. There's bound to be the dumb tourist stuck down a hole on occasion."

"Says the tourist stuck in a hole. I'll leave the suit for Imogen to speak to Rhyll," Ileana replied.

"Maybe go over those sketches, see what I'm heading into." Rhyll leant forward and began swimming; breaststroke was the only option in the suit, and only inches from the ceiling. Eventually, she was close enough to see details. "It's blocked."

"Is it the end of the tunnel?"

"It is if I can't open it," she grumbled.

"That isn't helping. Is it a stone slab like the other one?" her mother asked.

Rhyll groped around the blockage. "It's too smooth to be stone. It's ..." She wiped away some of the muck on the surface.

"Rhyll?" her mum called, a tinge of concern in her voice.

Rhyll had her faceplate hard up against the door. "I think it's orichalcum."

"The whole door?"

"Seems so." Her fingers ran back and forth over the surface, starting from the top and working down. "There's a film of slime or something over it, but it has the same sheen and feel. And ... I can feel a depression!" Her gloved fingers worked around the central area.

"What? For the sun-disc? Have you got it?"

"I do, but it's not circular; it's like a cross ..."

"No cross in ancient Egyptian culture, dear," Imogen said, pondering. "Could it be an ankh?"

"I'm back on the shelf," Cat informed them. "I'll climb up now. Keep us posted."

"Will do."

"Have you got that ankh with you?" Imogen asked.

"Of course. I'm a well-equipped tomb raider."

"You do love pants with lots of pockets."

"See, it's practical, not just a crazy fetish. Tell that to Daniel next time you speak to him." Rhyll slipped off her pack to retrieve the ankh, feeling for it in the gloom. She hooked the strap over her shoulder and turned her attention back to the door. "Here we go." She pushed the ankh into the depression. It didn't seem to fit. When she released it, it slipped from her gloved fingers.

"Crap!"

"What?"

"I dropped it." Rhyll struggled to get lower, but the buoyancy of the suit made it difficult. She inverted and pushed off the ceiling with her feet, arms groping blindly in front.

She felt other things down there in the murk. A bony hand suddenly came into view. "Fuck!" she shrieked. She pushed away from it in shock. "Sorry about that. There's a skeleton down here!"

"A skeleton?" Imogen really sounded worried now.

That doesn't bode well for me! She redoubled her efforts to search for the ankh.

To the side of the tunnel she felt something firm: a fallen block. She held onto it, using it as an anchor, and sifted her other hand through the silt and sand on the floor, feeling under the bony remains of some poor sod who'd gotten stuck here. *Did he drown or starve?*

"Got it," she said finally. Realigning herself with the door, she rubbed the depression to remove the crust of accumulated muck and tried again.

There was no blue flash of light this time and she didn't become bodiless like in Peru. Rhyll felt a subtle vibration as the ankh snicked into place, much like a magnet clings to iron, fusing to the surrounding surface. Nothing happened.

"Rhyll? Anything?"

"Not yet." Rhyll held her breath, waiting, feeling the door. "I can feel a vibration. Very faint." Her vision started to clear. "Hey, the water level is dropping."

"That's a relief." Her mum's voice did sound less stressed compared to a few minutes ago.

"The water is halfway down my face now. Wherever it's going, it's going fast." She kept a running commentary. "Chest ... waist ... thighs ... shit!"

"What now?"

"More bones! It's like a graveyard down here." On the floor around her she found many bones and other skeletons of various sizes and shapes as she scanned the floor with her torch. "This is weird." She lowered her cowling now the water had almost gone, and breathed in the air, surprised at its dry freshness. *If the water reached the ceiling, where did the air go? Where is it coming from now?* She pondered briefly and looked up. Sure enough, there were small holes placed along the ceiling.

"What's weird, chica?" Cat asked.

Rhyll returned her attention to the floor. "Some of the skeletons are in robes ... some are in western clothing, but really old-school."

"Arabs and some earlier European explorers from long before records were kept."

"Or they've been keeping secrets longer than we expected."

"Or that too. Cat's with me now."

"Good." Rhyll got on her hands and knees and delved through the scattered remains on the damp floor. Some of them were wedged where the wall and floor joined. Pulling one away revealed the low slots along the base of the side walls, with the tell-tale indication of water flowing over the built-up silt. "I found the drains."

Close to where she was kneeling she spied a pouch on one of the trouser-wearing skeletons. She grabbed it as a grinding sound from behind startled her. There was a rush of air. It made an eerie and deep whistling sound; going by the ruffling of her hair, air was being drawn into the new space.

"The door's rising!" Rhyll said in an excited voice. "Lara Croft, eat your heart out." Rhyll chuckled as she put the pouch in her pack and stepped to the exit.

"What can you see now?"

"Patience, Mum." Rhyll laughed, relived there was an exit. She looked down at the widening gap. "The sand was built up a few inches on the tunnel side only. It's dry on the other side."

"Which indicates that door may have been down for a long, long time."

Slowly, the door creaked upward high enough that she could get through without having to crawl. The breeze had reduced substantially, as did the sound. "I'm now looking at a large chamber."

"Careful the door doesn't drop on you," Cat warned.

"Not that I could stop it, it must weigh a ton." With trepidation, Rhyll scampered through. "I'm in. All good here." *So far.*

The door didn't budge, and she felt foolish for her nervousness. "As far as I can tell, this chamber is a large rectangle. The torch doesn't reach the end, and barely reaches the sides. There are columns running the length on each side. I should be directly under the Sphinx by now."

"There's a reference to the Hall of Records," her mother was saying. "You're further along than we guessed."

Rhyll continued down the centre, describing what she was seeing. The ceiling was easily ten metres above her, vaulted, and like she'd seen in the Vatican, covered in paintings, illustrations, depictions of people and animals. "The artwork here's very much intact. Nearer the middle, there are ... seven columns forming a circle around a tall pedestal." She walked around it, running her hands gently up and down the smooth surface. "More orichalcum." The columned pedestal itself was almost a metre tall, and on a large crystalline base, smaller but similar to the crystal columns she'd seen back in the Erdany mine.

"It sounds like there's more orichalcum there than has ever been discovered!" Imogen pointed out.

"I don't have anywhere near enough pockets," Rhyll quipped. "Seven's an odd number."

"A mathematical genius if ever I heard one," Cat muttered.

"I meant, smartarse, it's *unusual* having an odd number to form a circle."

"Why is seven significant?"

"Beats me." Rhyll shrugged. "Seven diamonds; seven chakra points ... This is supposed to be the *throat chakra*, by the way."

"Why the throat chakra?"

"When I know, I'll tell you." Rhyll continued her examination.

"Then there's Temple of the Seven Rays," Imogen added.

"You mentioned them yesterday," Cat said.

"An ancient religious order supposedly from Atlantis. It's where the emerald tablets originated, so they say."

"Like this one?" Cat asked.

From the sounds of the conversation Rhyll could hear through the suit's commlink, her mother was repeating the story of the tablets. She got on her hands and knees to crawl around the crystal base. There was nothing overly significant around it, and it didn't glow at her touch.

Disappointed, Rhyll stood and diverted her attention nearer the top of the pedestal, which was about a foot above her head. As she looked up and stepped around it, a hole in the shadow of the deep fluting became visible when her light moved across the surface. Further inspection showed there was just the one hole. Shining the torch through the gap showed it went deep, but when she reached around and waved her hand on the opposite side, there was no indication the light went through.

Rhyll then stretched up to see if she could pull herself to check the top; as she did so, the pedestal shifted. In surprise she let go before it toppled, thinking she may have already damaged it. *I do weigh more than I look. A lot more.*

"What's happening, Rhyll?"

In satisfying her curiosity, she had neglected to keep the others informed about her progress or keep everyone else in the loop.

"I'm probably breaking stuff."

"What?"

Rhyll wanted to see the top, and went in search of something to boost her to a sufficient height. As she wandered, she updated them on what she found.

Scattered to the side of the hall outside the circle of columns she came across several blocks that had fallen from the roof. They were about a foot wide, half that in height and roughly two feet in length. Too heavy to lift, but she managed to flip them over and over until she had several lined up, creating short steps. She rested briefly between each one, wiping the sweat with the back of her hand. *Maybe it's time to lose the suit.*

"Keep going. I'm making notes as you go," Imogen said.

"The columns themselves are covered with inscriptions, but not all hieroglyphs." She paused. "Anyone recall the writing on the screen in the UFO?"

"Same as the HUD in our suits?" Cat questioned.

"Yes. The writing looks very similar."

"So the same aliens — or from the same species — may have been here before?"

"Prior to collecting to you guys in Brazil, we stopped by here first. Q said he found the Giza Necropolis coordinates in the ship's database. It must be true, otherwise it's too coincidental."

"I don't suppose he said how long ago?"

"Didn't say, and I didn't think to ask." Having rested sufficiently, she could now stand on the corner of the crystal base and examine the top of the pedestal. Her footing was precarious, at best, as the base was smooth and not much wider than the pedestal; she feared toppling it if she exerted too much force.

There was dust, grit, and a slot. She tried to stand on her toes to look, but felt herself slipping. Adjusting the positioning of her feet, she groped around the top. The slot was about two hand widths long and three fingers wide. As her fingers explored the depth, she noted two sides angled in, but she needed greater height to push her hand in deeper. As it was, she couldn't feel the bottom. However, the two narrow sides angled in from the top ... like an upside down triangle. *What does that shape remind me of? A prism, perhaps?*

Frustrated, she had to retrieve the prism from her backpack, and then climb back, reaching upwards to place the object on top of the pedestal.

There was no indication, from what she could see or feel, which way the crystal artefact was supposed to go, so she inverted it and hesitated. *No little rune carving like the diamonds.*

"Mum, tell me about this prism; the one I found under Lake Titicaca."

"Okay ... Amaru Muru used the sun-disc as you did, and we can assume he travelled to the same caverns. I've seen your video and tapes of the caverns, but not completely analysed them yet.

"Muru was a high priest of the Temple of the Seven Rays, and the prism refracts light into its various components—"

"Why the *Seven* Rays? Surely there are more colours in the spectrum?"

"True. Blame Pythagoras: he came up with the number seven as being prominent in nearly everything in the natural world, like the seven colours of the rainbow. It's the same with the human world: seven deadly sins, seven notes in an octave — if you don't count *doh* twice. The correlation of the seven colours and the seven chakras, can only be guessed at for now. Lucky number seven, seven churches in the book of Revelations, seven days in a week ..."

"And we have seven columns here ... Here goes." She carefully slotted the prism into the niche. "It's a perfect fit!" *So perfect, I can't get the damn thing out now!* Her fingers tried to pry it out, but there was nowhere for her to grip and she didn't have her penknife to lever it out. But the placement was so precise, she doubted the blade would fit.

Not sure whether she had done the right thing or not, she climbed down and hoped she didn't need the prism for another task. Despite her care, the pedestal twisted again. *Rotating?*

Dolt! She re-examined where the pedestal joined the base.

There was the thinnest of gaps, as if the pedestal wasn't firmly fixed to the base. She carefully bent down to look, but couldn't ascertain what mechanism was used to allow the movement.

With a two-handed grip, she turned the pedestal. While it was initially an effort, once it was moving the rotation was smooth — almost frictionless. *But if that were the case, surely it'd slide off.*

"The pedestal rotates, and the prism is stuck in the top." She told the others what was happening. Rhyll stood back, hoping something would present itself.

Nada.

"Anything else?" her mum was asking.

"I'm only halfway down the hall." She continued her exploratory walk, describing more details as her torch revealed them, working her way to the end. "Guess what."

"Is it bad? Did you break something again?"

"No, it's good. There's this large crystal platform at the end of the hall."

When she reached out to touch it, it began to give off a dim blue glow. A familiar sensation of calmness coursed through her body.

"This is it!" Rhyll squealed in relief. Her voice echoed in the darkness and she could hear the others whoop in excitement over the commlink.

"Congratulations," her mother said.

"Thanks to you and Dad." Rhyll double-checked for the familiar shallow, body-shaped depression in which she would lie; it was probably covered in several centuries' worth of grit and dust.

Looking beyond the platform, she saw she was almost at the far end of the hall. Sand drift had completely blocked off the doorway in the centre.

"Not sure how I'm getting out. The eastern entrance is blocked. Maybe in the spacesuit I could dig my way out." *Assuming I can dig through forty metres of sand in an hour.*

Rhyll removed the spacesuit and placed it on the floor, then took her blouse off to wipe down the surface, holding her breath as the dust settled. After that, she leant forward and blew the small amount of dust and grit out of the niche situated at the neck. *The throat chakra.* She took the blue diamond out of her pack and after checking the rune inscription was on the base, she slipped it into place. The light began its familiar slow, rhythmic pulsing.

Picking the suit up, she placed it on the pedestal so the commlink was near her mouth. Rhyll then kicked off her boots and removed the remainder of her clothes, folded them and put them on top of the suit. She turned, sat on the platform and slid back over the cool smooth surface until she felt the depression, then she swung herself around and reclined

"I'm lying down now," she told them. "The platform's glowing and pulsating as the others did. I don't know how long I'll be out, but I'll call you the moment I wake." As she relaxed she looked up at the ceiling, noticing a possible exit directly above. *Probably where all the grit came from.* "There's a hole in the ceiling." She yawned.

"Love you," she heard her mum say as drowsiness took over.

Like the previous times, there was an overwhelming urge to close her eyes. She didn't resist and was inundated with vision after vision — as if those images were waiting for her return.

22

OTHER THAN THE GLOW FROM THE PLATFORM, IT WAS MOSTLY DARK when Rhyll recovered. She had forgotten to turn off the torch. "I guess I can always recharge it," she muttered.

"Rhyll?" Her mother's voice sounded full of relief.

Rhyll turned to face the commlink. "Mum? How long was I out?"

"At least three hours. Are you okay?"

"All good, but are you alright?

"We're all fine now. Ileana has returned with some equipment and she and Cat are looking for ways to get to you. Campbell's Tomb is still full of water."

Rhyll described what she had gone through while unconscious. "The visions started coming back, then I woke up." She sat up, working her way off the platform, stretching to get the kinks out of her back. As she did, the pedestal came to life, the bright light almost painful to her dark-adjusted eyes. "The central pedestal's glowing!"

She quickly pulled on her clothes, while the light threw her shadow on the far walls.

"The orichalcum's glowing?" her mother asked.

"No, the crystal base is."

When she didn't hear a reply, she realised the suit was needed to communicate. Rhyll quickly went back to the crystal platform and spoke to her mum while she pulled on her boots and then the suit.

"What does that mean?"

"I've no idea. I've not seen this setup before." Rhyll walked around the base, looking it up and down as she buttoned her blouse. "There's a beam of light shining out of the hole. The centre of the pedestal must be hollow; it's the only light source."

"Is the beam of light coming from the crystal?"

"I can only assume so, but while the crystal is white, the light is brown or tan."

"Interesting ..." Imogen said softly, as if distracted or facing away from the commlink. "Oh by the way, the electrical interference has lessened." It was her turn to update her daughter on progress while she was unconscious. "Our phones pinged about an hour ago; a message from Dan to confirm to us he has heard from the Bedouins and they are on their way. They must have sensed the change too."

"What about the drones?"

"They are here and there, but there's been no change in their activity. I don't think they know yet."

"They'll definitely know as soon as the hoverpod lands. Maybe Dan should hold off landing until I get out? It could be hours, days even."

"As to that, I can't say."

Rhyll started to rotate the orichalcum column. As the light moved, she glanced down at her chest, watching the gradual change of colour on her suit. She stepped behind the pedestal, out of the beam, and slowly moved it, watching the ray of light through the dusty darkness, like the beam of a lighthouse in the fog.

"It must be the prism refracting the light from the crystal base. You thought the base was hollow," her mum responded at the news.

"Now the beam is yellow. I think it only shines on the columns," Rhyll continued. "Between columns the beam isn't bright enough to reach anything, but when it gets to the next column, it's a primary colour. We're on green now." Rhyll walked around slowly, turning the pedestal with her. "Blue, violet and ... violet? One of those must be indigo. The same colours as the chakra and diamonds."

"And they only show on the columns? Where exactly?"

"I'll go and look." Rhyll left the violet light shining on the column and ran over to check. "The violet diamond goes to Tibet ... but there's nothing here that resembles Tibet in any way."

"So it isn't a map?"

"Just a lot of lines of alien-looking squiggles. Funny, they look something like those on the HUD."

"Hmm ... It *must* mean something."

"I agree. Seems to be a lot of effort to mean nothing."

"Can you take notes?"

"No tablet." Searching her pockets for pen and paper, she patted the small rectangular shape in her calf pocket. "Wait, I *do* have my phone. Argh! How could I forget? I could have videoed everything before."

"Do it now."

"I hate myself," she muttered. She dragged her phone out.

"Rhyll, you've never had a life like the average teenager," Imogen tried to reason with her. "You hardly ever use one ... Ken and I rarely did, so it stands to reason it wouldn't occur to you. Kids today can't think unless they have one in their hands, or an earbud constantly playing music."

As Imogen talked, Rhyll videoed and took pictures of everything illuminated. She then ran back to the pedestal and repeated the process, back and forth until every column had been completely recorded. Then she took several minutes to scan the platform and the entire hall, though it was still quite dim.

"I'll try to send them to you ... Bugger! Barely any signal." She moved around the area to check. "If the colours don't match what we know about the chakra locations, what do you reckon this is showing then?"

"Going by Ken's notes and the myths — and sometimes I think it's the same thing — it could lead to the locations of the other emerald tablets. Remember, the chamber you're in is believed to be the Hall of Records. The knowledge there is supposed to be greater than the library of Alexandria."

"And they'd tell us about Atlantis?"

"And much more, yes, if there's any truth to the myths."

"Cool." There was a faint ping heard in the background.

"Message from Cat," Imogen said. "She's at the front of the Sphinx. She says there is a hole similar to Campbell's Tomb, but smaller. She also says 'Well done, chica'."

Smiling to herself, Rhyll returned to the glowing platform to pull on boots and socks "The white crystal pedestal is beginning to fade." Remembering her torch was flat, she held it in her hands and started charging it.

In the silence, she heard a rumble. "Can you hear anything?" she asked her mother.

"Nightjars, I think."

"Nightjars?"

"Definitely not pigeons."

"No rumbling?"

"No."

"Where are you now?" Rhyll asked.

"After you got trapped, we all climbed out of the tomb and I'm now wrapped in a sleeping bag, sitting on the Sphinx side of the causeway, drone spotting. Should be a nice sunrise soon."

The rumbling changed tone, but it hadn't stopped. It came from the far end where she'd entered. Rhyll took a few steps towards the centre before it dawned on her: the slab that had dropped must now be rising.

Rhyll ran back and climbed onto the platform. She grabbed her spacesuit, stepping into it as water flowed swiftly over the floor like a tide. "There's water coming in here!" she reported.

"From where?"

"From where Cat and I separated." By the torchlight, it had churned up the sand and dust and was now a dirty, brown roiling mess. Bones and skeletons had been dragged along with it.

Making sure her phone was secured in a pocket, Rhyll climbed down and started to walk back to the first tunnel. She had been in more powerfully flowing creeks, but having this amount of water while underground in the dark was unnerving. Again she kept her mother updated on her progress.

"Cat and Ileana will meet you back at Campbell's Tomb."

"Great." Rhyll's mind kept working.

The other puzzling thing was that the orichalcum door had sealed this chamber off for many centuries, yet now it remained open to let all the water in. *Was it designed to do this?* With the drainage holes near the door, she assumed so. *Had she activated a trap, or was it always going to happen?*

"I'm leaving the Hall of Records and passing the orichalcum door."

After going under the strange alloy door, she paused in case it dropped and she might retrieve the ankh ... but it stayed up. She could no longer hear the rumbling, which she surmised had been the slab trap rising. The water flow had also increased. Tapping her shoulder, she brought the cowling up before the suit was inundated.

Turning, she waded up the tunnel with only the torch light to go by and ran through the sequence of events prior to her going to sleep and waking up. Nothing obvious came to mind; the crystal pedestal had glowed the moment her feet came off the platform, and faded shortly after she completed the rotations. *Was it timed? Was it always going to happen after a certain sequence of events took place, to stop others from accessing the secrets of Atlantis?*

The going was much tougher now. She felt something entwine her legs. Her searching hands gripped the rope that Cat had left behind. "Thanks, Cat." Pulling herself against the flow, Rhyll reached the slab that had blocked her exit. It was now up in its original position, allowing the built up water to flow through.

A few tiring minutes later she was inside the circular columned area, what they thought may have been the Tomb of Osiris. Now moving to her left, crossing the flow was made trickier with the eddies churning around the columns. Her boot slipped and if not for her grip on the rope, she would have tumbled back towards the Hall of Records. Even so, she did slide back a few metres.

Regaining her footing, she struggled against the flow until she reached where the shelf should have been. It was still there, but now underwater.

Where did all this water come from? "There's a hell of a lot of water here now," she said to her mother.

"Cat and Ileana should be there shortly. Are you okay?"

"Tired, but almost out."

"Almost there, chica," Cat said.

"Dan and Nala are heading back, too. Now the signal is better, Dan can monitor the hoverpod's progress here as good as anywhere else."

"Lovely." Rhyll was now concentrating on climbing out. Cat, in her foresight, had knotted the rope and left it dangling. Even with the aid of the knots, it was a slow, gruelling climb, and she was exhausted by the time she reached the chamber with the alcoves for the sarcophagi.

Faint circles of light played high up on the far wall. *Cat and Ileana's torches.* She retracted her cowling, as they weren't in their suits and wouldn't be able to hear her.

She tapped her shoulder and called out, "I'm down here."

"We're coming," Cat said.

Rhyll stumbled to the base of the next shaft. Shining down on her, their two headlights were a welcoming sight.

"Put this under your arms and hang on, chica."

A loop of thick strapping was lowered. "Thanks, Ileana." Rhyll slipped one arm through, then the other. She tucked it under her arms and gripped it tightly.

"Haul away." As they heaved on the line, she started walking up the roughly hewn walls.

"Merde, you *are* a heavy one, chica," Ileana called down.

"Be nice." She laughed. "It must be the suit."

"Of course. We won't judge," Cat said.

"Maybe *you* won't." Ileana joked.

23

"FOUR DOWN, THREE TO GO," NALA CONGRATULATED RHYLL WHEN she and Dan returned to the group, who had made themselves comfortable within the Temple of Khafre. "I hear there was a bit of danger?"

It was dawn, with a brilliant, clear sky. They'd lit a small fire, more for brewing tea than to provide warmth for themselves. The Temple of Khafre — or its ruins — was now row upon row of massive stone blocks. Where they hadn't toppled, some still formed archways.

"Nah." Rhyll shrugged it off. "The Tomb of Osiris and its connecting tunnels began to flood after a slab blocked the flow, and when the door opened, the water rushed back down the tunnel."

"You mean the pyramids *are* connected underground?" Dan asked.

Rhyll nodded. "Seems so."

Imogen filled them in on some of the details Rhyll neglected to mention. "As I've been telling her, these ancient tombs — whether here, or Brazil ... or anywhere — can and do have some unpredictable and intricate traps. The builders took the burial of their monarchs seriously, believing very much in the afterlife.

This is why so many of the tombs have the various vaults of gifts and food, so when their monarch returns in the afterlife, they have their treasures with them."

"Still, well done you." Nala hugged her friend. "Can you sense anything now?"

"Yes. I can sense as much as I would under normal conditions as far as the electrical interference."

"You mean it's still there?" Dan looked puzzled. "How are we getting signal?"

"It's diminishing. The interference is quickly fading from this point, and outwards. I believe it's fading faster than the actual death wave. Now it will all soon be like the other areas, giving only a slight loss of signal and sporadic interference."

"That's good news. More good news is that our hoverpod is about ten minutes away." Dan put his pad down. "And my battery is going flat."

Rhyll placed her hand on the pad and asked, "How many Bedouins are there?"

"I'm not sure, but I suspect as many as they could fit without affecting their pod's ability to fly. No doubt with safety protocols and over-engineering a pod could carry at least double the recommended passengers, but I don't know what they've got. They do have ways and means of flying here themselves. From our brief conversations with their translator, I gather they have access to more pods."

"Bedouins in hoverpods?" Rhyll sounded dubious.

"Don't forget, for the most part the pods are AI-controlled. Once the coordinates are punched in, the Bedouins just have to ride in it — and not touch anything."

"Our druid friends in the UK drove cars," Nala reminded her.

DAN'S HOVERPOD ARRIVED AND HE PROGRAMMED IT TO LAND IN front of the temple on a large, flat area. Shortly after, seven more pods landed in quick succession nearby. It was an interesting sight, seeing these hoverpods surrounded by ruins ... a sort of juxtaposition of ancient and modern inventions.

The doors opened and the nomads emerged in their traditional garb, and it was from the clothing that Rhyll realised there were a few women present as well. Many of them appeared bewildered by their recent experience, but under the guidance of a couple of their leaders, calmed down as they gathered in a group, glancing at the westerners but moreso at the young redhaired girl. Their subdued mutterings could be heard over the susurration of the constant wind.

Rhyll stepped forward, arms out, palms facing them. "Barakat ealayk waeallaa 'aslafika. Amana al'ard tahibukum jamiean," she intoned her normal greeting; this time she inclined her head slightly. It felt the right thing to do.

"You speak Arabic?" Cat said, utterly astonished as the gathering of Bedouins dropped to their knees, then bent forward to put their foreheads to the sand. They stayed this way for a full minute in silence, despite the wind blowing sand around them.

From the look on Ileana's face, she felt the same as Cataleya; both stared at her, mouths agape.

"Nope," Rhyll answered. "Same as I can't speak fluent Portuguese."

"What did you say to them?"

"Bênçãos para você e seus ancestrais. A Mãe Terra ama a todos vocês."

"Blessings on you and your ancestors. The Earth Mother loves you all," Cat translated.

Rhyll nodded. "It's the same one I always use, though I think the translation differs slightly with some dialects. I don't know why, but it just came to me the first time and felt so right, so I've used it ever since."

"Chica, you surprise me every day." Cat shook her head.

Rhyll blushed and laughed quietly. "Me too."

The group of robed men and women stood and moved closer

to touch her respectfully, awe in their eyes. Like the locals did in Amarete in Peru. It felt odd to her, but she sensed no ill intent. It's the least she could do for these people who believed she was a messenger from Gaia.

It calmed and inspired them.

"Asalaam 'alaykum." The woman who acted as interpreter stepped forward and introduced herself as Yasmeena al-Rahim. She bowed low.

"Wa 'alaykum as-salaam," Rhyll replied with a bow of her head, looking admiringly at Yasmeena's robe. Although earth-coloured, it was such a fine-looking garment decorated with hundreds of beads woven into the trim.

"It is an honour to meet you, Earth Carer." Yasmeena stood straight, matching Rhyllien's height. "With respect, you should now leave this place. You are too valuable, and possess ancient and secret knowledge that — in any other hands — could bring us all great peril."

"Ancient and secret knowledge?" Rhyll asked, puzzled. "To be honest, I don't know what I found."

"Some of our people — those able to feel these things — tell me you have found the great hall and activated the shrine of *Djehuti*."

"*Djehuti*?" Rhyll looked to her mother.

"I think she means Thoth, the Egyptian God of wisdom and knowledge," Imogen told her.

Yasmeena nodded. "A God of many things. I think the word is ... *esoteric*. He was the recipient of much information from all over the known world — and some of the unknown world; knowledge we are not yet ready for. Our concern is others will try to take this from you. It would be" — she searched for a word — "catastrophic?"

"If you mean really bad, then that would be the word." Rhyll nodded.

"Yes. Very, very bad."

The sound of much buzzing reached their ears. As one, the

group looked up at the dozens of drones now approaching the area.

"Take cover," Cat ordered, ushering Imogen to the nearest archway.

Within a few minutes the Bedouins had scattered to various parts of the immediate area. In moments they were barely visible, as their garments blended with the surroundings.

"What are they doing?" Cat asked, apprehensive with so many strangers bearing weapons — most with powerful rifles.

"They'll try to take out any drones that come too close," Yaasmeena told them.

"Nala, stay here and do what you can. Ileana, come with me." Cat started jogging to the roadway, where she grabbed a discarded bike. Her companion joined her; regardless of the bike size, all they had to do was coast down the road.

"Where are they off to?" Dan asked.

"No idea, but with Cataleya, whatever it is will be good for us, bad for them." Nala pulled out her gun and cocked it.

"At least the link to the Cloud works." Dan gulped, then started taking photos.

In moments, the air was full of gunfire echoing off the walls of the temple. Imogen covered her ears while Nala kept close eye on her charge, standing between her and anything else. If a drone ventured too close, even passing by and not paying attention to her, she aimed and shot it out of the sky.

"You're a pretty good shot," Rhyll praised her.

Nala only nodded in reply.

Rhyll realised she was not allowing for any distractions. *Good woman*. She glimpsed something descending, then realised it was coming from a great height and was much larger than the drones. "Hoverpod coming!" She pointed.

A short time later, three more pods appeared.

"Looks like they've been waiting for this to happen to get here so quickly," Dan observed.

"Surely they couldn't have pre-empted it? *We* didn't even know what was going to happen."

"Yet here they are." Dan started taking photos of the nearest pod. "Hey, they're from ICON! I recognise the logo."

"What? How?" Rhyll asked, perplexed.

"I don't ... Wait. Maybe they were the ones who hacked into Stradjek's pod, so they'd know you had planned to come here at some point. They have the resources, financially and technologically, and they've been around since the beginning; remember the one we found at São Lucas? They're probably pretty pissed with you for stuffing up their plans in Area 53."

"And pinching their UFO."

"And Q said it was satellite surveillance that detected him. Takes a lot of clout to pull that off."

The gunfire continued unabated. Drones dropped out of the sky, but more were zooming in from the further reaches of the city. Some of the nomads had already turned their attention to the nearest hoverpod, suspecting they were the greater threat.

One of the ICON pods began rotating. Suddenly, bright bursts came from a turret in its nose.

"Shit. Lasers!" Dan kept taking photos as Rhyll pulled him behind a large block.

An area where several nomads had been training their rifles on the pod was blasted. Two of the three nomads fell, the third managing to duck behind cover.

Rhyll buckled over, their agony hitting her like a truck. She gasped for breath and dropped to her knees, wiping away unbidden tears.

"Rhyll's been hit!" Nala screamed.

Dan looked over, shock written on his face.

"No. I'm okay." Rhyllien stood, bracing herself against the pillar. Sweat beaded her brow.

"We can't hope to compete with lasers," Nala yelled, aiming at the cockpit. Each shot left a small spiderweb on the window, but didn't penetrate. "Damn."

The turret swivelled towards her.

Dan let go his camera and dived, knocking her to the ground as the block where she was standing took the hit. Chunks of the ancient stone flew in all directions, and the laser left a scar of fused rock where it had hit.

Rhyll was still catching her breath as the wave of empathic pain subsided. She had to do something as more laser fire blasted the area around her. Relaxing her mind was difficult with everything going on around her: the cries of pain, the retaliatory yells of defiance, the gunfire ...

Falteringly at first, she reached out, much like she had in Area 53. In her mind's eye, the pod was now a glowing ball with various shades of intensity. She recalled that this was how energy appeared, and she directed her thoughts at what she knew must be major electrical wiring, imagining electricity from each cable arcing to the next... and *pushed*.

Rhyll gasped at the stabbing pain between her eyes. What she had done was not totally unlike what she'd accomplished in Area 53; though it was still electrical wiring, it had been at a much greater distance.

Opening her eyes, she saw the pod began to slowly spin as it descended rapidly. It landed askew on a pile of ancient rubble, then rolled onto its side.

"Did you do that?" Dan asked Nala in shock.

"How the hell could I do it with you on top of me?" She thumped him in the chest as he rolled off. "Besides, the power-pack is in the back; I couldn't hit it from this angle."

"Who, then?"

They turned to Rhyll, noticing she looked deathly pale.

"Rhyll?"

She smiled wanly. "Something I picked up in Area 53. You two get Mum to our pod."

Smoke wafted from the interior of the downed hoverpod as the hatch burst open. Dark-clad men appeared, and climbed out, some limping or holding their arms. Six in all, they tried to shelter behind the craft but the nomads were spread around the area. It was no good as protection. Firing randomly with their automatic weapons, they attempted to find more suitable cover.

The nomads fired at them. Three more mercenaries were hit before the remainder were out of sight.

Originating somewhere to their south, something streaked across the sky, taking out a second pod.

"Cat!" Nala and Dan echoed each other as they climbed to their feet.

"She must be at that cop station near the Marriott," Dan added. "Ileana was impressed with their armoury."

"Now is a good time to go, while they're busy dodging missiles," Rhyll suggested.

"I'm so glad she's on our team," Nala said, as Dan turned to help Imogen to her feet. She had been sitting nearby, under the overhang of a low wall. "And you too," Nala added, looking at Rhyll.

"I'll be with you shortly."

Imogen hesitated, looking to her daughter.

"Mum, remember, I'm supposed to be resourceful. I can't do that worrying about you here. Go. I need to concentrate."

Dan gently encouraged the ageing professor towards his pod, guiding her through the inner sanctum of the Khafre temple.

Nala kept a close eye for any further threats from above, and a closer eye on Imogen's progress.

Pushing the pain away, Rhyll closed her own eyes again to work on the third pod, now moving closer to the direction of the missile launch. As Dan surmised, it looked like it was heading towards the Marriott.

She had to do more than short a few wires if she was going to remove the threat completely; a downed pod simply meant mercenaries hiding in the rocks waiting to shoot at her friends.

Towards the back was a an intense glow. It was energy, but felt different. *Energy is energy.* Like in all previous incidents, she concentrated at what it would look like if it expanded, and *pushed* with her mind.

There was a sudden brightness.

The rising sun was dimmed briefly as the powerpack of the large hoverpod blew up; the brilliant flash expanded in all directions, as did the fuselage and shrapnel, falling to the ground over a wide area. A did the bodies.

Did different energies cause different consequences?

Shocked at the damage she'd caused, the throbbing of her head bringing tears, she lost vision momentarily. It took seconds for blurry images to reappear from the fog of her blindness. She knew there was at least one pod left. The bright flashes indicated its lasers were firing at some point out of sight, in the direction of the hotel.

Rhyll decided it best to lay down for this one; she didn't think she'd be standing afterwards. She tried to relax, giving up on pushing the pain away, but took several deep breaths before she began focusing on it. Overpowering tiredness hit her.

She couldn't do it and lay there, moaning.

Another streak burst from the ground, and the last pod exploded seconds later.

As this was going on, the nomads had continued to shoot at the drones. When the last pod dropped from the sky, there were cheers and high-pitched ululations.

The sounds of the sheering faded as she lost consciousness.

24

"LOOKS LIKE YOUR GIRL HAS SUCCEEDED AGAIN, SO YOU'RE BOTH OFF to Tibet."

"Remind me why we're doing it, and not your military wing?" Tyrone queried, sounding like a whiney child.

"You're doing it to prove your worth to us. Either one of you may fail, meaning you aren't as resourceful as we'd like our associates to be."

"And why is *he* doing it? I thought he had been with you for years."

"Benjamin has shown much promise, but disappointed us lately. Like you, he needs to assure us of his true worth. Only then is his future with us guaranteed. Do this, and you'll have the full backing of the Illuminati."

"And why Tibet? Surely you can nab her anywhere."

"As surprising as it is, Rhyllien's quite formidable. We now want her alive, and she will be less stressed when she thinks there will be no attacks. That's where you come in—"

"In case you haven't noticed, everyone dies in the death wave," Tyrone laughed nervously. "Why would I risk certain death?"

As they were talking, she was escorting them into a large room.

"These are from our R&D labs, based on what data we got from Area 53." She showed them the new version of the EMF suits, explaining their function. "Our suits are superior to the ones on Earth because in space we can do many things that they can't."

Tyrone and Williams looked over the two suits curiously.

"Isn't Area 53 run by ICON?" Williams asked her.

"We let them think they are, but we have people everywhere. At least fifty per cent of corporations employ a few of our colleagues; some are quite high up now." Aitana was enthused by the success of the Illuminati indoctrination. "We even have one on the ICON board" — she paused, realising she'd said too much — "and if that information ever passes your lips, you will die by my hands."

Tyrone shared a worried glance with Williams.

"Care to share how we're supposed to do this?"

"I'm sure you'll come up with something once you find them; too much planning without knowing all the relevant details is tantamount to failing. However, we will give you all the information you need to work these suits, and how to go about getting extracted. I should add, if you haven't got the tablet and artefacts, then the extraction will not be taking place."

"When do we leave?"

"You'll both be shuttled to Earth in one of our spacepods. The onboard AI will have the coordinates and as soon as you've completed your training you'll be gone. We have another gadget here, too." She moved into another room with a bed resembling an old MRI. "You'll put these mesh nets over your head — lucky your hair is short — and then one at a time will lay on this." She indicated the bed. "After roughly an hour, it will have embedded all the information you need to work the suits and the extraction process."

———

WHEN RHYLL CAME TO, SHE RECOGNISED THE INTERIOR OF A hoverpod. Though her vision was blurred, she could feel it was a luxurious one. She was slumped in a very comfortable chair which was reclined to an almost horizontal position. Her head throbbed as she glanced down. She was in her clothes, but not the spacesuit. In front of her, four heads were close together poring over a map on the screen. Beside her, but on the other side of the pod, was her mother, also reclined and asleep.

After taking a few minutes to heal herself, she levered the chair to a sitting position.

"Hi guys," she whispered, so as not to wake her mum. "Nice ride, Dan."

The four heads turned to her in surprise, all smiling when they saw her, greeting her quietly. Nala came over and held her hand.

"What's happening and where are we?" Rhyll asked. Through the wrap-around windscreen, outside was all rugged, mountainous terrain with patches of deep green and other patches of snow.

"We're heading to Tibet and the next chakra point. It's closest out of the three remaining locations; Uluru would be the least populated — and that's next on our itinerary — and Mount Shasta the largest but also the furthest."

"What happened in Giza?"

"Now, that's an interesting story. Sit down, have some food and drink and we'll tell you."

ONCE RHYLL HAD USED THE ONBOARD BATHROOM TO FRESHEN UP, she sat and a table slid from the side of her seat. Nala brought out some heated food and cool drinks.

Imogen had woken, and after relieved hugs, the group recounted the last four hours.

"The Bedouins took out the bulk of the drones, then skirmished with the two dozen ICON security troops that landed."

"I have to say," Cat added, admiration in her voice, "they are very good at doing what they do on their home turf. I almost felt sorry for the troops."

"The more interesting part," Dan said, "is some powerful people are on our side—"

"Or more precisely, not on ICON's side," Nala interrupted. "They took out the remaining armed hoverpods. We have no idea who or why. From what we can tell, it was from a satellite laser."

"How did you do what you did to the pods?" Dan asked her.

Embarrassed, Rhyll described briefly what she had learnt about manipulating electricity — and other energy — in her escape from Area 53.

"Did Q have anything to do with that?"

"Only after we found each other. He flew the pod, then the UFO, and you know the rest."

RHYLL DROPPED THE EMERALD TABLET IN FRONT OF THEM. "AS I said earlier, different dialects translate the same words differently. Compare these squiggles to those on the column, and also the pictures of the HUD."

With the emerald tablet in the middle of the table, the group passed her phone around to get a quick comparison. It was true, while there were subtle variants, on the whole the squiggles on the tablet, HUD and columns were almost the same.

"Those aliens had not only been here before, as Q had assumed, they must know about Atlantis," Rhyll concluded.

"Myths do say aliens were here first. If we had the other tablets and found someone to decipher them ... it could possibly change our entire history," Imogen said.

"Q's presence would've been handy now," Rhyll muttered.

"Be warned, there'll also be a lot of opposition if it's found out what we're doing," Imogen cautioned. "As we've discovered over time, the powers that be don't appreciate change; they've staked their reputations on a particular ideology built on the foundations of a particular history. To find it was all false — not as they claimed — will ruin them. And they'll stop at nothing to prevent that from ever reaching the ears of the population."

"In our future Earth, they won't be around, and definitely not in a position to oppose it."

"True. As long as we act before they do."

THE END

Continued in Book 4

GNOSTIC

Please consider leaving a Review
Help other readers find this urban fantasy series by leaving a
review on your favourite blog or website. Even simple ones like
'I loved it' really help with a book – and an author's – success.

ACKNOWLEDGMENTS

I'd like to send a huge thank you to both:

Belinda Crawford who created the covers; https://designedbyboots.com

Noel Osualdini for his excellent editorial assistance.

My original beta-reader crew: Peter J Aldin, Stephen Kerwin, Aaron Cordy, and a big welcome to Karl Martin, Heather Stone, Doug Switzer and Scott Burnard for all their perseverance and politely pointing out my failings.

And finally but most importantly, my wife Morag for putting up with my absent-minded rantings, and all my friends. I'm slowly learning what that glazed stare means.

ABOUT THE AUTHOR

Andre Jones was born in Wollongong, NSW Australia and currently resides in Melbourne with his very understanding Scottish wife, a British Shorthair cat, and more recently, a Jack Russell Terrier pup.

As a child he devoured the works of Enid Blyton, Tolkien, McCAffrey, Asimov, Heinlein and Bradbury just to name a few. As a young adult, he got lost in the many and varied roleplaying games, including MERP, GURPS, Harn, Skyrealms of Jorune, good old D&D *(and its many variants)* and Traveller … and spent far too much time on video games like Skyrim.

He wore many hats including; Security Officer, Police Officer, Park Ranger and finally as a Petty Officer in the Royal Australian Navy for 18 years *(sadly, his role-playing stopped there for too long)*.

As a Navy Veteran, his retirement has provided the opportunity to write, roleplay, draw and potter to his heart's content.

ALSO BY ANDRE JONES

Death Wave Chronicles

RELIC

DRUID

SPHINX

Seven Portals Series

City of Bridges

Shadow of the Tower

Ripples in Time

Please consider subscribing to my website ... I even send out newsletters now and then.

https://www.andrejonesauthor.site